Through the n

Book one

Copyright Victoria L Short 2022
The right of Victoria L Short to be identified as author of
this work has been asserted in accordance with the
Copyright, Designs and Patents Act 1988.

British Library Cataloguing in Publication Data.
A CIP catalogue record for this book is available from
the British Library.

ISBN: 9798444480205

This is a work of fiction. Names, characters, businesses,
organizations, places, events, and incidents either are the
product of the author's imagination or are used
fictitiously. Any resemblance to actual persons, living or
dead, events, or locales is entirely coincidental.

For Poppy

What if stars are not what we think they are.
Maybe the light of a star doesn't come from distant suns,
but from our wings as our soul turns into an Angel?
Maybe our destiny calls to us and there is a world
beyond our world where we are all connected. What if we
are part of a great and moving plan? For even time and
distance are not what they appear to be.

Caroline/Carolina

1

The image in the puddle.

It was quite a normal morning despite the rain fall and nothing out of the ordinary stood out that would make me think this was the day that my life was going to change. Apart from the fact I chose to drive a different route into work today. I favoured a more picturesque scenery; down winding curved country roads and freshly cut fields of green and gold.

I drove past the village golf course and a little row of old seventeenth-century farmers' cottages, all still in use, with a wonderful variety of flowers which filled their front lawns. Just ahead, I could see the old wrought iron gates that had once been the entrance to Debden Manor. I smiled to myself as I think back to my childhood.

As a young girl I would often sneak out of the garden. I would climb over our back fence and get lost in the forest behind and hidden in the depths was the footprint of the old house.

I would often play in the old crumbled down ruins and just beyond there was a lake with an old, gnarled oak tree, both had stood the test of time. I would often gaze into the murky waters trying to seek the answers to why I felt so at home here among the rubble and overgrown vegetation. My younger sister Claire found me there once gazing into the dark depths and I'll never forget the look of horror on her face.

'I don't know why you come over here to play,' she

said, 'If Mum knew she'd go crazy!'

'I like it here,' I said stubbornly.

I knew I shouldn't go down to the lake; it was like the forbidden fruit; it could never had tasted sweeter to anyone other than me, but I went there all the same. I would often find myself sitting on its banks leaning back against the trunk of the old oak tree. It was shallow around the edges; I could see pebbles on its brownish bed and a weeping willow tree on the opposite bank. I always had a sense of peace and tranquillity whenever I visited this place, which was until I turned fifteen when I first heard the voice.

'Caroline, find me.'

It was like the wind carried the voice across the water. After that day I never went back.

For years after I heard his voice in my dreams, not every night, occasionally from time to time. I could almost feel his breath on my face as he spoke. The voice was soft and velvety, it hung in the air around me, even long after I woke.

The rain continued, and by the time I pulled up outside work it was teeming down so I made a quick dash from the car park to the servants' entrance of Copped Hall.

I had an infinite closeness to this old house with its rigid symmetry of yellow brick and white stucco pediments. Windows and doors with decorative headers and the arched grand entrance with its Palladian architecture alongside its whimsical gothic theme. The house was built within a grand landscape setting, perched high on a hill looking impressive from a distance and my job was to restore and keep the gardens as they would have been.

I shook out my coat and hung it on the back of the door in the small lobby. Mark, my supervisor bumped in behind me, almost crushing me into the opposite door.

'Morning honey bunny.' He air-kissed both my cheeks. I just loved his little endearments and quirkiness.

'And how are we on this wonderfully miserable day?' He placed his umbrella in the old wrought iron umbrella stand and hung up his bright yellow raincoat. Reminiscent of my childhood glossy rain-mac that I use to wear, along with my bright red wellies.

'Morning, Mark, and I'm fine, thank you for asking.' I was always pleased to see him; he always had an abundant amount of energy no matter what time of day.

He glanced down at my scruffy appearance. 'You look superb as ever, darling.'

I followed his gaze. 'Why thank you.' We both laughed.

'I don't think I'll get much done outside today,' I added, 'so have you got anything that needs sorting out?'

'Glad you asked, I was coming to find you anyway, to ask a big favour.' He gave me a huge grin.

I glanced at him, a little doubtful and wondering where this conversation was going to take me.

'Okay, I'm all ears.'

He clasped his hands together quite dramatically and continued.

'You know we've put a reward out for locating the lost wrought iron gates for the front of the drive?'

'Yes,' I said, as a rush of excitement ran through my body.

'Well, nothing has come of it.'

'Oh, that's a shame.'

I couldn't hide my disappointment.

'Anyway, we are trying desperately to find old gates that we can restore, and I was wondering if you had any ideas of where we could find some?'

'Really, that's such a coincidence, I drove past the old entrance to Debden Manor this morning, and the old gates are still there.'

'Debden Manor, hmm.' He put his finger and thumb on his chin and narrowed his eyes, you could almost see the cogs of his brain working. 'Do you think we could use them here?' he asked, hopefully.

'I don't see why not; they are literally hanging off, and I reckon if you make a few calls, you could get them.'

'It's worth a try.' He turned and walked away.

'How's Steve?' I shouted after him.

'Grumpy as ever, but I still adore him,' he said, 'I'll let you know the outcome later,' he called back as he closed his office door. Steve was Mark's husband of ten years, he was tall, blonde haired a typical rugby lad, so you could imagine his parents surprise when he brought Mark home to meet them. They have been inseparable ever since.

I smiled to myself as I made my way towards the staff room to grab a cup of tea and a Danish pastry, which was made by Ms. Hughes, the estate secretary, every Friday.

As I walked into the staff room, I found her bent over the large dining room table placing her home baked goodies out for us all.

'Morning, Mrs. Hughes.'

I must have startled her because she twisted around quite quickly.

'Oh Caroline, you made me jump!'

She placed her hand over her heart and chuckled.

'Sorry, Mrs. Hughes, I didn't mean to.'

'Pish.' She waved a hand towards me. 'Never mind me, Mr. Hughes is always saying I jump at the silliest of things.'

'And how is Mr. Hughes, still enjoying his retirement?' I said, as my eyes scanned the selection of pastries.

'He drives me up the wall, and is always underfoot,' she said cheerfully, 'that's why I've taken to working three days a week rather than two. I told him he should join the local bowls club.'

'And did he?'

'No, don't be daft, he would sooner potter around in his garden and take Copper for long walks. Here, take a plate.' Mrs. Hughes passed me a delicate white China plate with gold edging around the rim, decorated with red and pink flowers.

'I heard from Alan that you were here late again last night.'

Alan was the estates head gardener, and he took me under his wing and helped me expand my knowledge.

I floated from job to job after I left school, then one day I happened upon Alan one afternoon when the estate first opened to the public, we got chatting and not long after I started working with him. That was six years ago, and I haven't looked back.

Mrs. Hughes had that uncanny ability to tactfully distract the conversation away from herself and onto me; I loved her dearly, but she could be a bit of a busy body when it came to my love life. She busied herself with pouring the boiling water from the kettle into the flowery teapot that matched the plates.

'How many times have I told you; you need to get out and meet a nice young chappy,' she said as she placed a bright pink tea cosy over the top to keep in the heat.

Even though I had preferred my own company growing up I had four good girlfriends. All married. I was Auntie Car-car, the one that spoilt their children, but incredibly happy to give them back at the end of the day. I was the friend that listened to all their troubles and woes and the friend that babysat at the drop of a hat.

I had a great relationship with my sister Claire, she too was married with children. Our parents had retired and spent half the year cruising around the world and the other half playing golf, so we rarely saw them. Not that I blame them. They had worked and saved hard. Although they never missed birthdays or special events and when we did all get together it was filled with laughter and warmth. We were a close family, although I was always looked on with certain amount of pity because I was still single at the ripe old age of thirty. I had never found that connection but somewhere deep down inside I felt like I was missing someone.

'You know me Mrs Hughes; I like my own company. Anyway, I haven't found any nice young chappy that would be worthy of me,' I said, feeling comparatively pleased with my answer.

She tutted to herself and went back to the task of making the tea. I was debating which pastry to have, apricot or cinnamon. Sod it, I took both. I picked the cinnamon first, and bit into the flaky pastry.

'Ooh, my favourite, delightful as ever, Mrs. Hughes.' Crumbs fell onto my cardigan, and I absentmindedly flicked them onto my plate.

'Glad you like it. Tea?' she said merrily.

'Mmm, yes please.' I was grateful for the diversion.

She passed me a cup of tea and I took a sip. 'That's lovely, nothing like a good cuppa in the morning, thank you. You certainly know how to look after me.'

'You're welcome, honey, that's what I'm here for and I will always be looking out for you,' Mrs Hughes added as she walked towards the door. I thought her comment was a little strange, but I shrugged it off.

I walked over to the large window and sat down on the plush two-seater sofa that was nestled in the bay and sipped my tea. I stared out of the window and watched the rain fall over the countryside. My eyes glazed over, and I became lost in my own world of knights, kings, and damsels in distress. I harrumphed under my breath at my overactive imagination as I envisaged myself dressed in a colourful gown from a bygone era, walking around the grounds of this old manor.

The noise of the door opening brought me back to reality, and Mark thundered into the room with excited energy. 'We've got the go-ahead.' His face gleamed with enthusiasm.

'Blimey that was quick,' I said, 'you don't hang around!'

He nodded, letting his brown hair fall across his forehead. He pushed it back automatically.

'For the time being I just want you to go and check them out and, arrange with the owner a Mr. Thorn when it's convenient to take them.'

'Now?'

'Well, finish your tea and cake first,' he said as he made his way towards the pastries. 'Mmm, I love a Friday.'

*

I went in search of Lee and Dean, our heavy-duty lifting boys, and found them in the car park, lifting some ornate stone flowerpots from the pickup truck.

'Hey, boys, got a job for you both if you wouldn't mind driving me to Debden Manor?'

'What, the old farmer Parker's place?' Dean said as he jumped down from the truck.

'Yes, that's the one. Do you know, I haven't heard it called that in years?'

'What are we going there for?' Lee asked, as I watched them struggle with a large pot.

'The gates. We've been given permission by the owners to use them here.'

Lee parked the truck just outside the entrance to the old estate, it was still raining, but not quite as heavily. I jumped out of the truck and was greeted by the owner.

'Mr. Thorn? Hi, I'm Caroline, I've come from Copped Hall.' I extended my hand.

'Yes, it's nice to meet you.' He took my offered hand and squeezed it gently.

My pulse raced through my body.

He held it for a few moments longer. He was remarkably handsome, not pretty, but rugged, and I had a strange sense of deja-vu as his thumb brushed the top of my hand.

'Have we met before?'

'No, I don't think so. I would remember such lovely copper hair.'

He must have felt embarrassed by his comment because he released my hand quickly and cleared his throat.

I watched him closely as he zipped his jacket further up to his chin.

'Dreadful weather,' he said changing the subject.

'Yes, awful, but a typical June. So, you're cool with us taking the gates?'

I was trying to remain light and casual, but my insides were jumping around like a bunch of baby kangaroos.

He waved his hand in the air. 'Yep, help yourself, they're on my list of things to do here when I eventually get round to it, so you're doing me a favour.'

My mouth went dry, and I lost all train of thought. I must have been staring at him because he cleared his throat to get my attention.

I blushed. 'Sorry, so when could we take them?'

He shrugged his broad shoulders. 'Whenever you want, but whilst you're here you might as well take them now. If that's convenient with you all?'

'These hinges look like they've seen better days, we might have a job getting them off,' said Lee as he inspected the gates. 'We might damage the wall.'

'That's fine, there's not much left of the old wall, so it's coming down anyway,' said Mr Thorn.

Lee and Dean nodded in agreement and took to the task of preparing the tools for the removal of the gates.

Mr. Thorn placed his hands into his pockets. 'So, I'll leave you to it,' he said, as he shuffled from one foot to another. I could tell he wanted to be on his way.

'Umm, yeah, great, thanks for that, we really appreciate it,' I said, feeling a little awkward.

He gave me a dazzling smile, and my stomach whirled over slowly as I leisurely perused his body. He was six feet something, lean, but muscular I imagined, underneath his quilted jacket. He wore his dark hair short, shaved at the sides and back, but kept the top slightly longer. It had been gelled back to keep his unruly curls in place, but what really drew my attention was his eyes, I couldn't shake off that feeling of familiarity; I knew him somehow. We said our goodbyes, and I watched him walk back down the way he had come.

Then he stopped. 'Caroline.' He started to walk back towards me.

'Yes?'

'Would you like to look around the estate, whilst you're here.'

'Really? Um, yes, I would love to.' I shouted over to Lee and Dean, 'Boys, are you okay if I leave you for a bit?'

'Course,' Dean said, 'you go ahead, it's going to take us a while to get these off.' He started to hammer at one of the rusted hinges.

It was beautiful here in the countryside. Broken sunlight peeked through the grey clouds as we walked down the gravel driveway. At least the rain had stopped now. I listened to him talking about the land and its history.

'These old crumbled down ruins and land was once owned by Nicholas Trevilian, who, according to local history had been beheaded for helping the Prince of Wales, escape, after the failed Royalist uprising in 1649.'

I was too polite tell him I knew it already. However, I was happy to listen as his rich, velvety tones washed over me.

The road itself wound its way through an avenue of blossom trees, and the subtle aroma filled my senses as I took in a deep breath.

'It's quite intoxicating, isn't it?' He flashed me a wide smile, which showed off his even white teeth.

'Yes, it's quite breath taking,' I said as I looked around at our surroundings.

The sun hung just above the trees on the left as we rounded a curve, and we passed an old outbuilding that had been abandoned for years but was still standing. We had explored it one summer, Claire and I, looking for wartime souvenirs or old bits of pottery from bygone eras.

My majestic old oak tree on the banks of the lake came into view, I smiled at my memories. Then another, more intense memory flashed before me. The oak tree looked almost the same, but not quite as tall, and the branches were much lower and stretched only a little way over the water's edge. I had a vision of sitting beneath the tree on a hot July day, with a small child who looked at me with love. The unusual memories I was having of this place made my insides tighten as I recognised certain parts of this estate, not the memories of playing here as a child, but older, deeper. An uneasy queasiness overcame me, and my head started to spin.

I heard Mr. Thorn's voice in the background as I tried to clear my focus.

'Are you okay?' he said as he took hold of my hands.

'Caroline, are you feeling alright?' His face wore a worried expression.

'Sorry, I came over a little strange.'

He had callused hands and broad shoulders that came to those who worked hard for a living, and I noticed he had faint lines around his blues eyes and a small scar on his left cheek. But it was his voice that un-nerved me, deep, but soft and occasionally gruff which seemed to hang in the air when he spoke to me. He sounded and felt familiar.

'Do you want to sit down for a bit?'

He helped me over to a rickety wooden bench, and I sat down very gingerly as his gravely concerned blue eyes roamed over my face.

'You must think me a trifle silly,' I said as the first flushes of warmth entered my cheeks.

'No, not at all, have you eaten something this morning?' he asked kindly.

The soft breeze tickled the loose strands of my hair around my face, and he absentmindedly tucked a bit behind my ear and casually brushed my cheek with his thumb, then looked aghast.

'I'm sorry, I don't know what came over me, I'm not normally this forward.' He said as he quickly put his hand down.

'And I'm normally quite healthy, and don't often have silly bouts of female dizziness.'

We both laughed, which helped break the thick tension that was radiating around us.

'So, what made you buy this run-down plot of land?' I asked with keen interest.

'I have always been quite fascinated with this old estate, ever since I was a small boy. My dad would bring me camping, and we would always pass through here.'

'Are you from East London?'

'Yeah, that's right.'

'I could tell by your accent. My grandparents were born in East London and then moved down to Debden in the fifties for slum clearance.'

'So, you're an Essex girl through and through.' He chuckled as I nudged him with my elbow.

'I loved growing up in this small part of Essex, not many people know it's here,' I said.

'I find it refreshing and peaceful and not so many cars.'

He glanced down at me. 'Anyway, enough about me, what do you do for a living?'

'Believe it or not I'm a gardener.'

'Really, I would never have thought.' He laughed as he looked down at my muddy wellies and stained jeans.

'What made you choose this line of work?'

'My dad really.'

I explained to him that I would often follow my dad around prizing information from him. I collected his flowerpots, stacked them in the greenhouse, watched him prune and weed. In springtime I would help him plant seeds into the little flowerpots made up of cardboard ready for his summer bedding. Dad was a keen horticulturist and his passion flowed onto me and over

17

the years he taught me everything I needed to know about all types of flowers, plants, and vegetables, even down to the medicinal purposes of everything that could be grown from our soil.

'Nature is our best provider,' dad would say.

'Yes, I agree with him,' he said as he looked at me with

an intense stare.

I shifted a little uncomfortably on the bench. What was the matter with me? My heart was racing, my blood was pumping fast through my veins, and I had a sudden instinct to put my hands on the side of his face and kiss his wonderful soft full lips. Much to my mortification I leaned in and put my lips on his, and he accepted my kiss wholeheartedly. I eventually pulled back, and by the time I had recovered my breath he spoke.

'Well, that was rather unexpected, but pleasant.'

Deeply embarrassed, I rose awkwardly to my feet, and he followed and came up alongside me. I glanced wildly around, looking for a way out.

'I'm so sorry…um, I don't know what came over me, I've never done anything like that before.' The awkwardness of my actions were flapping under my breast like a panicked flock of chickens. If the tables had been reversed, would I have been so accepting?

He took hold of my hand. 'You have nothing to be sorry about, I welcomed your kiss and I very much enjoyed it.'

I cringed inside. I needed to get away. 'I think I need to go now, I bet the boys are wondering where I am.'

Disregarding my efforts to free my hand, he held me firmly in his grasp.

'You don't have to go; I haven't showed you around yet.' He shifted closer towards me, clearly amused, with one corner of his mouth quirked up.

I stood hastily. The back of my knees brushed up against the bench.

'No, I must go.' I said as my body tightened from my head to my toes. I tried to pull my hand away.

'I'll walk you back up.' He let go of my hand.

'No!' I spoke out too sharply and regretted my actions. 'Sorry, it's fine, really. I know the way back, and you probably have loads to do. It was nice to meet you.'

'Nice to meet you too, Caroline. Maybe we could go out together sometime soon?'

'After what just happened?'

'Why not.'

'Okay, you know where to find me.'

Despite the general awkwardness, I smiled and waved back at him.

*

The lads were trying to get the gates off, but without much luck; the hinges had become so rusted over time that they would not budge.

'Looks like we've got to take part of the stone away,' Lee said.

'Will that work?' I questioned.

'Should do,' said Dean, 'it's better than trying to lift them off the hinges.'

He passed Lee a bolster chisel and hammer and they started to knock the stone away around the hinge. I turned away to avoid the chunks of brick that were flying everywhere...

'Watch out Caroline!' Lee shouted out.

A searing pain exploded at the side of my head. I lost my balance and fell to my knees. Did something hit me? I tried desperately to stay focused. Then I noticed a large chunk of stone lying on the floor next to a dirty puddle of water.

A few drops of my blood landed in the centre, and it sent circular ripples to the outer edges. My brow creased in confusion as I looked at myself in the reflection of the water. It was just a shallow, muddy puddle caused by the rain, yet the image was so clear. Almost like I was looking into a mirror. Although I recognised myself, I looked slightly different. My hair was the palest of blondes, with streaks of curly gold running through, not my usual auburn, and it was piled on top, in a tight bun with ringlets draped round my shoulders.

Suddenly the wind picked up. *Caroline come back to me.'* It was the man's voice from my dreams.

The wind swirled around me like a cyclone, with the leaves following in its wake. I felt sick, my mind tried desperately to urge my body to move, but it didn't want to obey. My fingers started to buzz, and I had a deep sense of urgency to touch the image that stared back at me…Before I had time to think it through, I felt my hand move.

The sounds around me became distant, my head spun, and my vision began to blur. I felt as though I were falling, or I was being pulled down into a darkness, not fast but in slow motion. I lost all-natural sense of my body as I floated down into oblivion. One would describe it as a sensation of weightlessness, like being pulled under the water and unable to resurface. I had no power over my body or my mind as I lost awareness of both.

2

Misplaced in time

The warmth of the sun on my face woke me from my state of unconsciousness. I tried to open my eyes, but they were puffy and sore, and I could see the pink brightness of the sun through the thin veil of skin that covered them. Slowly I sat up, and very carefully opened my eyes. The sun was so fierce I had to shield my face from the glare. My head was fuzzy and thick, so I clutched my hands to my forehead and closed my eyes for a few seconds to calm the dizziness. The spinning slowly subsided. Almost instantly I realised I wasn't in my own clothes. Gone were my wellie boots and jeans and in their place was a long, satin, royal-blue dress, and dainty matching slippers. What was going on? Had someone played a prank on me? I remember getting hit in the head, but nothing after until now.

'Hello,' I shouted. Nothing, not even a giggle.

I checked my pockets for my phone. No pockets. My hands searched the ground, looking for my phone. Nothing. I crawled to a standing position and leaned heavily on a large tree trunk. I breathed in large amounts of fresh air to quell the sickness. My body felt like I had been pulled inside out and every which way possible. Although nothing had changed, nothing seemed to have happened and yet I was experiencing a feeling of overwhelming terror so great I seemed to have lost all sense of rationality. I closed my eyes and shook my head hard to clear the fog of confusion, not that it helped. I wasn't quite sure what this would achieve. As my focus returned, I realised I was standing outside the gates of Debden Manor where I had stood only moments ago, but they were no longer old and rusty, but newly painted black with gold flowers. The driveway continued beyond the gates, and from this distance I could see the house with its huge lake. What the hell was going on? I was surrounded by a thick forest, and in front of me was a little dirt track, which must be a road of some sort. My mind was in turmoil. Chaos of emotions ran through me. One could only describe this as a feeling of displacement, of being somewhere else far from home. Lost almost, but I wasn't lost, I was standing in the middle of Epping Forest in the heart of my little Essex village of Debden. I ran towards the gate and held on for dear life, willing myself to return to where I had come from, but there were no winds and no dizziness. Nothing. All I could hear was the pounding of my heartbeat in my ears. I stood quietly for a moment. I heard nothing but the sounds of the forest. Then from the distance I heard a rattle of a cart and the whisper of human voices. I turned towards it and walked down the dirt track hoping to find some answers. After five minutes or so, I approached a hill to my right with a dense copse of trees. There was a little wooden signpost to my left, with crudely carved out handwriting on it: *Rectory Lane*. I stood in a state of bewilderment. This was the main road I travelled daily to get home, but it didn't look like a road now just a dirt track with wheel and horseshoe tracks. I blinked several times to clear my vision. I held up my hand to feel my pulse, beating a little fast but steady. I seem to have all my abilities, but something wasn't right as I stood staring as the little wooden sign. Fear ran through my body like a freight train hurtling towards its destination.

Get a grip, Caroline. I looked up and took in a few deep breaths to calm myself.

The sky was so blue with long swirls of puffy white clouds and the air smelt different, it smelt of summer and damp earth. Had I travelled back through time? But that was utter nonsense! Time travel was impossible… Or was it? Looking around at my surroundings I knew deep down I was in Debden, but the question was: *when?*

I could see St Nicholas's church, as it stood in the middle of the Rectory Lane; like a well-meaning and kindly grandfather, it was the center of activity in the village. From the church, the houses ran down either side, half-timbered cottages with overhanging upper stories, and thatched roofs made from heather or straw. Tiny dormer windows with obscure glass were surrounded with honeysuckle and ivy. The gardens were covered in blooming flowers, delphiniums, lavender, and hollyhocks that reached past the windows and blossom trees were in full bloom. There were only a few people scattered around, since it was mid-morning, and I imagined the villagers were hard at work at this time of day. The only idlers were a few cats and dogs, and children who were too young to learn a skill. On the opposite side of the road, further down, I could see a blacksmith's cottage with his adjoining shop. There was a large inn built of soft red brick, over which hung a great sign painted with a crude golden lion that swung out over the street on an elaborate wrought iron arm. Fear consumed me; what had happened? Was I dead? Or was this a dream? My rational mind was telling me this could not be real, but in my heart, I knew I was no longer in my own time.

It was beautiful and peaceful away from the twenty-first century; gone was the hustle and bustle of the cars, and Debden as I saw it had such an aura of prosperity, which was something I would never have imagined. I always assumed that village life in the seventeenth century would be poor and dirty, but this was the total opposite of what I expected. Everything about this village seemed of solid ease, with plenty of food, warmth, and comfort.

My stomach twisted with fear and tears filled my eyes. I blinked to clear my vision and a single tear rolled down my cheek. I wiped it away with the back of my hand. Crap! This was real, but how? And why?

This wasn't possible! You got stories like this in books, and on television, but not in real life.

The beauty of the village I'd grown up in was so different, yet still remarkably familiar. I noticed the rest of the cottages, they appeared to be occupied by hands men and their families, who probably divided their time working on the large estate of Debden Manor, as well as their own homes. It seemed to me that this little village didn't depend on the estate for work, it appeared to be quite self-sufficient, and its occupants seemed to have their own economic existence. I was so totally absorbed in my own thoughts, that I did not notice the cart until it pulled up beside me. I heard a kindly, yet familiar voice speak to me

'Mistress Carolina, what are you doing so far from home?'

I lifted my head up. 'Mr. Hughes?'

I stared at him, confused. Brows raised, he glanced at me strangely. He was dressed in Seventeenth century clothes, and I knew for certain that this was real. I could see relief in his eyes as he jumped down from the cart.

'No, my lady, it's Mr. Carson...' His fluffy white eyebrows met in the middle. '...the head groom on your father's estate. Are you feeling well, Miss?'

Think, Caroline! 'Hmm ...no, I had a bad bump on my head, and I don't seem to recollect where or who I am.'

By the expression on his face, he was just as confused as I was.

'Your mother has been extremely worried.' He walked towards me. 'You have been gone most of the morning.'

I stood there somewhat bewildered and scared; I didn't really know what to do. *If he knew me, then shouldn't I go with him?* This whole situation was becoming stranger by the minute. Mr. Carson held his hand out.

'Come, Miss, let's get you home.'

Dazed by the rush of recent events, I obediently followed. My cold hand touched his warm palm. Ouch! I pulled my hand back from his grasp. A huge surge of energy ran through me like an electric shock, it worked its way up from the tip of my fingers to my head. My mind rushed with images of this life. Carolina Sackville's memories had downloaded at such a speed into my mind that I couldn't hold on to reality as I started to fall.

'Caroline, change your fate and make amends to stop the wheel of time.'

It was the last thing I heard before I blacked out.

*

'I want to know how long my daughter is going to be unconscious for, Doctor Reed.'

'Lady Sackville, as I stated two days ago, your daughter will awaken when she is ready.'

'This is sixteen forty-six, we are no longer in the dark ages, doctor, and your profession has come along in leaps and bounds. Surely you can give me some sort of explanation?'

'Unfortunately, I'm at a loss. She appears to be well, with only a slight bump on the head, but nothing that would cause her to black out. Maybe she is suffering from the vapours, or her menstrual curse is somewhat off. I'm vexed to say.'

'My daughter has never suffered with the vapours, and never complains when she has her flowering.'

Somewhere in the back of my subconscious I could hear these two-people arguing, their voices were getting louder as I slowly became conscious.

'By your leave please, the two of you!' I said as I opened my eyes. 'Mrs. Carson in the kitchen can probably hear you both!'

A blonde, blue-eyed woman in her early forties rushed over. 'Oh, my little darling, how are you feeling now? you gave us all such a fright.'

'I'm truly fine, mother.' *Oh my god, how's this possible?* I sat up quick, in shock.

27

Warm hands touched my shoulders and gently pushed me back into the soft pillows that had been plumped up for me.

'There you go, my darling.' She scrutinized my features with a worried look about her.

My thoughts raced. I was one and the same person, but I had two different memories... Here and now, I was Lady Carolina Sackville, born the thirteenth of January sixteen-twenty-two, to the Duke and Duchess of Henage. The only daughter of Lady Anne and Lord John Sackville. I had grown up in a privileged home. Spoilt. Pampered. Indulged. Lady Ann placed her hand on my head.

'Are you truly in good humour, Lina?' she said with concern in her eyes.

I was the one that was panicking now.

How do I have all these memories?

The doctor picked up my hand to feel my pulse. I had totally forgotten he was still here. I was startled.

'Hmm,' he grunted under his breath, as he checked my vitals.

'Well, ev'rything seems fine; I shall be back in a day or two to see how you are feeling.' He placed my hand back down onto the bed and patted it, 'til the morrow then, ladies.'

Lady Sackville pulled a cord near the fireplace, and a bell rang in the distance. The door opened and a young girl no more than fourteen entered.

'Sarah, would you kindly show Doctor Reed out, please?' Lady Sackville made her way back towards me.

'Yes, my lady.' Sarah curtsied and bobbed her head. The doctor bowed and took his leave as he followed her out.

The dialect was strange and so vastly different, but I understood them so well and they understood me. It was as if a switch had been turned on in my brain, and every word was so clear.

'We must get you well Lina we have a big day on Saturday, you are meeting your betrothed, Lord Trevilian.'

Her eyes twinkled in excitement as she sat on the side of my bed.

'Debden Manor Trevilian…you mean Nicholas?'

Lady Sackville peered at me rather oddly.

'Don't you remember, darling that you were once betrothed to his brother Christopher from birth, but he…'

'Drowned in the lake years ago, yes I remember now, and I was supposed to marry him four years ago.' I finished. 'Thank god I know my history,' I said without thinking.

'Are you sure you feel well, darling?' Her brows drew together in confusion.

'I'm fine, pay no heed to my ramblings, Mama. So, I'm to meet Lord Trevilian, then?'

'Lina, what has gotten into you? Are you parched? Would you like a drink?' She stood and made her way towards my bureau, and the selection of drinks.

'Umm, yes, water please.'

She turned around rather abruptly; her eyes were like saucers. 'Water? Since when do you drink water? She walked back towards me and placed her heavily jewelled hand on my forehead.

'What would I drink then?' My memories of being Carolina were vague, it's as if I had been asleep for a long time and they were blurred.

'We have wine, which you always drink, or we have cider and perry.'

'Crap. I forgot we can't drink the water, I'll have…' The look on her face made me falter.

'It's not right this talk of yours, Lina. Whatever ails you? Anyway! She waved her hand through the air as if she were dismissing my comment. 'Enough of this silly talk, how do you feel about having some food with your wine?' The thought of food made my stomach growl. *When did I eat last?*

'Food sounds nice, thank you.' I smiled warmly.

She pulled the cord by the fireplace and waited impatiently.

'Where is Sarah?'

I could hear my mother tapping her foot in frustration.

'She's showing the Doctor out.'

'I'll just have to go down and tell Mrs. Carson to plate up some food for you, I won't be long.' She flounced out of the room in a whirl of satin.

I snuggled back in the warmth of the cosy bed, with the fluffy feather pillows surrounding my head, and for some unexplained notion I felt comfortable and safe, and before I realised it, I started to doze a little.

I wasn't quite sure how long I had been sleeping, until a knock at the door woke me. My head still fuzzy, and my voice was thick with sleep.

I cleared my throat. 'Enter.'

My door opened, and a gentleman in his early fifties walked in.

'How are you feeling, my darling girl?'

I recognised this man, my father, my teacher, my confidant.

'I'm feeling well, Papa, a little confused and extremely tired.'

I looked at him closely as he walked towards me. Lord John Sackville was of a good stocky build, not very tall, probably average height for the men of this century and he was very handsome for his age. He had dark hair that was going grey around the temples, and he wore it short, but not too short because the curls of his hair touched the ruff of his collar. He had hazel-coloured eyes that looked kind and knowledgeable, but the strangest thing of all was, I adored him. This whole situation was odd, maybe I was going to wake up soon and realise this was just a terrible dream.

John Sackville leaned down and kissed my forehead. I was comforted by his presence.

'We were so worried about you darling,' he said as he picked up the chair from my dressing table and placed it next to the bed. 'Please try to remember to tell us where you are going next time.' He sat down and took hold of my hand and I noticed that his fingers too had rings on them, although not quite as many as Mama's.

'I'm so sorry Papa, I went for a walk after breakfast, and I just got further and further away. You know me, I get so lost in my own little world.'

'It's good that Carson found you when he did, my darling.' He gave me half a smile and patted my hand.

'Good old Mr. Carson, I was awfully off with him, would you apologise for me?'

'Of course, I will, but you will see him soon enough, I'm sure.'

'Thank you. Papa would you be terribly offended if I retired for a little while? My head still hurts, and I need some rest.'

I wanted to be on my own, as I didn't know quite what else to say to this man, whom I adored, but who also seemed like a stranger.

'Of course, darling, I only came up briefly to check on you before I go out.' He stood and straightened his doublet.

'Not away on business again?' I questioned him.

'No, just down to the cottagers, some dispute over property borders and cattle. He leaned down and kissed my forehead. 'Sleep, rest and I hope to see you at breakfast on the morrow, if you are feeling up to it.'

'Of course, I'll be down.'

He picked up the chair and placed it back in its rightful place. 'Goodnight, my darling girl,' he said as he opened the door.

'Goodnight, Papa, see you in the morning.' I waited for the door to shut before I lay back down. My head pounded, my eyelids were heavy, I could no longer keep them open as I drifted into a deep sleep.

I stood alone in a place that was so different, full of colour with a strong fragrance of mixed flowers. I had a deep feeling, one would describe it as a mixture of calm, confusion, and an overwhelming sense of loss that I couldn't quite place. In the dream state of my mind, a voice spoke to me.

'All will be well; you will find your way back soon.' A kind old gentleman appeared before me, more like an apparition, the haze of a soul or an angel maybe.

'Sorry, I don't get your meaning?' I said as he started to walk away. 'Wait, please I don't understand!' He paid no heed and continued to walk towards the bright white light. 'Wait don't go!' I shouted out in my sleep, which woke me with a start.

I sat up and looked around my room, nothing had changed. I was still in 1646. The loss I felt in my dream followed me to my conscious state. For the first time in my life, I had no control. No control over my own destiny, or over my fate, and I had no clue what to do next. Tears rolled down my cheek, I swallowed down the lump of despair that had lodged in my throat.

Why had this happened? Has my soul been misplaced in time? I seem to be re-living an earlier life. But why? What was the reason for this?

I dried my eyes with the cuff of my nightgown and swung my legs out from under the cover. I got out of the bed, ignoring the food and drink that had been left for me. I must have slept for longer than I had thought; the evening had settled swiftly.

My room was dark, except for the flicker of a candle by my nightstand, and the low embers of the dying fire. I picked up a fur robe that had been thrown casually over the chaise longue and placed it around my shoulders and walked towards my Juliet balcony. I opened the double doors, and the crisp, cool air caressed my face and shoulders, banishing the last lingering trace of sleep.

Feeling chillier, I tugged at the fur robe bringing it closer beneath my chin and as I leaned further over the small balcony, I had a recognition of where I was: my home was Copped Hall, maybe I was meant to be here. Smiling to myself as looked up, I noticed the stars had come out, the moon was high, and the sky was thin and transparent. In the background I could hear the quiet country sounds of the crickets, a croak from a distant frog, and the whir of tiny gnats.

No longer tired, and extremely excited. I rushed over to my wardrobe. The dresses hanging there were full of colour and spirit, far too fiddly to put on in a hurry. I grabbed a dark blue dress and pulled it over my head, then I put on rough brown leather boots and wrapped a knitted shawl around my shoulders and waist and tucked it into a worn leather belt. Picking up the candle, I left the comfort and safety of my bedroom... I could walk around this house with my eyes shut. I knew every knot and indentation on the handrail as I descended the great staircase, even down to the steps which creaked. Missing a few here and there, so not to disturb the household.

I made my way towards the back of the house to the kitchen, where I would often sit and watch Mrs Hughes roll out her pastry for our Friday morning treat, but this was no longer Mrs Hughes kitchen. I passed through the kitchen into the scullery and placed my candle on the sideboard to open the back door.

The candle gutted and I was shrouded in darkness until I took a step out into the night. The shine from the moonlight surrounded me. From where I stood, I could see the historic English yew trees and the large privet hedge rows, which offered plenty of shade from the sun. I marveled at the glistening fountain and a pathway that was lined with a mixture of herbaceous flower borders as it heads towards the privy garden, which had stunning symmetrical patterns and a variety of plants which I had helped Carson plant many years ago. I re-discovered the magic of a little hidden pond; I peered over the edge and saw the freshwater fish swim lazily backwards and forwards in the moonlight. I remember so clearly feeding the fish with Mama.

My fear now became curiosity and at this moment, in this crazy new time, I found a sense of peace. Almost as if I really belonged here.

The wind picked up around me, and with it the travel of noise, which disturbed my thoughts. Muffled voices seemed to be coming from the direction of the chapel, and curiosity got the better of me and I followed the sounds. Sneaking into the chapel, I hid between the pews and watched as three men conversed.

'I have had word that we have been beaten at the Battle of Stow,' said the small, dark-haired man who was dressed quite finely.

A tall man, half-hidden in the shadows spoke. 'Sire, I'm sorry to hear that, I should never have left Lord Astley…this was the last hope for Oxford, without the numbers they will not stand another attack.' His voice was familiar, but I couldn't place it; and it was far too dark to see his face.

The thin small man spoke again. 'I need to get to a Scottish garrison; they will have the numbers.' He sighed heavily. 'I never thought I would see the day my kingdom would turn on me.'

'Where is your son, sire?' I recognised the voice that spoke, it was my father.

The short man took off his hat and wig. He ran his hand through his short dark hair.

'He has fled the capital with Buckingham, I have sent word that he is to join his mother Queen Henrietta-Maria at Tyne, there awaits a ship to take them to France.'

'What of young Henry and Elizabeth?'

'I had no time to get them before the Earl of Essex's troops rounded on them.'

My father placed his hand on his shoulder for comfort.

The tall man in the shadows spoke again, his voice was soft and velvety, but it held authority. 'They will be safe sire but used as puppets against you.'

'That is my fear, but Cromwell will see no harm to the children. I must get out of England, if Essex or his men capture me, I will be imprisoned.' He placed his wig and hat back on his head and buttoned up his coat.

The man in the shadows spoke again. 'I'll round up my men, and I'll send word to my family, and your loyal friends, sire.' The flicker of the candle shone on his face slightly as he stepped towards the light, but all I could see was dark hair and beard.

'Tell them to watch themselves, Nicholas. Cromwell will be out for blood if he cannot find me.' The small man said with dejection. I watched as my father summoned one of his men. 'Go and wake Lady Sackville quietly, so not to disturb the rest of the house, and relay a message to her. Tell her we are defeated, and we are taking the King north for safety.'

The young steward bowed his head. 'Yes, My Lord.'

'No, John, stay here,' the tall stranger said to my father. 'There is no need of you to join us, just carry on as

36

normal your family has not been implicated and as far as Cromwell and Essex are concerned you are loyal to them,'

I tried to push Carolina's memories to the front of my subconsciousness. They're sketchy at best, but I think I have travelled back to the end of the English civil war and from my calculation it must be around March 1646. The King, my father and the tall dark-haired man took their leave and disappeared towards the back of the chapel. A noise behind made me jump.

'Oh, what have we here, a peeping tom?' That was the last thing I heard before a searing pain shot through my head.

3

A mistake made

I woke to the suffocating confinements of a cloth that was wrapped around me, and the weight of the man, whom I assumed was the one who had knocked me senseless. He was pressing the straw bundles down upon me, the rope-bound ties restricted any movement. I was tied so tight my arms were pinned to my sides and my hands started to go numb.

The straw was sticking into my scalp through the rough wool hood that had been thrown over my face, my ankle and hip were pressed down hard against the boards, and beneath me were mounds of straw so thin that they offered little or no padding whatsoever; with every jolt of the cart, the pain would shoot up in both areas.

I don't know how long I had been in the cart, but even if it were a short journey, I would be left black and blue. I managed to wedge my hand under my hip to give me some degree of comfort, but the pain in my bones was unbearable and I longed for the cart to stop.

Hearing hoofbeats in the distance lifted my spirits; surely, I would be rescued soon?

The morning had clearly broken through, because instead of a dark blur I could see a light blur. I waited for the rider to overtake, but no such luck, my hopes where cruelly dashed when a sharp jolt to the right took the cart from the main path onto a much rougher terrain.

We travelled some distance, which felt like forever, and bile surged up in my throat and for the first time in my life I began to pray because, in my heart, I knew there would be no escape. Minute after minute, around and around in my mind was a jumble of thoughts on how I could get out of this situation.

The horses slowed and, in the distance, I could hear the unmistakable sounds of an encampment of men. *Remember your self-defence Krav Maga classes, these seventeenth century idiots won't know what hit them...* The cart came to a jarring halt, and my captor shouted out.

'I have brought you something, men!' My blood ran cold. Completely blinded by the hood, I felt my captor pick me up and toss me over his shoulder. He then stood me on my feet, and roughly pushed me forward. My legs were so numb and cold I couldn't stand up, and I fell hard to the floor. My captor cut my ties and pulled the hood off my head, and I stood again, half in defiance, half in fear.

'What have you brought us, Stefan? I hope it's something good to eat.' The men at the camp laughed as I looked up at the dark-haired stranger who had spoken. My breath caught in my throat. Oh my god, he was handsome. A fleeting image of happier times with this man flashed through my head, but how was that possible?

'I caught this woman eavesdropping on your conversation back at Copped Hall,' said my kidnapper. 'We cannot let her go, she might be a supporter of the roundheads, and the last thing we need is her telling them where we are heading,'

'Well, while the wench is here you might as well have some fun, just be sure to silence her permanently when you are done, we don't need her talking.' The tall dark-haired stranger turned to walk away, and I realised that, despite being the subject of their talk, as a person I was completely forgotten by that point.

My fear became rage. 'Don't you bloody touch me!' I brought my fists up to my chest, ready to fight anyone that came close.

A voice in the crowd of men spoke, 'Hark the mouth on this one, I know what to stick in it to shut it up.' They all roared with laughter.

'I'll bloody well bite it off if you come anywhere near me.' The men fell silent.

'Have you ever heard a wench talk like that?' said another voice.

Despite my bravery and confidence, I was more frightened than I'd ever been in my whole life, and I hadn't the vaguest notion how to get out of this predicament.

My mind conjured images of them raping me or the other unthinkable thing was to murder me. Terror gripped me, like a steel vice.

The one they had called Stefan grabbed and pulled my shawl off my shoulders, then he ripped the back of my dress down the middle with a small knife.

My karv maga kicked in.

'You bastard.' I grabbed him in a head lock, kicked his feet from underneath him and put his own knife to his throat as he laid beneath my feet.

'Anyone comes within a foot of me, I will slit his god damn throat, is that understood?'

A whoosh of breath left my body as I was lifted into the air totally forgetting to watch out behind me.

The tall stranger held me at arm's length, and I struck out behind me with my foot, kicking him hard in the groin. The impact nearly doubled him over.

'You little bitch!' He tried to mask his pain and fury, but it was apparent for all to see.

'Let me go, you bloody bastard!' He dropped me flat on my behind. I stood and flung my hair from my face; I was furious, and I went to go for him again.

'Enough!' he shouted, everyone in the encampment stopped dead in their tracks, even nature obeyed as an unearthly silence fell over the clearing, but all I could hear was the pounding of my heart. Squeezing my eyes shut I waited for the blow, which didn't come.

Half fearful and half curious, I slowly opened my eyes. He was huge, more so up close, his hair was dark brown, with gold strands here and there, which looked like the sun had kissed the tips and his strangely coloured eyes, cobalt blue in his bearded, haggard face. His cloak was billowing out behind him in the wind, fury danced across his features making him look almost satanic.

His shoulders were wide, arms bulged with muscle, he looked like he had just stepped out of a Mills and Boon romantic novel.

I would often take myself off to my bedroom to read. There in the solitude I would experience the delicious excitement of being loved and courted by a dashing, handsome nobleman who would steal my heart with just a glimpse. I would lie back and imagine myself the heroine, changing the plots to suit myself, but never changing my imaginary hero. He would be strong, masculine, and forceful, but kind, patient and humorous. He was tall with thick curly dark hair and wonderful blue eyes that could be seductive and knowing. And of course, my imaginary hero would become my husband. A jolt of recognition, those eyes I have seen them before, he was my hero from my dreams, always. Fear, excitement, and wonder bubbled to the surface. His voice pierced my body like a shot of adrenaline through my heart. It brought me back to the present.

'Stefan, this is your mess, deal with it.' His face was devoid of emotion.

My fear became anger, how dare he dismiss me, without consequence.

'He will not *deal* with me, and you will take me back home! I'm no wench or kitchen maid, my name is Lady Carolina Sackville, daughter of the Duke of Henage, and I demand you return me henceforth.' I stood my ground glaring up at him.

He roared with laughter and crouched down to my level. We were almost nose to nose.

'Prove it,' he said arrogantly.

I faced him head on, I was not going to cower down to him. 'I shouldn't have to prove anything; my word is enough.' However, my bravado was starting to slip. How could I prove it? It's not as if, in the seventeenth century, we carried a driver's licence or a passport.

'If you are Lady Carolina, let's hear your proof. Follow me. Stefan,' he barked, 'give her your cloak.' I felt Stefan, my kidnapper, drape his cloak over my back, and I tightened it closer around me, more for security than warmth. Picking up my forgotten shawl on the ground, I followed the tall stranger into a tent.

'Your majesty it appears as though we have a noble lady in our presence.'

I entered the tent. King Charles 1st was sitting bent over a small table, writing a letter, and his face was etched with worry as he turned around. I was literally struck dumb; I was standing in the presence of the King of England.

'Your Majesty.' I curtsied.

A line appeared between his brows as he sized me up and down. 'What's going on Nicholas?' he said.

Then it all fell into place. Lord Nicholas Trevilian, fourth Earl of Essex. Oh my, that's who Carolina Sackville was betrothed to. I chuckled to myself when I realised.

Nicholas's expression hardened. 'Laughing matter, is it?' He turned towards me irritated.

'No, I just find it extremely strange that today was the day I was supposed to meet you.'

Judging by the look on his face I'd taken him back slightly.

'I see,' he said, rather abruptly 'Well, anyone in the household would have known that.' His eyes narrowed towards me. 'Anyway, that's still not proof enough.' He said as he half turned towards his King.

'I am Lady Carolina, but those close to me call me Lina, and never in the presence of staff,' I said as I tugged the cloak tighter under my chin. 'I was born on the thirteenth of January, sixteen-twenty-two, I'm the only child to John and Ann Sackville.' He stood glaring, waiting patiently for me to finish.

'And we were supposed to marry four years ago, but because of this stupid bloody war, it was put on hold.' I concluded, feeling rather superior in my knowledge.

Nicholas rubbed his chin, looking mildly embarrassed about my outburst. Charles looked aghast at my comment, and I realised my mistake.

'I apologise sire, but I find myself in rather an unlikely and uncomfortable situation,' I burst out.

The King placed his quill down upon the paper, he leaned back into his chair and sighed heavily. He was silent for a time.

'I know it was bad judgment on Stefan's part,' he said at length, eyebrows raised, 'but pray madam what were you doing up wandering around the grounds past twilight?

'I was in an accident and unconscious for two days, when I woke, I couldn't get back to sleep. I find solace and comfort in our garden, especially since I helped plant them, hence the reason I'm dressed the way I am.' I started to ramble; I knew I wasn't going to get out of this predicament anytime soon. 'I'm twenty-four, considered an old maid, I had the privilege of having a tutor, my father taught me everything, even small sword fighting. I ride. I hate needlework and musical instrument playing. I hate conventional boring women's work. I love to read. I write. I…I…I—'

'Stop!' The king raised his hand.

Nicholas interrupted him. 'Enough prattling, woman, until I can send word to prove who you say are, you will remain under my protection, is that understood?'

'Why can't we turn back, damn you?' I shouted back at him.

In the heat of our bickering, Charles spoke up.

'Because, my dear Carolina, I have lost my fight with the parliamentarians and I'm currently on the run for my life. If we were to turn back, we would be caught, and you, my dear, will surely be put on trial with the rest of us, because if you are in the company of the king then you are a traitor to your country.'

'I see.' I felt a hollowing of my stomach at his words. 'How long will I have to remain?' I spoke.

'Until we get to where we are going.' Nicholas interrupted.

I met his eyes head on. 'And where is that!' A stab of pain hit my chest. I needed to be back near Debden Manor, so I could return to my own body and my own century.

'Never you mind.'

For the space of a moment, I wondered wildly what might happen to me if they took me far away. Would I ever get back? Tears of fear stung my eyes. I took in a couple of deep breaths and blinked several times. I didn't want these men to see my tears.

'Well, Lord Nicholas, it seems I'm in need of a dress since your man sliced it open,' I replied through gritted teeth.

'I have needle and thread; you can sew it yourself.' He walked towards the entrance of the tent. 'Follow, now.' He pointed to the floor by his feet.

My eyes popped like saucers and my mouth dropped. Unbelievable, how dare he speak to me like that?

'Why you—'

'Enough!' I was cut off mid-sentence by the king. 'I grow weary, please leave me,' he said as he waved us away with his hands. 'Lady Carolina, we have a long journey ahead and we can only travel through the night.'

He picked up the forgotten quill and dipped it into the gold ink pot. 'And Nicholas...' he spoke but never looked up. '...she is in your care, since she is meant, if proven, soon to be your wife,' he said firmly as he began writing again. We had been dismissed.

'Yes, sire.' Nicholas bowed his head.

My manners totally being forgotten by this point, it was my turn to interrupt the King.

'Your Majesty I'm terribly sorry, but pray where shall I sleep?' The king didn't even move, it was as if I were no longer in the room.

Nicholas spoke for him. 'With me, in my tent.' His churlish behaviour was not lost on me as I glared at him with an icy contempt. We took our leave of the King and, tight lipped, I followed Lord Nicholas Trevilian.

I could hear the small sounds of the camp's activity as we made our way towards his tent, and he lifted the flap aside so I could pass through.

'Well, I suppose this wouldn't be considered inappropriate, as we were supposed to be married next summer,' I quipped.

'You, my lady have too much to say for yourself. Ladies should be seen and not heard, so be quiet until you are spoken to.' The breeze stirred the lose wisps of hair around his face, and he brushed them back absentmindedly.

'I beg your pardon. Who do you think you are talking to?' The blood was pounding thickly in my ears.

'You. And I have been inconvenienced enough today, so please be quiet, I have letters to write and plans to make, and I don't need you prattling on,' his mouth was

46

set in a hard line, and I knew then that I had overstepped the mark.

He dropped the tent flap and it hit me on my behind. Sticking my nose in the air, I walked over to the makeshift cot and sat down, and he threw something in my direction, I looked up.

'Needle and thread to stitch your clothing.'

'Prick!'

'Beg your pardon?' He frowned at me.

'Nothing.'

*

We sat in silence. I was trying so hard to mend my dress but doing an awful job of it, while Nicholas sat at his desk and brooded over a letter he was writing.

I became increasingly conscious of his body, and every so often I would lift my eyes to his direction. I watched his fine, long hands write with a feather quill, seeing his torso twist slightly as he dipped it into a pot of ink and the graceful line of his neck and shoulders as he bent his head to continue writing.

Once or twice, I thought I saw his gaze linger on me in the same way, a sort of hesitant eagerness, but he quickly glanced away each time, hooding his eyes.

After what seemed like forever, he rose from his chair and walked over.

'Give me that,' he said curtly. 'I cannot concentrate with you huffing and puffing over this task.'

I gave him my dress; he took a seat next to me and I watched him closely as he stitched it up. He was astonishingly handsome, his beard was neatly trimmed, his cheek bones were high and wide, either side of a strong roman nose. He had the darkest, bluest eyes, and the thickest eyelashes, that I had ever seen. His hair was long, just touching the collar of his coat and tied with a leather strip at the nape. A few loose curls escaped as he bent his head, and my hand itched to tuck it behind his ear. I'd always thought the men in this century were short, but he must have stood at least six feet. This man was rude, brutish, and lacked good manners at times, nevertheless I was drawn to him.

'You must be Carolina because any serving maid would know how to stitch.' He raised a derisive eyebrow at me and continued with the task.

'Does that mean I can go back?' My spirits lifted slightly.

'No.'

'Why?' I demanded.

'Because I cannot be sure.' His eyes dropped back to his task. He continued to sew.

'How long will it take to reach where we are going?' He gave me a hard stare. I shift uncomfortably on the cot. After a moment my eyes rose slowly to his face. It seemed all too easy to get lost in his beautiful eyes, I think to myself. He cleared his throat to draw my attention. I felt the flush of heat on my cheeks, embarrassed at being caught staring at him.

'Sorry. What were you going to say?'

'Eight days or so, depending how long we can travel through the night without drawing too much attention.'

'What happens once we get there?'

He ground his teeth together and I could tell he was trying to keep his temper in check.

'You ask too many questions. Here's your dress, it's mended. He threw it at me and stood.

48

'Get some sleep, we have a long hard ride ahead of us.'

'Jerk,' I muttered under my breath.

His head turned back to me rather abruptly. 'What did you say?' he scowled.

'Nothing.' I forced a fake smile.

'Go to sleep.'

'Where pray tell, do you propose I sleep?' It was my turn to be churlish.

'On the cot,' he replied through gritted teeth.

'And you?' I raised a single brow.

'Next to you, because if you think I'm sleeping on the floor, madam, think again. Unless *you* prefer the hard floor or sleeping outside with the men.' His expression hardened while he waited for my answer.

'No.' I met his stare full on as I raised my chin in defiance.

'Thought not, now sleep.' He turned away, throwing the tent flap open in frustration, and stormed out.

The minutes passed and became an hour, my fear turned to wonder as I thought of Nicholas, and finally, blessedly, to exhaustion. Curled up in the furs, my eyes drifted closed.

*

The camp stirred to life, just as the sun set below the horizon. I had slept no more than a few hours. I shivered beneath the fur robes that Nicholas must have put over me. Not from the cold, but in anticipation of the long, arduous journey ahead. The tent flap was thrown up and Stefan walked in, which made me bury my head further beneath the covers. Hidden from view.

49

'My god Nicholas, she's a beauty! That glorious hair, the fairest I have ever seen. Those piercing green eyes, and that skin smooth, white like alabaster. I should love a taste of that little morsel. You're one lucky man.'

'What say you, my lady, am I your lucky man?'

The deep velvet baritone of Nicholas's voice had me peering out from under the covers, and I smiled from ear to ear.

Stefan turned his head over to where Nicholas was looking, and he turned a bright shade of pink.

'You might have warned me!' He looked aghast.

'And spoil the look on your face right now?' The rich sound of Nicholas's laugh warmed me inside.

'Please forgive me, my lady.' Stefan bowed his head in my direction.

'It's quite alright, nice to hear I'm pleasing to someone's eye.'

What the hell was the matter with me! I glanced over at Nicholas, he frowned making little slash lines across his brow, he held my gaze.

What must he think of me? I must remember not to be too forthcoming with my words.

Stefan coughed and cleared his throat.

'My Lord, the horses will be ready shortly,' he changed the subject quickly.

'Good, we will start our journey within the next hour, I want to wait until we are under the stars before we set off.'

'I'll ready the men, what about the tents?' Stefan questioned.

'Leave them,' Nicholas said as he waved a hand through the air. 'Tents will only bring attention, no matter how far we're in from the road.'

'What about the King?'

'He knows, I have told him he will have to rough it with the rest of us.' Nicholas said rather dryly.

Stefan left the tent and Nicholas rose from his desk; he turned his attention towards me, his dark blue eyes were serious and watchful. 'I'll leave you to sort yourself out, and I'll be back for you when it's time.' With that last remark he left the tent.

*

Two hours later the tents were dismantled. I stood in the empty encampment surrounded by darkness. I was told I would be riding between two guards. I suppose they thought this would stop me fleeing.

The world around me became an unreal blur of noise and dust and inner confusion. I didn't know where I was going, or where I was, or even *who*, I was. My whole world had changed, and my life was spinning out of control.

I thought of myself as a reasonably intelligent woman, but now at this moment I found myself longing, watching for a glimpse of Nicholas. I could think of nothing else. What was this growing fascination, this *obsession* with this man I hardly knew and the one that held me captive?

Was my mind conjuring up some hidden girlish, naïve delusion that he would sweep me off my feet like a knight in shining armour, declare his love like the stories I had read from my books or those from my dreams. I started to become angry as I tried to put the distasteful and silly thoughts aside.

We kept an easy pace so as not to tire the horses. Several times, Nicholas rode past me on his black destrier, clad in black from his tall boots to his cloak that draped around his powerful shoulders, it billowed out behind him as he rode. He was quite the most frighteningly, overpowering, handsome man that I had ever beheld, a deadly stranger hellbent on dragging me across England, away from my home and further away from getting back to my own time.

Not quite sure how long we had been riding for, having no watch or phone was like losing an extension of my right arm. The men picked up the pace and rode the horses harder as the sun started to peek out over the horizon. We steered clear of the main roads, and I had no sense of where we were. The sun was almost up, the horses began to slow as we turned off from the makeshift path and trotted deeper into the forest.

'Halt, we will camp here for the day, and remember, be quiet and stay low, last thing we need is undue attention,' I heard Nicholas shout from the front.

The men started to make camp as the dawning sun burst forth upon the forest, sending long streams of light through the gaps of the trees, but not quite enough warmth to banish the morning chill. Looking up through the trees I could just see the morning sky, it was bathed in spectacular hues of pinks and the last dark grey-blue edges of the night.

Rather than sit idle, I decided to see to the care of my horse, and after taking of her bridle and reins I started to unbuckle the saddle from underneath, I struggled a little with the heaviness of it, until unseen hands appeared from behind me.

'Here let me help,' came the deep rumbling voice of Nicholas.

'I can manage.' My voice held a note of defiance.

'You are tired.'

'So are the rest of the men.'

My lack of height was a hindrance, I couldn't quite get the lift of the saddle off my horses back.

'The men are hardened to these conditions, you are not.' He tried to brush me aside.

'Because I'm a woman, is that what you mean?' I exploded. I knew I was being rather obstinate, but to be honest I was too tired to care.

'Sheathe your claws, Lady Sackville, you have made your point.'

'I'm not making any sort of point.'

'Are you trying to pick a fight my lady?' he sighed with exasperation.

'No, I'm sorry, I'm not trying to pick a fight, I'm just very tired.'

I took a deep breath in and exhaled sharply. What I really wanted to say was I'm fiercely independent and I can look after myself. But I knew deep down this was not so.

'It was a long night, over yonder there is a pile of furs, take a few and lay your head,' he spoke casually enough. Then he pointed to where the furs lay.

'I have my horse to rub down.'

I saw his fingers clench and tighten. His knuckles stood out white against his sun-bronzed skin, and I knew I was pushing his patience.

'I'll get one of my men to do that.' He puffed out a large amount of breath and closed his eyes. Briefly.

'They'll be pleased with the extra work I bring them.' I knew I was being rude and childish, but I couldn't help myself.

'They will do as I ask.' His change of tone stopped me in my tracks. I knew I was fighting a losing battle, but I was too exhausted to argue any further. I just had enough energy to make it over to the trees.

My arms ladened with the furs I found a nice, secluded spot, just far enough away, but still close enough for security and peace of mind. I placed a thick fur pelt on the floor over a soft mound of moss and I lay down with my back towards the trees, pulling the other pelt over my body. I placed my arm under my head for support and I slowly drifted off to sleep, whilst listening to the soft sounds of nature and the bustle of the men making camp.

*

'Why is my daughter still attached to this machine?' My mother's voice came through crisp and clear.

'We just want to keep monitoring Caroline.'

'She has been like this for two days now, will she wake up?'

'She is well, but we are baffled, the only sign is the bump on her head, but the scans have come back clear, Caroline will wake up when she is ready.'

'What can cause this, doctor?'

'We really don't know. Caroline seems to be in a state of paralysis, her body is asleep, but her mind is awake.'

'So, she can she hear us?'

'MUM?' I sat up, confused and totally unfamiliar with my surroundings, and disturbed the person next to me.

'My lady, are you well?' Nicholas's concerned blue eyes rested on my face.

The fog of sleep started to clear; Then I remembered where and who I was.

'I thought I was back home at Copped Hall asleep under the shade of our yew trees, and I thought someone was calling me.' How could I tell him it was my Mum from the future?'

'Did you know that's your mother's favourite place to sit when she used to visit? I would often read her favourite sonnet by William Shakespeare.' A blurred memory became suddenly clear.

'The Phoenix and the Turtle,' we both said in unison. Nicholas stood abruptly; I was taken back in surprise.

'What's wrong?' I questioned.

'Lady Sackville, my apologies, you are who you say you are.' He bowed his head.

'Of course, I would not lie,' I said, as recognition dawned over his face. I could see the mountain of guilt build up behind his eyes.

He ran his hand through his thick hair.

'Your parents will never forgive me,' he said, as he started to pace back and forth in agitation.

'I'm sure they will understand. Does that mean you can take me back now?' I said hopeful.

He stopped pacing; his throat worked as he swallowed.

'No, Lady Sackville.'

'Please, we are past the formalities, it's just Lina.'

His eyes softened as he glanced at me.

'Our town of Essex is for parliament all the way, and if I turn back and anyone of my uncle's men get a whiff I will be arrested, they will torture the information out of me as to where the King is fleeing to, and I cannot take that risk, do you understand.'

My heart lifted 'Oh, well then, looks like I'm stuck with you for a time,' I said jokingly.

His eyes flickered quickly to my face; I think he was unsure how to take my last remark. I gave him an impertinent side-ways smile and he relaxed.

Insofar as wanting to go back to my own time, I was secretly glad I was still going with him because, if truth be told, I wanted to be near him. The only way I could describe this pull he had on me was that it felt like I had a magical rope that was tied to my waist, and it kept pulling me closer and closer towards him every day I spent in his company.

'Please excuse me, Mistress Lina.' He inclined his head and left me sitting there wondering what my fate would be now. My eyes never left him as he walked towards the King and Stefan, he must have said something to the King, because Charles glanced over at me and nodded in my general direction.

I was trying to busy myself with folding the fur covers when I heard the leaves crunch behind me. I turned around and found Stefan hovering. He swept me a bow, it was so low it made his ponytail flop over the top of his head and hang over his forehead.

'My lady,' he said, 'I would sincerely like to apologise for the misunderstanding I brought upon you, I do hope in time you can forgive me.'

'You can stand now, Stefan,' I said, as I crossed my arms over my chest and waited for him to straighten himself up.

'I really do not know what else to say, my lady, but I will forever be in your debt.' His face reddened with deep embarrassment.

'Please do not worry yourself, I understand where you were coming from, I suppose it was strange finding me snooping in the church past midnight.'

'Snooping?' He gave me a blank look.

'I meant eavesdropping,' I corrected myself and went back to the task of folding the fur covers. I must try to remember not to throw twenty-first century words into my conversations.

'Anyway, I accept your apology, Stefan, no harm was intended.'

'Thank you, my lady.'

A young boy, no more than sixteen, hung back slightly behind Stefan, and he cleared his throat. 'Excuse me, my lady, Stefan,' he coughed nervously into his hand.

'What is it, Alec?' Stefan asked.

'The King has requested the pleasure of my lady's company.' He smiled shyly.

Damn, that can't be good, can it? I turned my head towards Stefan and curtsied.

'I take my leave off you now, sir,' I said as Stefan gave me yet another bow.

'Good day to you, my lady.'

I walked past the bereft young man, and followed the young boy called Alec towards the King. I curtsied. 'Your Majesty.'

'Please sit, Mistress Carolina.' He gestured with his hand for me to join him.

I sat down opposite the king, on the fur covers that had been laid upon the grass. I noticed how much he had changed over the last couple of days, he looked old and tired, with the weight of the world upon his shoulders. I busied myself with straightening my dress as I waited for him to speak.

'Would you care to sup with me?' his kind but wary eyes searched my face.

'It would be a pleasure, your highness, thank you.'

Alec gave the king, then me, a plate of food. I waited for the King to eat first.

'Please eat, do not mind me,' he said, as I watched him pick the food up with his hands.

Which would this be, breakfast or evening meal?

I thought, and not before time. I was ravenous.

Our food consisted of stringy fowl and a slab of stale bread, not the best fare, but when you're hungry anything tastes good.

'I understand from Nicholas that you are whom you say,' he looked kindly up at me.

I put my hand over my mouth 'Yes, sire,' I mumbled with a mouth full of food. I swallowed it down quickly, before his next question. It was quite dry, and the food lodged in my throat, I coughed and patted my chest. The king nodded to the boy. Alec soon passed me some wine to wash it down with.

'This puts us in quite a predicament, your reputation has been compromised,' he said, as the young lad passed him some wine. He took a sip and passed it back.

'Once all is explained to my parents, I'm sure it will be fine,' I said faintly.

'If you were my daughter, I would not accept any apology from Lord Trevilian, he has taken you from your home, and put you in the most unsuitable position.'

He broke off a piece of the bread and popped it into his mouth, chewed it thoughtfully for several seconds and swallowed the dry bread. He gestured to the boy for more wine.

'Well, technically he didn't take me.' I faltered as he eyed me over the brim of the cup.

'I mean to say, sire, he did not take me personally. It was his man,' I corrected.

'And yet, it was *his* man and because of this, you both shall be wed much sooner than planned,' he said finally.

'Pardon? It's too soon sire. We know nothing about each other. We have not had a proper courtship and, and…' I was struggling to find the words, as I found myself in this unsettling new predicament.

'Silence.' He put his available hand up to stop my tirade.

'I have a mind for a wedding, and that's my final order, as your king.' His mouth set in a hard line, and I knew there would be no persuading him. Yes, I was extremely attracted to Nicholas, but not enough to be his wife, maybe the other me would have been happy, but then the other me wouldn't have gone walking around the grounds past midnight and got herself in this fine mess.

Our food finished, and plates cleared away, I sat staring into the flickering flames of the fire. The red and gold colours danced before my eyes, it was hypnotic, and my eyes started to feel heavy. The king turned and started a conversation with one of his men, and I knew then I was being dismissed.

'May I take my leave now, sire?'

He nodded. 'Yes, go rest your head for a time, because it won't be long before we start on our journey again.'

I took my leave of the king and walked over to my spot under the ash trees. I was unable to go back to sleep, so I sat in a daydream, thinking about my life now. *Would I ever go back to my own time?* Or was I here to stay, and if so, for what purpose? Maybe I was in a dream where my body was still asleep, and my mind had conjured up some alternate reality.

I picked up a sharp twig and stabbed my finger. 'Ouch, damn!' I said aloud. Blood. Hmm, and it hurt. No, seems real enough to me I thought, as I sucked on my finger to stop the blood. Surely if I were in a dream that wouldn't have hurt.

The snap of a twig made me look up. Nicholas was making his way towards me.

'What are you doing?' he asked as he took a seat next to me.

I quickly flung the stick away. 'Nothing,' I said, and wiped my finger on my dress.

'So, the king told you?'

'Yes, he has made it quite clear.' I blinked several times as I could feel tears welling in my eyes.

'I'm sorry if this displeases you.' The muscle in his jaw twitched as he saw my unshed tears.

'No,' I said shyly. 'This does not displease me, but we hardly know each other, and it feels like I have been thrust upon you since the day you lost your brother.' I lied; how could I tell him the real reason for my sorrow? If I married him, then it would be even longer before I got back to Debden Manor, to my own time and the thought of never seeing my family again would break my heart.

He spoke and broke me from my thoughts.

'Trust me Lina if I did not want to marry you I would not,' he assured me.

Was he feeling the same towards me as I him?

How can love be instant? I'd also thought love at first sight was impossible, but here and now I know this isn't so.

I was a little taken back as Nicholas picked up my hand and placed a kiss upon it. His mouth was soft, and his beard tickled the tips of my fingers. At this moment I secretly wished he would brush his lips against mine.

Suddenly, another image flashed in my mind of me kissing Mr. Thorn in the grounds of Debden Manor, just before I was hit on the head.

Why would the image of Mr. Thorn pop up now? I was clearly more confused now than I had been before.

The rich baritone of his voice broke my spell, and I was drawn back to the present.

'Sorry, you were saying?' My mouth drew back in a smile.

'I said when we reach Barnwell, we will take up the residence of Duke and Duchess of Gloucester, both loyal to the crown. I have sent word ahead and they will be expecting our arrival in a few days, hence forth you will have the comforts of a bed.' He laid his hand on my shoulder for a moment, then he removed it rather quickly, forgetting his place, though it seemed to bother him more than me.

'Finally, the comforts of a home,' I said, trying to appear bright and cheery, 'and no more stringy fowl and stale bread.' But the worry must have been clear.

There was a short silence which was broken when he sighed and began to talk. His voice held a calm assurance as he squeezed my hand, his touch seemed to soothe my worries.

'We will be married at All Saints Chancel, four days from now.'

His touch worked on me, and I felt instantly better, if still apprehensive.

'Where's Barnwell?' I asked in curiosity.

I drew my legs up to my chest and wrapped my arms around them. I perched my chin on my knees and raised my eyes towards him. Nicolas's eyes turned dark, and he swallowed a few times before he answered me.

'Just south of Oundle, beautiful little village.' His voice trailed off as his face took on a vacant look.

'I had many happy times growing up there.'

Nicholas had let his frosty exterior slip, and I got a glimpse of the man he used to be before this godawful war. He had a gentleness about him, his frown disappeared, and his mouth softened with a knowing smile, but it was fleeting.

'Try to get some sleep, Lina. You will need your energy for the hard ride ahead.' He dropped my hand. 'I will wake you when it's time to leave. His frosty appearance was back. He stood, and I watched him make his way towards Stefan.

We must have stayed longer because when I woke, I was surrounded by darkness. I lay for a time, looking up at the night. The sky was ambiguous, the clouds covered the moon and stars, trapping the light as it scattered towards the earth. I could hear the men in the distance, quietly preparing the horses for the next stage of our journey, and found it remarkable they could do this task, because each man could see no further than the nose in front of them. Orders were relayed in murmurs, from man to man, not shouted. The horses, still hobbled, would occasionally whicker, but apart from that, the dusk just held the sounds of the wildlife that came awake at this hour.

4

Barnwell

The rest of the journey to Barnwell passed without incident, if you consider riding thirty or so miles through forest and over rough terrain. In the distance I could just make out the Village of Barnwell, and the huge bulk of the manor house that stood, looming over the village atop a cliff with a broad bluff. At the bottom of the bluff, I could just make out the river, where it meandered from side to side.

Our surroundings were no longer quiet, there were people scattered about; poorly dressed and going about their normal routines, they moved across to the side of the road to let us pass. Nicholas and the King seemed to be oblivious to their hardship, poor, starving, and dirty. No wonder this country was at war.

Our horses clattered into the courtyard of Barnwell Manor. The estate was huge, it looked to be sitting on a few thousand acres, most probably farmed by the local villagers, and overseen by the duke.

Upon our arrival we were welcomed personally by the Duke and Duchesses of Gloucester. I stood slightly apart to watch as they greeted their unexpected guests.

Stefan took his leave, following the grounds man round the back of the house with the rest of Nicholas's men, whilst the King walked into the house with the duke, both deep in conversation.

Nicholas turned, took my hand, and brought me to his side.

'Lady Carolina Sackville, may I present Elizabeth Montague, my Aunt. Nicholas's expression changed, his features softened, as he looked towards his aunt, and I knew she was loved very much by him.

I raised my chin up to her face as she was much taller than I. Lady Elizabeth was beautiful. She had brown hair with threads of silver here and there, and the same blue eyes as Nicholas. She must be a good twenty years older, but barely a wrinkle touched her smooth skin. Her dress was dark blue velvet, and she wore diamonds and sapphires that twinkled around her neck and on her ears.

I smiled rather awkwardly at her, feeling awfully under-dressed in my stitched-up gown, my hair was a mess of knotty curls, and my face was dry and dusty from the ride up here. I must have looked a sight. The Duchess took in my dishevelled appearance, her eyes popped wide, and her mouth dropped open. Then a steel gaze locked onto Nicholas. She frowned and held up her hand.

'Stop talking, Nicholas,' she said somewhat sternly. She walked forward and took my hands.

'It's just Beth,' she said. Her kind eyes instantly made me feel at ease. 'You, sir should be ashamed of yourself, look at the state of her.' She sighed in disappointment.

'You should have sent one of your men out to get her decent travelling clothes, and why is your affianced travelling with you in the first place? You were only meant to meet her Nicholas, not take her!'

It was quite amusing watching Nicholas shift from one foot to the other, like a little boy caught doing something he shouldn't have, and for the first time he was lost for words. Nicholas with tight lips glared at his aunt. I think this was the first time he had been on the receiving end of his aunt's fury.

'You need not look like that, my boy.' She wagged her finger towards him. 'Don't forget, Nicholas, your mother and I correspond quite regularly.' She paused, crossing her arms across her chest. 'Well, I'm waiting,' she said tartly.

'For what, Aunt?' Nicholas's face took on an air of disbelief as though he were affronted by his aunt's comments. 'And let me remind everyone here whose fault it was in the first place.' His eyes shifted towards me.

'Don't bring me into this!' I jumped to my defence. Beth's face became stern as she frowned at her nephew. He had just dug himself a greater hole by his last comment and watching them square off at each other was like watching two bulls ready to lock horns. Nicholas towered above her, but she showed no fear and did not back down.

'Anyway, it has worked out for the best, we are to be married the day after the morrow,' he said, rather bristly.

Clearing my throat, I tried my best to break the uncomfortable exchange. The air around me was thick and tense and all I wanted to do was to get out of the courtyard and into a nice hot bath.

'Excuse me, Beth.' I smiled briefly at her as I interrupted their standoff. 'I'm extremely tired, very dirty, and in need of a bath and some refreshment.'

Nicholas looked over to me with relief in his eyes, and a look of gratitude passed between us.

Beth glared daggers at Nicholas and then turned her full attention to me.

'I'm so sorry, my dear Carolina, I'm forgetting my manners. Yes, you must be famished and in need of a good scrubbing.'

'Please, Beth, call me Lina,' I said looking down at my torn dress. My skin crawled, my scalp itched, and my teeth felt positively awful. The bath couldn't come any quicker.

Her expression softened. 'Very well then, Lina, please come with me and we shall draw you a nice hot bath and get you some decent clothes.'

I looked behind at Nicholas as we started to walk away.

'Never you mind about him.' She looked over her shoulder at him. 'Nicholas, the men will be in your uncle's study.'

Her fierce expression was back when she addressed her nephew, and, like an obedient little boy. Nicholas followed until we parted ways.

'Your parents must have been extremely worried, dear.' Beth took my hand and placed it in the crook of her arm, steering me away from Nicholas's direction.

'Yes, I imagine they were. Mother would have been beside herself, and knowing what my father's like he would have had search parties out looking for me,' I said as we ascended the stairs.

'How many days has it been?' she said as she patted my hand. I turned my head slightly towards her.

'Five, and I just hope my father understands.'

Beth scowled and blew out a large breath and shook her head.

'Well, my dear, the wedding will soften some of the blow, but I would not like to be in Nicholas's shoes when you do eventually go back home. Not only will he have your father to deal with, but he will also have his mother's wrath.' Her eyebrows all but disappeared into her hairline with her last comment.

We reached the top of the stairs and walked down a long corridor with family portraits hung on either side of the walls. She stopped at one. It was of two little boys sitting in a garden with a large dog.

'That was Christopher and Nicholas when they were boys.' Her eyes swam with unshed tears. 'This was painted here, not long before Christopher died.'

I leaned in further to get a closer look.

'Oh my, they look identical, they could have passed for twins!'

'Yes, they were so much alike, but quite different characters. Nicholas was always deep in thought, and you never knew what he was thinking, he always kept his emotions buried deep. Still the same really, while Christopher.'

Her voice trailed off for a few second as if she were remembering, she had a dreamy smile on her face, but it didn't quite match her sad eyes.

'Christopher wore his heart on his sleeve, he never stopped smiling. That was true of them both really, but when Christopher died Nicholas and my sister-in-law never really recovered.' She took a deep measured breath and exhaled slowly, her lips tightly closed as she stared at the picture.

A moment passed before she spoke again.

'Well, none of us has really. His death was so sudden and not long after my dear brother died.'

She sniffed and dabbed her eyes at the corners with her fingertips. My heart broke just a little for Beth, she truly felt like these were her boys too. I wondered if Beth and Edward had children of their own. As there were no other portraits of small children. I smiled affectionately at her and placed my hand on her arm. I wasn't sure if it was more for her comfort or mine. I just needed some physical touch. I longed so much for my own parents and my life before this mess.

'Look at me getting all sentimental.' She tutted and patted her chest, 'I'm so sorry dear Lina, you must be eager to get those rotten clothes and boots off.' She drew me away from the picture gallery and led me further down the corridor.

'Yes, very eager,' I said.

I was mentally juggling all the information she had just told me about Nicholas and his brother. Maybe that was why I had never seen him smile, not properly anyway, just half smiles that never reached his eyes.

*

Beth settled me nicely in one of the guest bedrooms, The room was light and airy, and decorated in soft blues quite different from the heavy colours of the present day.

I was surrounded by little trinkets and mementos, which sat neatly on Elizabethan style furniture, filled with cloth coverings to protect it from the dust and embers from the open fireplace. A beautiful delicate rug lay on the dark polished wood secretly waiting for the unsuspecting person to slide beneath it.

'I hope you will find this room comfortable, my dear.'

Beth walked over to the curtains and pulled them back. Sunlight streamed through the little obscure glass windows that where leaded with a triangle pattern. Small motes of dust whizzed off the material and floated above Beth's head before finally settling on the floor.

'This room rarely gets used; it is my sisters-in-law's room, when she has a care to visit.'

'Does she not visit much?' I asked.

'From time to time, but not as often as I would like.' There was a slight hitch in her voice, and I could tell she was trying to keep her emotions in check.

'However,' she cleared her throat and continued. 'I could say the same, I don't visit her often either,'

My thoughts drifted away for a few moments, thinking of my sister Claire and my niece and nephew. I too had that same problem, I didn't visit them often enough, even though they were only in the next village.

I snapped myself out of my thoughts and turned my attention back to Beth.

'So, you are as bad as each other.' I joked trying to lighten the mood.

'Pish.' She waved her hand in the air and placed the other on her hip. 'Don't mind me, I tend to get nostalgic and a bit teary when I speak about my family.'

She walked towards me.

'Anyway, how do you like the room?' she exclaimed going back to her cheerful manner.

'It's perfect, Beth, thank you so much, and I genuinely appreciate your kindness.'

'Oh, think nothing of it.'

She put her arms around me and rubbed her hands on my back for comfort. I breathed in her rose scent and closed my eyes. The feeling of sorrow washed through my body like a wave crashing onto rocks. I held onto Beth like my life depended on it. My throat tightened as I went to speak, but I couldn't find the words. Beth must have sensed my feelings because she pulled back and looked meaningfully into my eyes. My vision blurred through unshed tears.

'I just cannot believe what my nephew has put you though.'

She stepped back slightly and rubbed my arms softly as a mother would her child.

I finally found the words to speak. 'I'm fine, truly. No harm done,' I said with as much sincerity as I could muster. I wiped the tears away with the back of my hand.

'You, my dear are being far too kind towards him.

Her brow furrowed in thought and her tone was a little distracted.

'Honestly, Beth, it's all good. Anyway, there is no point dwelling, what's done is done.

Beth placed her hands on my cheeks. 'Wise words for someone so young.' She dropped her hands from my face and walked towards the door. Stopping, she gazed over her shoulder at me. 'I'll send up one of our maids to help you shortly, now rest.'

'Thank you.'

'Think nothing of it, my dear.' Then she disappeared through the doorway in a flurry of blue velvet and the last lingering traces of her rose perfume.

*

Sometime later I lay in a copper bath with cotton linens draped inside. I asked the maid why they were in there.

'The copper's cold my lady and it would quickly turn the water chilly,' she said with a puzzled expression. 'Do you not do this in your home then?' she asked.

'Umm, of course.' Little did she know how we washed in the twenty-first century, forgetting for a moment of how I bathed as Carolina.

'I shan't be long, my lady I'll just go fetch some more hot water for you.'

I heard the door shut as I leaned back in the tub. I closed my eyes and marveled at the sheer luxury of the warm water as it seeped through my aching limbs.

The chamber door opened, and the maid walked back in bringing the hot water, she poured it into the tub. The heat from the water slowly travelled up from the tip of my toes to my breasts. I sighed with pure pleasure.

'Do you need help washing, my lady?' she asked.

Really. Don't the rich wash themselves?

'No thank you,' I declined her offer.

'I'll take my leave now, my lady, if you need anything else pull the cord to your left near the fire and I shall return quick as you like.'

'Thank you, but I'm fine for the moment.'
She picked up my dirty, torn clothes, curtsied, and walked out of the room and left me to my own devices.

Picking up a small torn cotton cloth and the crudely mis-shaped lavender bar of soap, I lathered the contents into the cloth and slowly washed away the filth from the last five days of traveling. Not as much lather as I would have had from a sponge, but enough to clean myself. It was the trivial things we take for granted: shampoo, conditioner, toilet paper and a toothbrush, that I so desperately needed right now.

By the time I had finished, my water was grey. Pulling the cord next to me I waited 'til my chamber maid appeared.

'My lady.'

'Please, just call me Carolina,' I said.

She frowned at my suggestion. 'That would not be proper my lady, I would be dismissed. I raised my eyes towards the ceiling.

'Have you finished now, my lady?' she questioned.

'Yes, I have thank-you.'

She walked over to the wardrobe and took out a soft blue dressing robe. I stepped out of the bath, and she placed the robe around my shoulders.

'Lady Elizabeth has suggested you take a nap, so you will be nice and refreshed for sup tonight.'

She tried to gather the robe around me, but I shook my head and brushed her hand away slightly.

'That's quite alright,' I said as I gathered it close and tied the belt myself.

I was pleased I didn't have to go back downstairs; I was so tired and making idle chit chat was the last thing I wanted.

'Tell Lady Elizabeth thank you, and what time do we dine tonight?' I asked curiously.

'I shall come and get you ready my lady, no need to worry. I've got some broth and bread for you to eat before you nap.'

'Food. Thank god,' I muttered under my breath; she must had heard me because there was a small gasp that escaped her lips. I turned to her direction and was astonished to find a rather shocked expression on her face.

'Please, my lady do not take the lord's name in vain,' she said rather too curtly for my liking. Totally forgetting for a moment how religious this century was, but to be quite honest I was too exhausted to care.

I sat at the little table and chair by the window whilst I watched her set out the cutlery. She placed the bowl of broth on the table and poured the delicate rose wine.

The broth and bread were so tasty they were gone in minutes, and with the comfort of warmth from the wine, and fullness in my tummy from the broth, I felt wonderful. I uttered no protest as she turned down the bed covers; never had I seen anything so tempting.

'Is there anything else I can do for you, my lady?' she said.

'No, thank you, that would be all.'

'I'll be up to wake you for sup,' she said as she took her leave, but not before curtseying and bobbing her head in my general direction.

Snuggling down on the pile of pillows, I felt myself slowly start to drift away.

A haze of moving images that started to become clear.

'Please don't take her from me,' said Nicholas.

Was he talking to me? I was standing somewhere unfamiliar, a large field surrounded by hundreds of different flowers, the air was balmy, and the sun shone through pink clouds. I was distracted by Nicholas's voice.

'If you take her, how will I find her?' *Who was Nicholas talking to?*

An unseen voice spoke behind me.

'That's the game, Nicholas you know the rules. Sometimes you do and sometimes you don't.'

'Please let me say one last goodbye,' said Nicholas.

'Make it quick.'

Then the third layer of sleep hit me, the nothingness, just a black empty void of a dreamless existence.

*

'My lady, my lady, it's time to rise!'

I opened one eye reluctantly, just far enough to see the little maid as she loomed over me; for the first time in five days I had slept so soundly I couldn't remember for the moment, who I was, much less where.

'My lady, come now you must get up, you are soon to sup, and I have got to get you ready.'

I tried to nestle back into the warmth of the quilts, but her voice was still pestering me to get up.

Climbing out of bed with the quilt around my shoulders I headed towards the newly lit fire, and watched closely as the maid laid out the garments ready for me to put on.

I dropped the quilt from my shoulders and removed my nightgown; I felt a little uncomfortable while I stood naked waiting for her to dress me.

'What's your name,' I asked as she busily picked up my first garment.

'Clara, my lady,'

'How old are you, Clara?'

'I'm eighteen, my lady.'

So young, and most probably married by now, I thought to myself.

She dressed me from head to toe, starting with the white linen shift dress and white silk stockings, which were tied with an emerald-green ribbon at my thighs. On went the corset, bum roll, which was followed by two petticoats, the first one was a plain soft cotton and the second, a contrasting silk embroidered one.

My skirt was emerald-green satin, which Clara looped up at the side to reveal the embroidered petticoat underneath, then the matching green bodice, which was long waisted and dipped to the front, the neckline was straight and extremely low and it just about covered my nipples, which slowly rose up towards my shoulders. I felt quite exposed until she placed the collar and kerchief around my neck. On went the sleeves, they were full, slashed, and gathered into two puffs by a ribbon just above my elbow. *It won't be long before these clothes will be outlawed. No colours, just black and greys with white collars and cuffs. The puritan way.* I thought to myself.

On my feet I had matching satin slippers, a little pinched, but better than the heavy leather boots that I had been wearing. Lastly my hair, which fell in curls halfway down my back. Clara gathered the top part of my hair and braided it into bun on the crown of my head. Then she took the metal curling tongs from the fire and started to curl the sides and back of my hair into tight ringlets, which were left down to frame my face. She stood back to survey her handiwork with satisfaction.

'You look beautiful my lady; the green makes your eyes even brighter.'

'Thank you,' I said, as I turned to look at myself in the full-length mirror behind me.

Oh my, is that truly me? It was the first time I had seen myself since I woke up on the dusty road outside Debden Manor. Our features were remarkably similar.

The vision of Lady Carolina Sackville danced enchantingly before my eyes. I had an incredibly lovely face, with green eyes, porcelain skin, high cheek bones, perfectly formed eyebrow arches and soft smiling pink lips. Even though my colouring was different it still looked a little like me, but what struck me as odd was my eyes were still the same; almond shaped, with a slight slant at the ends. I touched my face in wonder but what struck me as odd, was the knowledge, the comfort, the acceptance. Carolina was no longer a stranger, she was me.

Following Clara out of the bedchamber and down the stairs, I seemed to glide effortlessly towards my Prince Charming and fairy godparents, smiling at the irony of my thoughts.

I walked into the Duke of Gloucester's library as the butler announced my arrival: 'Lady Sackville, your graces.'

All heads turned in my direction but I was more interested in the room. It was lined on two sides with bookcases, every shelf was crammed to bursting point. Ancient volumes, and hundreds of hand-sewn manuscripts, ledgers, worn leather bibles, and much more. The third wall was equipped with floor to ceiling windows, with French doors that led out to a large, railed-off patio. There were two large sofas opposite one another under the window, and a large, marble coffee table with gold gilded legs. On the fourth wall there was a large inglenook fireplace, and four armchairs which sat strategically around an Afghan rug which was center point of the hearth.

My eyes instantly found Nicholas, that familiar tingling excitement fluttered around in my stomach.

His eyes widened in surprise and pleasure, his Adam's apple moved up and down beneath his jabot. He was dressed in a snowy white linen shirt, with his trademark black doublet and breeches. God, he took my breath away.

I hadn't realised I had been holding my breath, until Elizabeth stood from one of the chairs.

'My dear Lina, you look absolutely ravishing, what say you, Nicholas?' She glanced over at Nicholas with a mischievous twinkle in her eye. His eyes seemed to devour me.

'Aunt, she looks good enough to eat,' he said.

My stomach turned in pleasure. I glanced up at him shyly under my winged lashes. My eyes half hidden. I didn't want to show him too much of the emotions he held over me.

With that remark Beth chuckled. 'Come, come, my dear, let me introduce my husband.' she took my hand and walked me towards the men. I curtsied to Charles.

'Carolina this is my husband Edward.'

I bowed my head and bobbed just a little.

'It's a pleasure to meet you, sir and thank you for your hospitality,' I said politely.

'The pleasure is all mine.'

Edward the Duke of Gloucester took my hand and placed a kiss upon it.

'Nicholas, what a lucky man you are, what a beauty you have.'

My cheeks flushed warm as the awkwardness crept into my face. The duke chuckled at my discomfort. I turned towards Charles.

'Your Grace.' I curtsied again, and inclined my head.

'Beautiful as ever, even in your finery.' He took my hand and kissed the back of it.

'Thank you, sire.'

Again bowing my head and curtsying.

Don't they ever get fed up with all this stuff and nonsense?.

Lastly, my attention was on Nicholas. He took my hand and held my gaze as no words were spoken between us. He kissed the back of my hand, but he lingered longer than was necessary.

Our silence was interrupted as the door opened and the footman announced that dinner was served. Elizabeth was in between her husband and Charles as they walked towards the dining room engaged in idle chit chat.

Nicholas held his arm out for me.

'Lina?' I put my hand through the crook of his offered arm, and we followed behind.

I felt his warm breath on my neck before he even spoke. He whispered into my into ear. 'There are no words to describe how you look.'

My breath coming a little short as I turned to look at him, our lips were almost touching. I couldn't help but stare at them. 'Why thank you, sir.'

I wanted so desperately to taste him. We were both lost in our own little world until we reached the dining room. We walked over to the table, but before Nicholas could pull out the chair for me, I pulled it out myself and sat down. Beth looked on in horror. Oops, I had made the biggest faux pas.

The food on the table consisted of roast chicken, sausage and raisin rolled in pastry, a selection of cheeses, with bread, and a game pie with leek and ginger. Wine was poured into my glass, I pick it up and drank it down.

'Mmm, that's so good, I needed that.'

All eyes turned to me and I realised my second mistake.

'So sorry, I'm rather thirsty,' I said with a lopsided grin. Nicholas chuckled and the conversation resumed.

The wine was sweet and quite strong, but enough to quench my thirst and after my third my head felt slightly giddy. Our food was served, I picked up my fork and looked at it with curiosity; it had only two prongs.

'Is everything okay, Lina?' Beth said as I pushed the fork into a piece of chicken.

'Yes, everything is fine, thank you Beth.' I popped it into my mouth. Mmm, so moist and tender, nothing like the chicken I usually buy from the hot food counter in Sainsbury's. I put another bit into my mouth and savored the flavour.

Every so often I saw Nicholas glance my way, I smiled at him, but he didn't reciprocate, he just looked at me, then carried on with his discussion.

'Charles, have you heard from Queen Henrietta-Maria?' Beth asked.

'Yes, my dear heart has fled to France and we have had word that she just made it through the channel, with Essex at her heels.'

Beth's hand flew to her neck. 'Oh my, that's terrible Charles. Any news from the young Prince of Wales?'

'He has fled with Buckingham, and hopefully he made the ship before it set sail.' He gave a huge sigh and picked up his wine and sipped it gracefully.

'Essex.' I looked up at Nicholas. 'Are you not the Earl of Essex?'

'Unfortunately not, madam, my uncle, Robert Deveraux is the third Earl of Essex and he deems me a traitor for siding with the King.' He carried on eating, and not once did his face show any sign of emotion towards his uncle.

'My brother is an idiot.' Beth sighed and put her hand on Nicholas's arm. 'This stupid war has put families against families, and uncles against nephews. When will it end?' she said, and loosened her hand from Nicholas's arm and went back to eating.

My gaze was directed towards the king. 'When you realise your people need a voice, especially the poor,' I said without thinking.

The room fell silent. All but the clank of Beth's fork on her plate could be heard through the silence. Nicholas glared daggers at me. I had committed the worst offence ever.

'Apologies for the woman, sire, they tend to speak without thinking,' said Edward. The duke glared at his wife, and Beth apologised to Charles. Nicholas, with venom in his eyes, expected me to do the same, which in my opinion was totally unnecessary.

'I apologise, sire, it's the wine talking.'

Forgetting for just a moment that woman are only second-class citizens and still such a long way to go before we got our voice.

'Do you think I want this war?' The King addressed me. I shook my head.

'People seem to forget what I have done for this country,' he said as his face twisted in pain.

Stupid man, I thought to myself. He has no concept of what he has done. Eleven years he has reigned and all he has done is levy the taxes, either for his wars or to refill his empty coffers when he became bankrupt. I turned towards Nicholas; I changed the subject quick.

'Will your mother be safe?' I asked.

'Yes, my mother is safe, just as long as she pretends to side with my uncle,' said Nicholas through a clenched jaw.

'Does he visit the estate much?'

'Luckily, no.'

I knew he was angry at me, because his responses were short and clipped and the atmosphere round the table was stifling.

'That's enough talk of politics and waring families.' Edward cleared his throat. 'So, Carolina are you looking forward to your wedding tomorrow?'

Edward couldn't have picked more of a delicate subject to hit upon. I hesitated, as no words came to mind.

'Of course she is Edward, what a silly question.' Beth answered for me and I inwardly sighed with relief. I was thankful for her intervention, as I wasn't not quite sure how to respond, but throughout our dinner the air remained thick and uneasy.

*

Dinner finished, our plates cleared, we all adjourned to the study. The men in deep conversation by the fire, whilst Beth and I sat on the sofa near the window.

'I have put together everything you need for the wedding, I know it's hard my dear not having your mother and father present, but Edward and I will do our utmost to make it a memorable day,' she said.

'That's fine Beth, I cannot thank you enough.' I tried desperately to concentrate on our conversation, but I was continually being distracted by Charles as he spoke much louder than all of us.

'I have written to Henry Holland, I have told him that Louis fourteenth has advised me to ride to Newcastle to meet the Scots, they have agreed to keep me safe until such time I can gather enough money to retake London, I have told Henry to meet me just outside Oundle,' said Charles.

My eyes kept diverting over to the fireplace. I watched as Nicholas poured brandy into three glass tumblers.

'When do we depart, sire?' he said as he handed one glass to Charles and the other to Edward.

'We have a wedding on the morrow don't forget, we will leave the day after.'

Holy crap, the penny dropped. Holland, along with Essex and Fairfax, will pay the Scots a sum of four hundred thousand pounds to hold the king captive, so he can sign a document to be King in name only. Charles gets to keep the luxuries a king is due. No longer to rule or govern England. Charles trusts Henry Holland but remembering my history, he repeatedly kept turning on the king. Holland chose whichever side was winning at the time, which at the moment is Cromwell.

What should I do? I had already altered history by being in the wrong place at the wrong time, how could I interfere now? I felt conflicted.

The knowledge that I could help stop this weighed heavy on my shoulders. When I heard stories about Charles in my history lessons he was just a fascinating historical figure that ended in tragedy. I couldn't separate myself from the story. I know him and the people around him I have come to care deeply about. The idea of us being captured and our heads rolling from our bodies sent a chill through me. My body shuddered slightly at my thoughts.

Somewhere in the back of my brain I could hear Beth talking to me.

'Sorry Beth I was lost in my own thoughts,' I murmured. My gaze now settled on Beth.

'That's fine, I imagine you have lots of those floating around.'

Little did she know, I thought to myself.

'You do not know the half of it. You were saying?' I said.

'I asked if you would like more wine, dear.'

'No, thank you, I think I've had my fill.'

She nodded towards the footman, he proceeded to re-fill Beth glass. He placed it back on the marble table.

'That will be all, Samuel, you may retire and tell the rest of the staff please.'

He inclined his head. 'Yes, my lady, goodnight.'

Beth smiled kindly at the young man. 'Goodnight, Samuel.' I waited for him to depart before I continued with our conversation.

'How long have you and Edward been married?'

'We will be celebrating our forty years together next July,'

'Wow. Forty years, what's your secret?'

She leaned closer and placed her hand on my arm. She spoke softly, so she wouldn't be overheard.

'Patience, and learning to speak when it's appropriate,' she explained.

I shifted a little awkwardly in my seat, as I remembered my outburst at dinner, I cast my eyes down to my hands with shame.

'I am so sorry for that outburst, my parents bought me up to speak my mind and I am a great believer in equality.'

My attention came back to Beth, her face was warm and kind and held no malice concerning my outburst at dinner.

'As I you, my dear, I had strong morals when I was noticeably younger than I am now.' She smiled. 'I too hated that feeling of being invisible and not being allowed to have any opinions save for my fathers, that was until I met Edward.' Her eyes wandered over to the fireplace and rested lovingly on her husband.

'I found Edward to be very forward thinking and he has always asked my opinion on matters of the estate and other problems that occurred throughout our married life.'

'So, really he does treat you like an equal?' I wondered.

'Yes, but unfortunately my dear only in private. Don't get me wrong he will often put me in my place, but it's my choice to disagree with him, much to say our life can get quite colourful.' There was an odd note in her voice, but she met my eyes with a smile.

'Do you think Nicholas will treat me the same?'

Beth was still smiling when she took her hand from mine and settled herself more comfortably in the sofa.

'Nicholas, although very set in his ways, he will always hear your point of view and he will always let you have your say. Whether or not he will agree with you is another matter, but like Edward and I, only voice your thoughts in private.'

I rolled my eyes at her last remark, which she didn't looked favorably on and I realised my mistake.

'I apologise Beth, you are just giving me some sound advice.'

'Our job as women is to keep the household running smoothly and to make sure everyone is in good humour, especially when children come along.'

I blushed at the thought, my god we are not even married, and the subject of children has been brought up.

'Do you and Edward have children?' Beth's face changed, one would describe it as grief, but it was fleeting, and she was back to her smiling self.

'No, Edward and I have not been blessed, but we have learnt to live with it.'

I felt her pain, to love and be loved by someone and not being able to have children and share that joy must be heart wrenching.

'I'm so sorry to hear that.' I truly meant it, because both Elizabeth and Edward would have made wonderful parents.

'It's fine, so don't upset yourself, we accepted it a long time ago, anyway we look on Nicholas as our son, although we would like to see a little bit more of him from time to time,'

'Well, I'm sure we can arrange that.' I smiled affectionally at her.

'That would be wonderful, mayhap you could visit us over the festive season?' she said with excitement. 'And bring my sister-in-law too, how delightful that would be.'

She placed her hands over her chest and leaned back against the sofa with her eyes half closed.

'That would be lovely Beth, but that's if things can get back to normal,' I replied.

I thought I saw a fleeting shadow in her eyes, though it was quickly hidden as she reached for her wine.

I didn't want to spoil her happiness; I knew things were only going to get worse in England over the next year or so and, if memory served, Cromwell abolished Christmas as he deemed it a pagan sin and it wasn't until the Prince of Wales was back on the throne in sixteen-sixty that England was able to celebrate the festive season once more. My head was starting to pound from the wine I had consumed at dinner and I needed some air.

'Would you mind if I took in a bit of fresh air. Do you care to join me?' I asked.

Beth took my hand and patted it gently. 'No, but you go head, all this talk of war it does get too much after a while,' Beth said kindly. 'Anyway, my dear, would you mind awfully if I retired now because I have such a long day on the morrow preparing for your wedding.'

'No, that's fine, you go ahead, I probably won't be too far behind you.'

We both stood. Beth took both my hands and leant towards me. She kissed my cheek and stood back to look at my face.

'It was awfully nice of you, Beth, to entertain so grandly.'

'My pleasure entirely. However, if you think this was grand, just wait until tomorrow.' Her eyes sparkled with excitement.

'I dread to think.' I giggled.

'Carolina, you are beautiful, kind and a bit rash with your outspoken thoughts, but my nephew will do well by you.'

I blushed amazed at her show of affection. 'Thank you, Beth.' I returned her kiss.

*

The moonlight spilled down the terrace steps onto the garden, I could still hear the men talking, but only in muffled tones. How could I stop Nicholas's fate? but *should* I stop it? or will it alter time so much that when I eventually wake up in my own body, will my time be the same? Or was this just a weird dream, that I couldn't wake up from? My mind was a mixture of emotions and logic, but which one should I follow? My head was telling me one thing but my heart another.

My feelings for someone I hardly know were so strong, that I couldn't allow Nicholas and his family to meet the axe man; the thought of losing him filled me with such an empty void. The only logical thing in my mind was I had to get him away from Charles, the king was the master of his own demise.

But how could I warn Nicholas about Holland and the dangers that would unfold? Women of this century should be seen and not heard, so how could I voice my political opinion, when I shouldn't have one? Look what happened at dinner. Maybe I should take Beth's advice, and speak to him calmly and in private.

I felt Nicholas behind me before he even spoke, he stood next to me and placed his hands on the concrete handrail, just close enough for our little fingers to touch, but we didn't.

'You're lost in thought?' he remarked.

Now's your chance to tell him I thought to myself, but before I could answer he spoke again.

'What is that nonsense you spoke at dinner?'

I sighed ever so slightly and turned my face towards Nicholas.

'Like I said, 'twas the wine talking.'

His eyes narrowed. My attention was drawn to his fingers as they drummed gently on the handrail. 'Is that so. Do you not agree with the Kings rule over England?'

'Yes and no.' I sighed and wondered where this was going.

'Explain?' he said rather briskly.

'Yes, I agree there should be a monarchy, but the king has lost touch with his people, 'it's not all about making the rich richer.' I reached out and touched his hand with mine. He withdrew his hand; I felt a sharp stab of pain in my heart.

He scowled. 'So, in your opinion this war is because we have to fund the poor?'

'I didn't say that, you're putting words in my mouth.'

Nicholas remained silent for a time; he turned to face me head on. He smirked and lifted an eyebrow at me. I so wanted to slap away that smug look on his face. I was starting to get angry.

'This war, Lina is not about the poor, or that they need a voice. Charles closed parliament down for fourteen years, and when he realised his mistake he re-opened it again. Parliament wants total control, and Charles to be king in name only. Cromwell wants to become head of state, and I guarantee that if he does, within ten years this country will be at an all-time low, and before we know it the people will be crying out for a king again. Therefore, my love, women do not run our country,' he said, all too self-righteous.

In my head I'm seething, how dare he, if only he knew that one day, we will have a female prime minister. In my view, man just cannot govern man, and I must remember that women have no political opinions, but everything he had said would come to pass.

I took in a couple of deep breaths to steady my temper, and turned our conversation towards other matters, otherwise I could just see us going around in circles, arguing on something that we would never agree on.

'I'm thinking about what Charles said about Henry Holland, you can't trust him.' I lifted my eyes to his face, searching for some sign of belief. I found none.

'Oh, here we go again. and why not?' His jaw clenched together in that all too familiar expression.

'There is no need to take that tone with me,' I said, as he puffed out a large breath and rolled his eyes skyward. I tried to stay calm as I continued with my lie.

'I overheard my father talking, and he said Holland will betray the King,' I said hoping to sound convincing.

'That just hearsay, Lina,'

'Please trust me it's not,'

'Since when are women born knowing about politics, or is it just you?' he said with a hint of mockery in his tone.

'I have not just sat around for six years ignorant of this war, I had little choice in the matter especially living in a house with parents who are staunch royalists, do you forget that I have two ears for listening? And just because I maybe in your estimation a lowly woman, I have a brain and I know how to bloody well use it. I do have my own opinions other than yours.'

'Someone woke up with a bad disposition this evening, tell you what, how about we just be on our guard and if anything is amiss, then maybe we will take your warnings.' He was laughing at me and talking down to me like a child and my hidden temper started to flare.

'If you don't take this warning seriously both yours and Charles heads will roll soon enough.' I barked.

'Stop your worrying woman, all will be well once we reach Newcastle.'

'The Scots will betray you,' I blasted out, Nicholas's forehead puckered, and his eyes narrowed.

'Pray, madam how do you know this, are you a spy for Cromwell?' His gaze was intent on me, and I could see the thoughts of my words working behind his high forehead. I clicked my tongue at such an absurd notion. 'Don't be ridiculous, me, a spy? If I am, don't you think you would have been caught by now?'

'How do you know this? His eyebrows rose higher. 'Did you dream this silliness?' he said in with scorn.

'This is not silliness.' My hand went to my forehead and I sighed heavily. 'How I know, I can't say, but whatever I say you must heed my warning.'

Nicholas's face underwent an astonishing transformation. From an expression of scowling perplexity, his face went completely blank and then resolved itself into an expression of doubt.

'Then you must be a spy and my suspicions of you were correct in the first place,' he said.

My face fell. 'For fuck sake Nicolas, for an intelligent man you have no common sense whatsoever,' I said, and poked him in his chest.

'Madam, what is coming out of your mouth is no better than filth from a common doxy.'

'So, now I'm a whore, am I?' I went to turn away but he grabbed my hands.

'Enough, Lina.' His voice bellowed through the silence of the night.

'There is no reason to shout at me when all I was doing was trying to talk to you.'

I tried to pull out of his grasp, but he tugged me into a fierce embrace and then he crushed his lips on mine, not gentle, not rough, but indifferent. My arms automatically entwined around his neck, I opened my mouth to receive his kiss deeper. I sighed in pleasure. Then suddenly, he ended the kiss and pushed me back gently.

'Go to bed, Lina and make sure you're ready by full sunlight.'

I walked away with unshed tears.

5

A marriage to bind

I could just make out the conversation that was going on outside my door. Well, just as much as my wine-soaked brain would allow.

'I cannot wake her up, your Grace.'

'Why ever not?'

'She appears to be drunk.'

'Drunk! This will not do, Clara, it's just after breakfast, how has she gotten herself in such a state?'

'It's my fault, your grace, she asked me to leave the bottle of wine, and I did,'

'It's not your fault, Clara, you were only doing as you were asked,'

'Your grace?'

'Out with it, Clara, I do not have all day.'

'Well, your grace, one is not prone to gossip, but there has been talk in the kitchen this morning.'

'And what was the kitchen staff gossiping about, Clara?'

'Lord Nicholas and My lady seemed to be having swords of words out on the terrace last night when everyone had retired, but the staff weren't eavesdropping, your grace. 'Twas so loud even the cook could hear them in the kitchen.'

'What were they quarreling about, Clara?'

'No one knows your Grace, but all they could hear was loud shouting from Lord Nicholas.'

'Good heavens, what is the matter with my nephew?'

'Your Grace, what shall I do?

'We sober her up, and I actually think we are going to need some help. Run down to the stables and get Stefan.

*

My mind started to wander, but I didn't care, I didn't even want to get up, let alone be married to someone out of duty. I wished I were at home, my real home, not this century, my century. I missed my parents, Claire, even my cats.

I missed going to the toilet, not some privy hole set in rock or a pot behind a screen. I missed my iPhone, my Bruno Mars CD, driving my car to work.

I shut my eyes tighter, 'please I want to go home, please send me back.' Dare I open my eyes?

I opened them slowly and I tried to sit up. That wasn't such a clever idea. I eased myself very carefully back down onto my pillows, I held onto to my head whilst rubbing the sides of my temples. *No such luck, I'm still bloody here.*

Tired and alone, I had this horrible feeling of being lost and everything was out of my control. Most days I had kept the fear hidden deep down, but today it resurfaced, like an ugly spot. The flood gates opened; I couldn't seem to stop crying.

'Mum, if you can hear me help me please!'

The door opened and Elizabeth, Clara and Stefan walked in. I closed my eyes quickly with hopes they didn't see me awake.

I felt Stefan lean over me, he sniffed the air around my face. 'Christ, she is as drunk as a doxy on London Bridge,'

'So, what do we do with her?' Beth questioned Stefan.

My self-pity was forgotten as I felt the warm quilts thrown off me. I was then jostled into the air over Stefan's shoulder.

'Clara bring a robe and a blanket and follow me,' he said.

I opened my eyes, I saw a harassed looking Clara running behind Stefan, she was trying desperately to keep up, I giggled.

'You have nothing to giggle about, Lady Sackville, you're in a whole lot of mess.' I could hear the angry undertones in Stefan's voice.

The chilly air hit me, I opened my eyes and I could see that we were in the garden and heading to where, I care not. Then Stefan stopped. Next thing I knew I was being thrown high into the air. I screamed just before I hit the freezing water of the lake.

'You bloody bastard.' I shouted at him.

Stefan shrugged his shoulders and laughed. I tried to stand, very dignified, but all I managed to do was slip and slide, rather unladylike, up the small bank of the lake, until Stefan gave me his hand. I reluctantly took it. That icy dip soon sobered me up as I pushed the hair back off my face. I pushed his hand away once I got onto dry land.

'That will teach you for getting drunk first thing in the morning,' he said with humor.

'Why thank you, sir for my icy bath,' I quipped sarcastically.

I was furious with Stefan. However, I suppose it was my own fault I thought to myself. Stefan swept me a low bow as I trudged past him with my nose stuck in the air. Clara rushed frantically over to cover my modesty from his prying eyes.

'Come now, my lady, let's get you warm and dry.'

*

I felt a little more human after a few glasses of sherry supplied by Ms. Jones the cook. I was functional and ready to tackle the chore of getting dressed for my wedding.

I scrubbed myself from top to bottom and it took three washes to get the pond smell from my hair, much to Clara's dismay. My skin was dried vigorously until pink. To let my hair dry I sat by the fire, which seemed to have taken forever.

Four hours later I sat on a chair by the fire, dressed in my full wedding finery waiting for Edward to collect me.

Looking at myself in the mirror. I had to admire the workmanship that had gone into this gown. It was made of heavy silver satin, with a baby blue over-skirt and bodice that fastened at the back with twenty or so tiny satin covered buttons, each embroidered with a silver rose. The neckline was low and square with puffed sleeves that tied below my elbows with a baby blue ribbon and silver lace cuffs.

The petticoat was silver satin with embroidered silver roses, which was on full display at the front and the baby blue over-skirt was gathered in ruffles and fastened at the sides. My hair was fashioned in the bun at the back of my head with my curls lose. To complete the look a diamond and white rose crystal hair comb was placed into my hair and a train of pleated blue satin was fasten at the back of my bodice between my shoulders. My heart was pounding beneath the tight corset and my mouth was completely dry, I suppose that was a combination of too much wine this morning and nerves.

A knock on the door broke my spell, and I stood and walked towards it. The satin swished effortlessly around my ankles despite the heaviness of the gown. Opening the door, I was greeted by Edward, the Duke.

'Are you ready, my dear?' His eyes glinted in pleasure as he took in my appearance.

'Yes, ready as I'll ever be,' I said apprehensively.

'You look beautiful, even as lovely as my wife when she wore this dress.'

'So, this is Elizabeth's gown?' I asked.

'Yes, well it was until she couldn't fit into it anymore, she used to wear it for special occasions.' Edwards eyes shifted around to make sure no one had overheard his words. He placed his finger to his mouth. 'Shush, don't tell her I said so.'

'I promise.' I crossed my hands over my heart.

'It's beautiful, I did wonder how this dress got made so quickly.'

'My wife never throws anything away, much to my dismay, but for this occasion her hoarding has paid off.' We both laughed as we exited the room.

Edward held his arm out as I climbed into the carriage, we didn't have far to go, the church was just a little away over the village. A few villagers seemed to loiter around.

'Don't they have anything better to do than watch a wedding?' I ventured to Sir Edward.

'Any excuse for the townsfolk to get an afternoon off work,' he chuckled.

As we walked into the church yard, we passed some of Nicholas's men and more villagers, they fell silent. The men took their hats off and gave me a sweeping bow as I walked past them.

One villager remarked on how beautiful I looked and others looked on smiling. I nodded graciously back.

Gregor one of Nicholas's men and Alec, Stefan's young apprentice opened the doors to the church.

Gregor's deep brown eyes slowly ran up and down the length of my body until they rested on my face, he nodded in admiration and of acceptance, as I was soon to be his mistress too. Edward held me tightly by one arm, probably to support me just in case I stumbled.

We entered the church, there were only a handful of people in the pews. They stood as Edward walked me down the aisle. Searching for Elizabeth and Clara as I needed a look of encouragement, I found them both smiling at me with pride. Looking ahead, I saw Stefan standing with Nicholas, and I wondered if he would have had a best man. Nicholas turned; my mouth almost fell open at the very sight of him. Gone was his beard, his hair was much shorter, and he was breathtakingly handsome.

Then the jolt of recognition hit me like a thunderbolt, it was Mr. Thorn, from my other life as Caroline Curtis. How was that possible? My mind was trying to rationalise this, but I could see no logic.

Nicholas stood waiting for me, the sunlight shone through the stain glass windows and bounced onto his thick curly dark hair, that swept the collar and ruff of his white shirt, his doublet was a dark navy velvet, and his breeches were of the same colour. Around his waist he wore a sword belt with a sword attached, which had a gold and sapphire encrusted hilt. His legs were encased in white silk stockings and on his feet, he wore black leather shoes with a gold buckle, his regalia was typical of the King's Cavalier. Well over six feet, broad and with such striking features, he was so handsome, it took my breath away.

Nicholas bowed as I approached, 'Your servant, my lady.'

Having no words, he lifted his left hand for Edward to place my hand into his.

My dad should have been doing this, but which dad? Both memories of me and Carolina are somehow so entwined I felt I was one and the same person.

But which one am I, Caroline or Carolina but wasn't I both and were Mr. Thorn and Nicholas both one and the same too? My mind was at sixes and sevens trying to fathom this bizarre twist of fate.

Nicholas walked me towards the waiting priest, never would I have imagined my wedding like this, especially four hundred years in the past.

We knelt before the wooden alter, Elizabeth and Edward took their places as our witnesses and the ceremony began. We stood when it came time for our vows, Nicholas took my cold clammy hand. I looked up to his face and I wondered if despite his casual appearance if he was just as nervous as I. He was staring down at me, his face showed no sign of emotion, I smiled up at him and the only sign of emotion I got was the pressure of his hand in mine. Nicholas tightened his grip on my hand, but only ever so slightly, it felt familiar, and it gave me the strength to carry on.

'I Nicholas take thee Carolina to be my wedded wife and there unto I plight my troth,' his voice was firm and confident, 'in sickness and in health, till death do us part.' Nicholas placed the cold heavy gold band onto my third finger of my left hand.

Oh my god it's my turn. No words escaped my mouth, and he gently squeezed my hand for encouragement.

'I Caroline, Sorry, Carolina, take thee Nicholas to my wedded husband. There unto I plight my troth. In sickness and in health. Till death do us part.'

I took the identical gold band and placed it on his finger. I vaguely remembered the vicar finishing the ceremony until Nicholas bent down to kiss me on my lips, his mouth was warm and soft, my stomach fluttered. We drew apart and everyone clapped. I smiled nervously up at him. Still a stranger but bonded by marriage.

I felt a small sense of relief as we walked out of the church and back towards the awaiting carriage. The villagers that had come to watch saw a happy wedding, although a small one, the congregation consisting, almost entirely of men all dressed as the Kings Cavaliers three women.

As we approached the house, the stress of the day and the last traces of alcohol in my blood caught up with me. Hence I found myself going giddy. 'I feel sick.'

'It's not that bad? he said smiling down at me.

'What's not bad?'

'Being married to me?'

'It's not you, it's me, I had rather a lot to drink on an extraordinarily little amount of food.' I smiled sheepishly at him.

He smirked a little. 'I did hear.' I could see the laughter hiding behind his blue eyes.

'Let me guess, Stefan.'

'Who else? And I understand you took a little dip.'

'A little dip, I call it a near drowning.' I laughed at the memory of it all.

'Are you feeling better?' I could see the concern in his eyes.

'Yes, better, although very overwhelmed.'

'Also I would like to apologise for shouting at you.'
His apology took me by surprise, I never expected it.

'It's fine, I should have been mindful of my words, so I apologise too,' I said as Nicholas picked up my hand and kissed the back of it.

'All is well now. Come, Elizabeth has laid on a splendid wedding breakfast for us.

*

We stood at the dining room doors, and I held my breath for a second as Nicholas placed his hands on the doorknobs to push them open. He turned and looked at me.

'Brace yourself.'

The doors opened and a second later the air was split with a thunder of cheers and applause. Waiting for the clamour to die down, he spoke to his men.

'Behold, my wife, the new lady Trevilian, mistress of Debden Manor.'

Looking around at the men who had abducted me, gone was the uncertainty in their faces and what I saw was loyalty. In a deep resonant voice that carried to all Nicholas spoke.

'Know that when she bids you, I have bidden you; what service you render her, you are rendering me; what loyalty you give or withhold, you give or withhold from me.

All the men stood, took off their hats, and swept me a low bow.

Words couldn't describe the feeling I had on hearing Nicholas's statement, and I knew each and every one of these men would lay down their lives for me.

They all cheered my name as Nicholas led me to the table, where Edward, Elizabeth and Charles waited for us to be seated.

After an exhausting morning, our wedding breakfast was much needed. Elizabeth was true to her word; she decorated the hall with a beautiful array of white flowers and the main table was laid with a snowy white linen tablecloth with flowers draped around the bottom like a table skirt.

Each place setting consisted of a large plate, a spoon, the funny two-pronged fork, and a napkin. I noticed the two center plates, which I assumed was for Nicholas and I were gold, further down the table they were silver, then the surrounding tables came pewter.

There was no disguising who was considered of higher rank. Obviously, equality was not something that this household pursued.

Nicholas took my hand and placed it on his arm.

'Come, let us sit,'

We sat side by side at the center of the table and I was surprised to see the King seated with a silver plate.

'Why does the king not have a gold plate like us?' I asked with curiosity.

'The gold is only for the bride and groom, the highest honor for today,' he explained.

'Oh, I see.' We smiled warmly at each other.

Everyone was seated, the noise around the room was jovial and relaxed, my concentration was broken when a servant brought an ewer and basin and a towel to wash our hands, and not just us, but every guest. We washed and dried our hands and waited for the food to arrive, my stomach growled.

'Hungry?' Nicholas whispered in my ear.

'Yes, I'm starving, did you hear my stomach then?' I blushed.

'I think everyone heard.' A bubble of laughter escaped his mouth.

'Stop it.' I laughed with him. I caught Elizabeth looking on, she smiled warmly at me.

'So, my dear, how does it feel to be married?'

I leaned past Nicholas, so I could get a better view of Elizabeth. 'Well, not a lot of difference really,' I replied.

'She will come morning!' shouted Stefan. I was a little taken back by his remark.

'If she walks fine, then he's done something wrong.' Young Alec shouted back, then he proceeded to get a slap at the back of the head by Sir Gregor. The men in the hall burst into laughter. God, I wished the wine would hurry up.

'Pay no heed, they are just having some fun, more for my benefit than yours, love,' said Nicholas.

The food finally arrived, and it was presented with great ceremony, but cooking like this deserves one, thinking to myself as I watched the servants place the food on the table. The first course of meat was brought in on enormous silver trays: Roasted mutton, veal, salted beef and finally the wine, which was kept cool in large copper tubs of cold water. Our wine was poured first into jewel-coloured, translucent goblets of venetian glass. I picked mine up and twisted the stem between my thumb and forefinger. I marveled at the workmanship.

'These are beautiful, Elizabeth.' I said.

'They were a gift from my father when I married Edward.'

I was greatly humbled by her kindness and generosity. 'Thank you, Elizabeth, you have made today wonderful, despite the rush and short notice.'

'As I told you, despite the circumstances and your family not being able to attend, I would make your day memorable.'

'You certainly have, I cannot thank you enough.'

'Pish.' She waved her hand away. 'Just enjoy your day my darling.' We raised our glasses to each other, and we sipped our wine. 'Mmm.' The wine was sweet, with an undertone of mixed fruit.

'You like the wine?' Nicholas whispered in my ear.

'Yes, very much, it's delightful.' I took another sip.

'Don't drink too much, I don't want you in your cups for tonight,' he said in a low soft whisper. With that my face went as red as the brocade curtains that hung by the windows.

The next course was fowl: Chicken, duck and capon tied together and cooked as one, turkey stewed with leeks and ginger, quail, pheasant, and woodcock. Next came fish: sole, turbot, whiting and eels. Every dish had been cooked in a sauce, all highly spiced and delicious. Vegetables followed, I received some strange looks because I put some chicken and capon on my plate along with the potatoes and vegetables. I leaned slightly over my plate and sniffed appreciatively; it seemed an awfully long time since our last meal.

'Why do you place all on your plate?' Nicholas questioned.

'Why, do you not?' I looked around and everyone was eating the meat first then the fish, the vegetables going untouched.

'It's strange,' he observed.

'No, it's not, if you try a bit of the chicken with the potatoes together, you get a whole new different taste, try it.' I placed a little of both along with a bit of leek on my fork and put it in his mouth.' His eyes widened as he chewed all the assorted flavors, and I laughed as he started to fill his plate with nearly everything.

'Don't mix the meat and the fish though, it won't taste all that nice.'

With every bite he chewed industriously, nodding his head and smiling at me.

'I would never had thought to mix my food,' he said curiously.

I picked up a pie of some sort, I took a small bite, then a bigger one.

'Mmm, this is delicious. What is it?' I said. Nicholas lowered his fork; he had just been about to put it into his mouth.

'Veal, minced with truffles,' he said and stuffed his fork into his mouth, chewed thoughtfully and then swallowed.

'Slow down, I don't want you vomiting on me later,' I said.

He smiled at me as he pick up a veal and truffle pie, he stuffed into his mouth whole and pulled a face at me. It was so nice to see that playful, loving side to Nicholas.

I never got to finish any of my wine because with every course finished a different wine was served. The servant would throw away the half-drunk wine, rinse the glass before filling it with the next. Next the salad arrived, crinkling my nose in disgust, because they had even cooked lettuce and violet buds. Everyone kept eating, but after a plate full of food I could manage no more, until the desserts came.

There were almond tarts, every fruit pie imaginable, along with a cheese board. How funny, that had never changed. The food had more flavour than I had ever tasted back in my time. Food was reared naturally, fruit and vegetables grown without pesticides, and the meat hadn't been injected with water to appear fatter. How far man has come, no wonder our world was slowly dying.

After our meal, the ewer of water was brought around again, because food was not only eaten with the spoon and fork, but with fingers as well.

Three hours had passed, our bellies full of food and wine. I was relaxed and worry free, then Stefan stood with a glass in hand, I leaned into Nicholas, 'I wonder what he's going to say next?' I said, feeling rather worried.

'Stefan will be on his best behavior.' He lifted a curl from my shoulder and rubbed it between his thumb and forefinger.

'Mmm, soft like silk.' He whispered under his breath.

His words melted my heart just a little more. We were both distracted until Stefan clinked a fork on his glass. He coughed slightly into his hand and cleared his throat.

'To the lady of Debden Manor, congratulations and be sure to make his life hell.'

We all laughed, and I picked my glass up and raised it as a thank you. More toasts were offered for our health and long life together. However, I knew that within the next sixteen months Nicholas's head would be parted from his body, unless I could put a stop to it.

I was enjoying myself immensely until I noticed our guests were expecting us to retire.

My suspicions were confirmed when Charles, remarked in a low, laughing voice.

'My god, Nicholas, if you are wondering when you can leave without causing a fuss, 'twas about two hours ago.'

Nicholas leaned down and whispered in my ear, 'I'm sorry to put an end to your evening, but if we don't leave soon, they will begin to talk, or the men will carry you up themselves.'

I smiled a little with uncertainty, and nodded in acceptance.

'Let's say good night to Charles, and your aunt and uncle, then we can slip out quietly.'

I stood as Nicholas pulled the chair out from behind me.

The thought of what lay ahead filled me with terrible nerves, I knew nothing about my new husband, only what history had told, and he knew truly little about me.

My face must have betrayed me, 'Come, love, there is nothing to fear, I'm no monster, I will be fair and gentle.'

'I know, I wouldn't think otherwise,' I said as I tried to swallow the nerves away.

We bade our goodnights and tried to slip quietly from the room, No such luck. There were cheers and claps, and ale tankards were banged on the table repeatedly. A thought struck me as I looked imploring up at Nicholas.

'Are they going to follow us for a bedding ritual?'

'Even if there was, there's no harm in it, anyway my love you are saved because it's an old custom and not many houses of the nobility adhere to those ancient traditions.

'Then why are the guests following us?'

Nicholas stopped to speak to Gregor and whispered into his ear. The giant nodded.

By the time we passed the table on the dais, my face was on fire from all the bawdy encouragement being shouted at Nicholas. As we started up the stairs I stole a frantic look behind me. Over my shoulder and much to my relief I saw that Gregor had stood across the stairwell with folded arms and legs positioned wide, obviously at Nicholas's order, to prevent them from following.

*

A little while later I was sitting on the bed, stiff, completely terrified, and fully dressed in Beth's burrowed gown and slippers. How in the name of God did this happen? I mentally asked myself. I went from trying to get the wrought iron gates from his home, to now being shut in a room, within an old stately home just outside Oundle.

I had been in this body for nine days and the fear I felt was nothing compared to the fear I felt now. At this moment I was in a state of generalized terror and helplessness.

Nicholas leaned casually against the fireplace watching me, and the air between us was heavy and silent. No words escaped me. I was a virgin, in this century as well as my own, exceedingly rare, but I had never found the right person. Do I invite him over? The air of embarrassment settled deeper and it was Nicholas who spoke first.

'You have nothing to worry about, Lina, I'll not be rough,' he pointed out reasonably.

My mouth went dry and I wrapped my arm around my middle. I laughed in spite myself.

'Well, I never imagined you would, but this is new for me. I sighed and contemplated my next move.

'Would you like to sit with me?' I asked sheepishly. I knew he wouldn't come over, or even touch me unless I invited him. I cleared my throat and patted the space beside me.

He nodded and walked over. I felt the bed dip with his weight. We were close, but not too close, there must had been a good ten inches between us.

'Would you like to talk?' His velvet smooth voice broke the silence in the room.

'Talk?' I smiled despite myself.

'Yes, why not,' he said.

I knew he was trying to make me feel at ease in his company. After all we were complete strangers.

'What would you like to talk about?' I asked.

'Anything you want.' He crossed his legs at his ankles and folded his arms over his chest.

'Don't you want to get things started?' My cheeks flushed with embarrassment.

'We have all night, there is plenty of time and I want you to feel comfortable with me, not scared,'

'I'm not scared.' But my face must have betrayed me because I was petrified.

He stood up and went to the table near the window. A bottle of wine and two glasses sat neatly on an intricate silver tray inland with gold flowers.

Nicholas poured out two glasses and came back, handing me one as he sat back down on the bed.

Nicholas raised his glass briefly. 'To Lady Trevilian, my wife,' he said softly. I raised my own glass and we both drunk together.

Nicholas tentatively reached out and took my available cold hand in his warm one, they were large against mine and his palm was calloused, I suppose this was from wielding his sword over the last six years. He stroked his thumbs over the backs of my hands.

'So, what shall we talk about?' He waited for my answer.

'How come it's just you and your mother?' I asked.

He studied his wine glass with some care before he spoke. 'My father died when Christopher and I were young boys.' I could see the grief hidden beneath his eyes.

'What happened to him?' I asked tentatively.

'He fell from his horse and broke his leg. The break went clean through his skin, the fever got hold of him and he never recovered.' His eyes flickered with emotion.

How far medicine has come. I remember breaking my arm falling off the back fence. It was soon easily fixed. Suffering from a break was minor, but in these times it could be fatal.

'What of your brother?' I asked.

Nicholas swallowed hard and the muscle in his jaw twitched. I knew I had hit a raw nerve.

'As boys, growing up, we would occasionally mess around near the lake and Christopher would often take himself off on his own, he loved to fish and this particular day I didn't want to go with him.' He paused for a moment. 'He took his net and an empty jam jar and headed down to the lake, that day he didn't come back. Twas late, supper was ready, so mother sent me down to get him, I found him head down in a shallow part of the lake.'

'Oh, Nicholas that's terrible, how old were you?'

'He was just Eleven and I ten. I pulled him out, but he had been dead for a while, he had a nasty gash on his head.

The doctor ruled his death as accidental drowning, my mother has never quite been the same.'

'No, I don't suppose she has. You either. You never expect to outlive your children,' I said.

'What is done is done, I cannot dwell on the past, I have responsibilities to contend with.'

I lifted my wine glass back and drained the contents. I stood and walked over to the table to get the wine. I picked up the bottle and sat back down next to Nicholas on the bed. He offered his glass, and I poured more wine for us both.

'No other cousins?'

'No, Elizabeth and Edward have never been lucky, and my bastard of an uncle married twice, he outlived both his wives, but left no heirs.'

Watching his face closely I could see his expression closed off when he spoke about his uncle.

'Eventually their lands and titles will be bestowed upon us.'

'Us?'

'You are my wife now, so what is mine, is yours and you will never want for anything. I will always keep you safe, hence on the morrow you will be sent back to Debden Hall with Stefan and a few of my men.'

I choked, spluttering the wine, and coughed until I felt his hand on my back. The cough subsided, breathless and red-faced, I turned around and crossed my legs underneath me. He now had my full attention.

'Pardon, no, I won't. I want to stay with you.' My face must have betrayed my emotions.

'Out of the question, Lina, you cannot travel with us to Newcastle.' His hand went to his forehead and he rubbed the sides of his temples. He sighed heavily.

'We have Essex and Fairfax on our heels, and if we are captured you will fall with us, the troops are not shy about killing women, even high-born ones, I will not risk your life.'

'Don't be ridiculous,' I interjected.

'Essex and Fairfax, on their orders, killed over four hundred women in Naseby. So trust me, they will not think twice. My uncle is a nasty vindictive man, and if he knows it will hurt me, then he will not hesitate.'

I placed my wine on the floor and put my hands on his arms. 'Don't go, let Stefan and your men take Charles.'

'No. If I risk my men, then I risk myself too.' He explained.

'Tell Charles to head to France, gather funds and a new French army, he will be betrayed if he stays in England, I warn you please, you are walking into a trap. Holland has paid the Scots four hundred thousand pounds for Charles and they will surrender him back to London.'

'Enough of this talk, Lina.'

'It's the truth. I promise you.'

Nicholas arched an eyebrow at me. 'What have you heard, and from whom?'

I could sense he was pulling away from me.

'I know things, I see things differently.'

The lie just seemed to roll of my tongue with ease.

'So, you say you are a witch then.'

Nicholas took my hands from his arms and leaned away from me, as though I had burned him.

'No, I'm not a witch, I just know how to help people with the right mixture of herbs and plants and I just see things differently.'

I couldn't quite believe the crap that was coming out of my mouth, but how can I tell him I was from the future, when my body had been born of this time? I couldn't even get my own head around it let alone convince a seventeenth century lord and a King's Cavalier.

'If you're not a witch then you're a spy for Cromwell.' Nicholas looked horrified at me, then the disbelief spread through his face.

Grabbing his hands, I placed them on either side of my face.

'Look into my eyes. Do I look like a witch or a spy? If I were a spy would I have agreed to marry you, and would you all still be safely hidden here in this house?

Please look at me Nicholas, truly look at me. This is me, nothing else. You see me. I'm your wife, your friend, your lover.' I swallowed hard as I said these words to him.

I leaned towards him and kissed his soft full lips. I pulled back and searched his face, there was a flicker of something, was he yielding to me?

I carried on. 'This is not for duty, or to convince you of who I am, this is just me submitting to you. I give you my body, my heart, my soul and I will never ever betray you. I know we have only known each other for a short time, but to me it feels likes forever, and the first moment I saw you, my love was instant.'

My breath went from slow and shallow to rapid and shallow and he hadn't even touched me yet.

'Stand up and turn around.' His eyes burned with desire. I obeyed.

I felt his fingers swiftly open the small little buttons that were attached to my bodice. The last one popped, and he threw it onto the chair opposite; his hands went to my waist and he pulled the fastenings to the petticoats. They fell to the floor in pool of white satin around my feet, stepping out I kicked them away. Standing in just my shift, he bent his head to kiss me, the kiss seemed to go on forever, while his hands roamed down my body, over my bottom.

Then he reached up hooking a fingertip in the neck of the shift, looking straight into my eyes as he drew it downward until his fingertip was deep in the hollow between my breasts. It stayed there, moving up and down, stroking the sides of my breast, while tiny flames began to shoot through my body making my breathing shallow and rapid. Then he pulled the ribbon at the neckline of my shift, it floated softly to the floor. Standing naked in front of him I felt a little shy, covering what I could with my arms.

'Stop, my god you are beautiful.' I could hear the longing in his voice, I knew he wanted me just as much as I wanted him. Nicholas's eyes darkened with desire, he swallowed hard and licked his dry lips as his hands continued to caress me, I stopped him.

'Now it's my turn.' I said.

Reaching up I unfastened his shirt, sliding my hands inside I felt his heart beating quickly in his chest.

I moved my hands up over his shoulders to push his shirt down to the floor with the rest of the forgotten clothes.

My tongue slowly caressed his chest feeling his hair and the soft mounds of muscle beneath my lips. He stood still as I continued with my exploration, his chest rising and falling with passion. He unpinned my hair, so it flowed down my back in thick waves.

'I want you so badly, Lina,' he almost whispered against my lips. 'I ache for you.'

'I want you too.' I pressed myself to the full length of his hard, unyielding contours of his body.

I could almost feel him trembling. My lips touched his forehead, his eyes, his mouth, sliding my tongue over his lips, feeling the warmth and smoothness of them.

I kissed his neck, his chest, circled his nipples with my tongue, I felt them harden in my mouth. I sensed the fire racing through his veins, I felt the rumble of his groan vibrate on my lips.

'Lina, can you see what you are doing to me,' he said.

I knew what I was doing to him, and it was delirious and wonderful, because I felt the same.

Walking around his body, my hands moved around his chest to his back, I placed feathery light kisses across his shoulder blades. All my fear and inhibitions melted away.

In one swift motion he picked me up and placed me gently on the bed. His hands slid down over my breasts, his tongue followed, which circled the pink crests until they hardened with pleasure.

With every slight movement my body twisted beneath his gentle assault, every sound I made the more ravenous he became.

My hands were tangled in his hair, then I ran them over his shoulders and back. My nails dug into his flesh. Then he moved down to the triangle between my legs, they fell apart on their own and he looked up at me and grinned, he teased and toyed with me, and delighted in tormenting me until I was more than ready for him.

He shifted up over me as I lifted my hips to receive him, his hardness coming into intimate contact with me. I felt the heat of him sliding slowly into my warmth then the sharp but brief tear inside of me.

A quick flash of an image almost like a camera shot came to my vison; I was being taken from his arms, screaming, and then I saw myself running towards a light. I gasped with the knowledge, and from the exquisite pleasure as he plunged full length into my welcoming softness, the image soon forgotten.

Wrapping my arms and legs around him, I was completely lost in incoherent yearnings to have him stay inside me forever. I lifted myself higher so I could feel him deeper within me, then slowly a building force began to race in a trembling fury along every nerve.

'Please, Nicholas.'

He steadily quickened the pace of his driving strokes, until that volcano of pure lust exploded from my very core. It tore a low scream from my mouth, which he covered with his own and in one deep thrust he poured himself into me.

'I'm home,' I whispered into his ear as we fell asleep.

6

We are betrayed

We were woken by a dull booming noise that echoed through the whole house. Nicholas was up in an instant, putting on his clothes.

'Lina, get up and get dressed,' he shouted.

'What's happening?' I said as I jumped out of bed.

I picked up the freshly washed gown that had somehow, mysteriously, appeared on the dresser overnight.

'He's found us.'

I could see the look of worry etched on his face.

'Who has found us?'

Another boom echoed through the house, I felt it vibrate through my whole body.

'My Uncle and his men.'

The fear started to build up from my stomach, the sort of fear I had never experienced, it's a fear you cannot describe, a fear that this could be mine or even Nicholas's last breath. I've changed history, I was somewhere I wasn't meant to be, and as a result the King and Nicholas have had to detour from their journey. This place wasn't written in history, but now it will be. Will this be their undoing? What had I brought upon Edward and Beth?

'Nicholas, what shall I do?' I could hear the harsh military rhythm of the gunfire, the noise appeared to be getting closer.

'Go find my aunt and make your way to the stables. Stefan will have the horses ready.'

My voice filled with panic. I unobtrusively, put my hand to my throat, I could feel the rapid beat of my pulse beneath my fingertips.

'Lina.' I heard Nicholas shout my name. 'Get moving.'

'Where are you going?' I took my hand down and drew in a deep breath. I needed to calm myself and think clearly.

'Lina, get dressed and go now!' Nicholas picked up his sword and pistol and half-dressed ran through the door.

I looked out the window and I saw a small army of men, some on horses and some on foot moving towards the house. I could hear shouting, muskets firing and swords clashing. The noise was deafening.

I quickly dressed and grabbed the shoes from the dresser, and I ran as fast as I could towards the stairs, where I was met by Clara.

'Come, my lady, the mistress has sent me to fetch you. We must make our way to the stables where Stefan is waiting to take you home.'

I stopped in my tracks. Did I hear correctly? I wasn't sure. 'What did you say?' I asked Clara.

'Stefan is waiting for you my lady; he is to take you home.' Clara took hold of my arm and started to pull me down the stairs.

I jerked my arm out of her grasp. 'I'm not going home,' I said in defiance.

'But, my lady, they are your Lord's orders and you must do as he says.' Her eyes looked pleadingly towards me.

'No, I do not, where is Lady Elizabeth?' I said as I barked my orders at her. Poor Clara she was torn between doing right by Nicholas and following my orders.

She only hesitated for a second. 'In the study my lady,' she replied.

I ran down the stairs towards the study. I shoved open the heavy oak doors just as Elizabeth turned at the sudden intrusion, her face was filled with fear.

'Carolina, you should be making your way towards the stables, please you cannot wait.'

I knew Nicholas had taken considerable pains to get me free from here and back to safety, but I could not leave without him. I pulled Beth away from the window.

'I'm not leaving, I'm going with him, and where is the King?

'Gone ahead with some of Nicholas's men.'

Beth kept glancing back towards the window, I knew she feared for Nicholas and Edward.

'Where is Edward?' I shook her slightly to get her attention.

'With Nicholas fighting off the soldiers, so Charles could escape.'

Beth's eyes kept darting towards the window, then back at me. I started to pull her towards the door.

'Please you must come with me, you cannot stay here,' I begged her. 'You will be captured, Beth.'

She hesitated and tried to pull her arm out of my grasp. I held on tightly. 'I cannot go with you; my place is beside Edward.' She cried.

How could I get her out of this house and away from danger? *Think, Caroline!*

'I have no idea how to get to the stables.' I lied.

The lie worked. Beth thought I was going to follow Nicholas's orders, so she didn't hesitate. She turned her attention to Clara.

'Go and hide with the rest of the staff, I'll take Carolina to the stables, but only come out when you know for sure they have gone, do you understand?'

'Yes, my lady.' Clara curtsied to her mistress, then turned and fled the study.

We took each other's hands and made a run to the back of the house, out through the kitchen towards the stables, my shoes forgotten in my hand until my bare feet touched the cold damp earth.

We both saw Nicholas fighting along with Edward and his men. We stood, unable to move as we watched Edward get a sword through his stomach, Beth screamed and brought the soldiers attention towards us.

From over the noise I heard Nicholas. 'Run, now!' he shouted.

Men with muskets turned and fired upon us. They missed. We ran as fast as our legs could carry us, shot after shot raining past our heads as we tried to flee the carnage.

My heart was pounding in my chest and the noise around us was deafening. My ears were ringing, normal sounds seemed to be cut off. All I could hear was my heavy breathing and the vibration of my footsteps thudding on the cold hard ground as we ran.

Beth let go of my hand. I stopped and turned. She stood staring at me with a blank look on her face, then she crumpled to the floor. Screaming I fell at her head, 'no... no...' no...' Sobbing as I placed her head in my lap. The back of her head was an open wound where a musket ball had entered. Panicking, I tried to stem the bleeding by putting pressure on the back of her head, but I knew this was a pointless task.

'I'm so sorry, Beth, this is all my fault,' I cried.

All of a sudden, unseen hands hauled me up and over a saddle. I sat across Nicholas's lap with my back to the direction of where we are going. I faced Nicholas; his body shielded me from the onslaught of the gunfire. I put my hands around his back and held on for dear life as we sped away from all the bloodshed which had been left in our wake. I looked over Nicholas's shoulder and could see Beth's lifeless form laying on the cold earth with my forgotten shoes. She lay a mere ten yards away from where her husband had fallen while her brother, the Earl of Essex looked on. He was staring back at us; he gave an order to chase and I watched his men as they took to their horses.

Nicholas rode the horse hard and fast, and we managed to lose them after a few hours.

*

With no recollection of how far or even how long we had ridden. I was in shock. I sat shaking uncontrollably, unable to stop. My clothes were soaked in Beth's blood, damp and cold, even with Nicholas's warmth I couldn't calm my trembling body. I felt a sense of cold isolation; it was as if winter had wafted through my body and penetrated deep into my bones. I glanced up from Nicholas's chest to his face, he looked wary, he stared at me as though seeing me for the first time. I put my hand on his face and he slowed the horse to a mild trot and pulled me hard against his chest, he held me so tightly I thought my ribs would crack under the strain.

He turned off the road to a cluster of trees, where he dismounted and tethered the horse. He lifted me off the saddle, and carried me to a grassy space behind a tree, he lowered me down just before his legs gave way beneath him and he collapsed in front of me.

I threw myself at him and he held me, I glanced up to a face so full of pain, he was fighting back the tears and the only thing I could do to comfort him was to kiss him. Notwithstanding, the fact that I was covered in Beth's blood, we took each other forcefully, silently, thrusting with an urgency so intense that I didn't quite understand. It was as if we were driven by a strength of need and this compulsion of ours was born from our fear.

This was no act of love, but a force of passion at the terror we had just witnessed. I think somewhere in the turmoil of our minds we thought this would bring us closer together. If only for a moment, to forget the horrors that we had witnessed.

Finished within moments we clung together, both messy, bloodstained and shaking in the warm sun.

'I'm sorry,' I whispered so quietly. I think it took him a moment to realise what I had said.

'It's not your fault,' he said, as his eyes glistened with unshed tears.

I hadn't known Beth and Edward that well, but for the brief time that I did, it was filled with warmth and kindness.

'It is my fault, if I'd have done as you had asked of me maybe, Beth and Edward would still be alive,' I said, as the tears flowed down my cheeks.

'You cannot think like that, we must move past this, it's all right, we're safe. I'm sorry for taking you like I just did.' He sat back on his heels and put his hands on my face.

'I needed you just as much.' I reached up to his hands.

'But so soon after, I could not help it. When I saw Beth fall and you after, I thought you had been shot too.'

He took in a large deep breath and exhaled slowly. 'The feeling I had inside was so overwhelming, the grief of losing you was too much to bare. I have only known you for such a brief time and…' He shook his head in despair as his eyes filled with tears. His hands fell to his sides, deflated and unsure what to do or say next. What could I do? All I could do was comfort him. I pulled him towards me and held him so close as I sensed his inner turmoil. 'It's alright,' I said over and over. I pulled his head up and looked into his eyes.

'I feel the same way, feels like forever.'

*

We continued our journey north, and the first farm we came across Nicholas paid a heavy coin for the purchase of the family's cart, along with food, drink, some fresh clothes, a pair of boots that where slightly too big and some woollen blankets. The farmer and his wife were neither supporters of the King or Cromwell, so there was hope we would not be reported if any Roundheads were to pass through.

We traveled slowly along the main stagecoach tracks. Nicholas said it was better to be out in the open as we would draw little attention. The Roundheads wouldn't expect us to travel so openly throughout the day, so we had little chance now of being caught. His main objective was to meet Charles in Newcastle. The few men he had left, he gave instructions that if they were to be separated, they were to make their way up to Durham. We stopped at every cottage, house, and village, first to stretch our legs and second to see if any of his men would be waiting along the way.

Cleanliness seemed to be lacking the further north we rode, animals and people lived in the same house and on the same sanitary level. Kitchen and privy slops were thrown from windows and the people were as dirty as the floor. Their clothes were course and stiff with grease and daily life. Disease was rife, faces were marked with smallpox, ringworm, sores that were open with pus.

We passed many a villager with disabilities and no one over the age of ten seemed to have all their teeth - those that remained were black as coals. The bread and stringy fowl we ate for lunch threatened to come back up, but what made me feel worse was that most of the illness I saw could be cured. Very few villagers I saw were over the age of forty, but whatever their appearance, these people were survivors and the healthiest of the heathy.

The weather grew increasingly bad the further we travelled, our pace became slower, the ride was terribly uncomfortable, the pain in my backside was bordering on becoming unbearable and stopping to stretch my cramped legs offered no comfort. I was beginning to miss the jarring of the horse, rather than the bumpy wheels of the wooden cart.

With a profound sense of relief, we reached Durham, the end of the line for the coach track.

We made our way up the cobbled street of Durham Road.

'That's where we will be spending a few nights.' Nicholas pointed to the coach house further up the road.

The Red Lion was set back a little from the road, a red brick building with stables on the side.

The house was two-storied, the oak frame ornately carved, and the soft red bricks were spread with vines. Each chimney was muffled in ivy and puffing with smoke. Honeysuckle framed the doorway, above which a horseshoe had been nailed for protection from witches. The stables next door had been whitewashed, the roof was covered in moss and yellow stonecrop. We walked into the stables and were greeted by a young man of no more than eighteen.

'What can I help you with, My Lord?' the young man questioned.

'Room and board for my horse?' Nicholas flipped him a silver coin.

'Wow. Thank you My Lord, and what shall I do with your cart?'

'Keep it.'

The young lad gave us a huge near toothless grin. 'Thank you kindly, My Lord.' He put the silver coin in his mouth to test it validity.

'You're welcome, boy, and if anyone asks you have not seen…' Nicholas didn't get a chance to finish.

'…Yep my mouth is sealed.'

Nicholas gave him a wink and flipped another coin his way. The lad was overjoyed.

'Look after him,' said Nicholas as he opened the door to let me pass.

'That's his wages for about two years,' I said as we walked towards the Inn. 'I hope he uses it wisely.' I was rather impressed with my husband's generosity. Maybe I had misjudged him.

'He should do, it will feed his family for a long time,' he said as he held the door open to the tavern.

We were hit by the delicious aroma of roasting hog, and my stomach rumbled and my mouth watered. Looking over to where the smell was coming from, I noticed a most disturbing scene; the spit was being turned by a dog in a cage. The dog and cage were placed above the fireplace and every so often the dog let out a low growl as a boy applied hot coal to his hind feet. This, I supposed, was to make him walk faster, all I could think was how barbaric it was. That poor dog.

'My god, Nicholas, Look! That's animal cruelty at its worst.' I exclaimed.

Nicholas's eyebrows rose as he studied me. 'Lina, have you not seen a turnspit dog before?' He smirked.

'Turnspit?' I replied with a certain amount of bewilderment and horror.

'The dog is bought for that purpose only, saves the boy falling asleep and the meat not being cooked the same all the way around. Hot coals on the dog's feet keeps the pike turning at an even keel, so the meat cooks evenly and the boy stays awake,' he stated rather matter of factly.

'I think that's terrible, that poor dog.'

Nicholas gave me a look of wonder and shrugged his shoulders. 'I'm sure he gets rewarded for his efforts at the end of the day. Enough about the dog, go and sit over there in the far corner...' He nodded his head in the general direction of where I needed to go. '...whilst I'll go and make the arrangements for food and lodgings.

As I sat quietly in the corner waiting for Nicholas I overheard two young maids talking behind me. I listened intently with a smile on my face as the two talked in hushed tones between themselves.

'I'm gonna do it, I'm gonna go with him.'

'But Nellie, you know what will happen. Look what happened to Margie, she got dragged down the aisle seven months later.'

'That's not gonna happen to me, I heard from Mrs. Philpot down the road that if you spit in a frog's mouth three times it will not happen.' The young girl called Nellie spoke a little more loudly than intended.

'Shush, Nellie.' Her friend twisted her head around to make sure no had heard her. I shifted along the bench more out of sight. I was intrigued to listen further.

'That's stupid Nellie, I 'have never heard nowt like that before.' Then she stopped and leaned closer.

'Do you think it would work?' she asked with excited energy.

''Course, but I have got to catch me a frog first,' said Nellie.

'My mother said pooh, she says nobody can spit three times in a frog's mouth,' Nellie's friend replied.

'Well, Sammy Morton says, she sees Lizzie Littlejohn do it,' said Nellie, with far too much enthusiasm.

'Uuds Lug Nellie. Lizzie said the same thing six months ago and look at the size of her now.'

'I've not seen her,' said Nellie,

'Course not, Mother chucked her out with Jack Clarke.'

I shook my head and silently chuckled to myself, old sayings and superstitions, no wonder girls got themselves into lots of trouble.

Nicholas walked back and took a seat opposite me, the girls conversation now forgotten.

'All done, we can either eat down here or upstairs in our room,' he said.

'I'd rather go upstairs; I need to lay down. I'm exhausted.'

'I'm not far behind you either.' He closed his eyes for a moment, then opened them and smiled tiredly at me.

'Come, let's go.' He took my hand as he helped me from the table, our hands remained entwined as we made our way past the young girls, I stopped and leaned down to them.

'Girl's just a word to the wise, no amount of spitting in a frogs mouth will stop that.' They blushed as I winked at them. All opened mouth and not a comment to be said.

'What was that all about?' Nicholas questioned.

'Ask me another time.' I smiled warmly up at my husband as we made our way to the stairs. As we went up, I heard some men below begin to sing, their voices roaring out in jovial good humour, all off key and out of tune:

King Charles, King Charles
When said and done.

King Charles, King Charles did run.
King Charles has lost his throne
King Charles all said and done.

At the top of the stairs, Nicholas unlocked the door and stepped back to let me go in first. The room was cosy and welcoming, I felt the tiredness of the journey drop away as I entered. The room was of decent size and in my opinion magnificent compared to sleeping in the cart under the stars, waking up damp and cold. The walls were panelled oak, dark and rich. The chimney piece, also oak, was elaborately carved with patterns of flowers and the embers from this morning's fire still glowed red with warmth.

The floor was bare, and all the furniture was in the heavy, florid style belonging to the early years of the century, the chairs and stools had been covered with thick cushions of sage green or ruby-coloured velvet, worn just enough to have acquired a look of shiny smoothness.

The bed was a standard double four-poster bed, with red velvet hung curtains that had seen better days, which could be pulled at night to enclose the occupants in privacy and warmth. A wardrobe stood against one of the walls, and a small table with a mirror next to it. The other side of the room was filled with two small windows, both dressed in more of the red velvet material.

Nicholas appraised the room and declared, 'At last some creature comforts,' as he sat on the bed and bounced up and down on it to test the softness.

I laid down on the bed and closed my eyes. I could still hear the men singing downstairs which filtered up faintly through the cracks in the floor. Nicholas had lent over. I felt his breath on my face. Opening my eyes, he kissed me gently on my lips.

'At least, my love, you shall have the comforts of a bed for the next few weeks,' he murmured into my ear as he laid down beside me.

'And the warmth of you beside me.' I turned on my side.

Nicholas settled himself more comfortably, turning on his back and cradling me in one arm, my head resting on his chest.

'I'm sorry, I have brought you into this, are you afraid?'

I raised my head up and saw the uncertainly on his face.

'Don't be sorry, and I'm not afraid. I'm with you and that's all that matters.'

'Yes, but…'

A rhythm of knocks at the door made Nicholas jump up. He walked to the door and knocked. Then another rhythm of knocks came from the outside, it was like a pattern back and forth. Nicholas quickly opened the door and a hooded figure walked in. He closed the door quietly behind him and removed his hood.

'Stefan, by god it's good to see you.' They both clasped each other, then they walked over to the table.

I pulled myself up and off the bed and made my way towards them both.

'I'm so glad you're unharmed,' I said to Stefan as I took hold of his hands. He looked a bit uncomfortable with my show of affection, but Nicholas took no mind as we all sat down at the table.

'How did you find us so quickly?' I ventured.

'I've been keeping a daily lookout, hoping to see Nicholas, and by luck I just arrived when I saw you both walk into the tavern.

'What's happened to Charles?' Nicholas asked Stefan, but by the look on Stefan's haggard face, we could tell it was not good news. Stefan clasped his hands together as he rested his elbows on the table. He put his chin on his hands as he looked to me then back to Nicholas.

'I handed him over to the Duke of Richmond, and then we heard they disguised him as Ashburnham's servant and slipped past numerous roundhead garrisons. Then Charles handed himself in at Newark to the Scots, but he has been betrayed.

My eyes darted to Nicholas, I felt my throat constrict as I swallowed up and down. I knew what was coming.

'Betrayed, by whom?' said Nicholas.

'Holland and his brother,' Stefan replied.

Nicholas looked directly at me. Questions were hidden behind his eyes, and once we were alone, I knew he would want answers. My mouth went dry and my palms became clammy.

'Tell me,' said Nicholas with a voice of steel.

Stefan continued. 'They both conspired with Essex and Fairfax, they bribed the Scots to hand over Charles, but before they hand him over, they wanted him to sign a document,'

'What sort of document,' asked Nicholas, but he already knew, because I had told him the night of our wedding.

'Cromwell wants him to be a King of consort, he is to retain everything, but parliament rules England,' said

Stefan. I felt Nicholas's eyes still on me, but I remained silent.

'What has he decided?' said Nicholas as his glance flickered back to Stefan.

'He won't sign, says he would rather be dead. If he cannot be a king to rule, then he won't be King at all.'

'So, what are they planning to do with him?'

I could feel the invisible crosscurrents of emotion radiating from him. I lowered my eyelids, indicating that I understood, and Nicholas silently nodded. Stefan continued hopefully unaware of the mounting tension between us.

'They're keeping him under close guard at Kelham House. Once he agrees to sign, they will most probably send him back to London, to Whitehall' said Stefan.

A knock at the door stopped the conversation Stefan stood abruptly and hid behind the door as Nicholas opened it.

'Your food, My Lord.' A young serving maid stood with a tray of our food, she peered in the room, I could tell by her face she had heard two male voices.

'I'll take it, thank you.' Nicholas took the tray of food off the young girl and kicked the door closed with his foot, he walked over and placed the tray of food and drink on our table.

'Come Stefan, there is plenty of food here for us all,' I said as I took the plates off the tray and placed them on the table. I changed the subject in hopes this would diffuse some of the tension in the room, and to delay the inevitable.

The food smelled wonderful; pieces of meat, stuffed with a mixture of breadcrumbs, with vegetables, onions, and herbs.

'Thank you, my lady, but no, I promised young Alec and Sir Gregor I would not be long. We are staying in an inn nearer to the town.'

'Oh, thank god they're safe, why don't you all come here?' I asked.

'We need to be close, the town is full of roundheads, which means we will have more of a chance at getting the information we need.' Stefan stood, and then nearly collapsed back onto the chair.

'What's wrong, Stefan?'

'I was shot when we fled Barnwell. The ball is still lodged in my shoulder.'

Why hadn't I noticed his deathly pallor beforehand? Probably because I was too preoccupied with my own troubles.

'Sit, let me see,' I ordered.

'No, my lady, it's fine,' More colour drained from his face as he tried once more to stand.

'No, you're not fine. Nicholas please tell your friend.'

'Do as she say's Stefan, no point in arguing.'

He reluctantly took his shirt off so I could inspect his shoulder, the roughly put together bandage had dried and had stuck to his wound.

'This dressing will have to be soaked off, then it will need to be cleaned of infection.' They both peered up at me.

'Infection?' Stefan looked worried.

Think, Caroline, they don't know what infection is.

'It needs to be free of the dirt, and the ball taken out. This is to prevent Stefan getting a fever.'

'Oh, fever,' they both said in unison.

Right think, Caroline, remember what I had been taught.

'Nicholas, can you go down to the kitchen and get me a large pot of water, clean bed linen, garlic, thyme, willow bark and if not, some chamomile or black pepper.' Nicholas hovered, not knowing what to do next.

'GO!' I barked at him.

He was soon back, with arms full of the ingredients I had asked for.

'They didn't have willow bark or chamomile, but I have plenty of pepper, garlic and thyme.'

'Good, put them on the table, now tear strips of linen off for me.'

Nicholas was busy making the strips whilst I put the pot of water on the newly stoked fire.

Whilst waiting for the water to boil, I crushed the garlic and thyme in one bowl and the black pepper in another. Once the pot was boiling, I added the crushed garlic and thyme and a few of the torn linen strips.

'Why are you doing that?' Stefan glanced over at me with a worried expression.

'It takes the germs off the linen,'

'Germs?'

Oh, crap. Looking over at Nicholas I noticed the tightening of his lips and the narrowing of his eyes. I knew he was trying to process everything.

I couldn't worry about that now, so I continued with my task. I gently pulled the bandage off as carefully as I could. The dirty dressing was still stuck, even after soaking it with the hot water. Droplets of fresh blood oozed out of the edges of the wound.

'I'm so sorry, Stefan.' I winced as I pulled the bandage completely off.

'It's fine, my lady, I have been hurt much worse than this. It is just a flesh wound.' he grimaced.

'Yes, but a deep one, come and lie on the bed, so I can get the bullet out. Trust me it will much easier if you did lay down.'

'Bullet?' Nicholas's voice vibrated around the room, I didn't bother to answer or even look up. Stefan still sat up and took no notice of me, it was as if he was waiting for permission from my husband.

'No my lady I shall be fine, this is where you shall be sleeping.'

'Please Stefan just do as I ask.' He took one look at my face and laid down without protest.

'Nicholas please can you pass me the brandy.'

Nicholas did as I asked without comment, he watched me closely and I could feel the undercurrent of emotions radiating from him. I had no time to think about what would lay ahead, I had to get this musket ball out.

'Now this is going to hurt, brace yourself Stefan.'

I poured the brandy onto his wound, and the knife. Stefan groaned through clenched teeth, but refrained from shouting aloud. I dug out the musket ball with Nicholas's small knife. The nasty part done, now I would need to apply some form of antiseptic paste to the wound. With a small amount of the garlic and thyme water I added the crushed pepper to make a poultice. After smearing a large amount of it on the wound I placed the soaked lined squares over it and then proceeded to bandage him up.

'This needs to be changed every day, do you understand?' I said to Stefan as I helped him on with his shirt.

'Yes, my lady, although my shoulder is starting to feel so much better already. Thank you.'

'Just because it feels better it doesn't mean you can do anything silly.'

'Yes, my lady.'

'For god sake, Stefan, please just call me Caroline.'

'Not Carolina?' Nicholas said as he pulled the chair out for me to sit down on.

'No, I prefer Caroline, come, let us sit, have something to eat and drink. You will feel weak Stefan but you need substance inside you so you can get back to town safely and in one piece,' I said.

'Yes, my lady, sorry, Caroline.'

Once I had cleaned myself up, I sat to join the men at the table. We ate the cold food and drank the warm cider that had been brought up earlier. No words were spoken.

After an hour or so the colour had returned to Stefan's face, gone was the ashen, sickly look, and in its place was a slightly pink complexion.

'Well, I must say, Caroline it's the best I have been all week,' he admitted.

'Good, I'm glad to hear it.'

'However, did you learn to do that?' Stefan asked with keen interest.

'I love gardening, I was taught by a wonderful man and he showed me that plants and herbs even flowers can be used for all types of things and I genuinely believe that while we live on this planet, our earth can sustain us. Food, medicine. Life really.'

Nicholas remained silent. He hadn't said anything to me, apart from the idle chit chat with Stefan concerning their plans to stay put for a while, with hopes that more of Nicholas's men would return, and to gather more information about Charles.

Stefan took his leave of us, with the promise of returning in the late afternoon for a fresh dressing.

I had dreaded this moment all evening. I watched Nicholas as he closed and locked the door, and I could tell by his body language that he was wary of me as he joined me at the table. I went to speak but he put his hand up to silence me.

'Stop, let me speak now. I have known of Carolina Sackville all my life, we only met on several occasions when we were both incredibly young. Yes I found her to be a beautiful little girl, pleasant and kind, well adverse in most topics, but extremely pampered and very, very spoilt and she would most probably faint at the sight of blood.'

I attempted to speak again.

'Let me finish!' His voice held authority and I knew it was wise not to interrupt him again.

'The Carolina of Copped Hall would have no knowledge of medicines, how to remove a lead ball, let alone know what types of plants that could take away pain and fever. Who are you?' Gone was the caring husband and in his place was the inquisitor, mistrusting and cautious of me. What should I do, tell him, or bend the truth?

7

The truth be told

The kind and loving man was gone, and the old Nicholas had returned. His churlish manner wasn't lost on me. I tried to take his hands but he pulled away. My heart broke a little knowing that somewhere in the process of helping Stefan I had lost Nicholas. How did I begin to tell the man I loved, when I couldn't even make sense of it myself? Everything overwhelmed me. The fear of not being able to go back to my own body and time.

He sat patiently waiting for my explanation, his blue eyes pierced my soul.

'I don't even know where to begin.' My lower lip quivered slightly.

His lips drew back in a snarl. 'Try,' he said, through gritted teeth.

'I'm Caroline Curtis, and Carolina Sackville. I have been born twice, actually many times, but I only remember two. Sixteen-twenty-two and Nineteen-ninety-two and if that makes me a witch, then I must be.'

My nerves took hold of me, I stood from my chair and started pacing the room.

'I was born three hundred and forty something years in the future, I haven't been born yet...well I have...but...'

Nicholas sighed in exasperation and he went to rise from his chair.

'Please, wait! I know it sounds strange but please be patient with me, that's all I ask.'

He sat back down, and crossed his arms over his chest and his legs at the ankles as he leant back in the chair.

'Since I was fifteen I have heard your voice, it whispers to me in my dreams, sometimes the wind would carry your voice even when I was awake. Not every night or all the time, but you have always been with me. Don't get me wrong it scared me half to death, but over the years I got used to it.' I caught his eye, but he still didn't answer, but made a small twitching movement in his legs. I took a step closer and continued.

'Then one day I was standing outside Debden Manor, your home...with you, a future version of you, and I think meeting you triggered something, a feeling so deep within me, something old but new. There was an accident and I got hit on the head...when I woke up.' I sighed and rubbed my clammy hands down the sides of my dress.

'I was in this body and this time, it looks like me, but it's not me, if that makes any sense. I wandered around for ages trying to find some sort of explanation, but I couldn't find one and I still don't have one. Then Mr. Carson our grounds man found me and when I touched him, Carolina's memories downloaded all at once into my brain and then I blacked out.'

'Downloaded, what is this word?' he frowned in confusion, it made little slash lines across his forehead.

'It's when information is sent to a computer.' I was rambling and I forgot for a moment that half of what I was saying he didn't understand.

'It's like her memories rushed into my memories. I'm one and the same person, both are me.' I stopped to take a breath. Nicholas remained silent.

'The only explanation I can come up with is that I think somehow my soul has traveled back to a past life. Does that make any sense to you? But what I'm finding difficult is that my memories of being Carolina are vague, it's like she has disappeared and I have taken her place. I'm struggle to find my way in this time. I don't say the right things, I upset you, I come across as spoilt, I don't know how to act accordingly to what is right, what is proper. I'm fumbling my way through this time and I'm doing a damn bad job of it.'

I searched his face for a sign of something. He never made a sound or comment. Nothing. I could tell by his face that he was trying to process everything I had said.

'Course you bloody don't understand, how can I convince you, a seventeenth-century lord, about astral plaining, the cosmic bloody universe, and past lives? I don't bloody well get it either, all I know is that I'm here, I know when you die, *how* you bloody die, I love you…. god knows why but I do…I can't save you…I can't make you believe me…I can't even show you this is real because I'm Carolina Sackville too…I'm stuck in a century I don't belong, in a body that's not mine…but *is* mine, and with a man who now probably thinks I'm either crazy, or a witch.'

I collapsed onto the floor and I buried my face in my hands. I sobbed like a baby, I cried so hard I didn't even hear him get up until I felt his arms go around my waist. He pulled me up to his chest and I cried harder making his shirt wet with my tears. He waited for me to calm down. My crying finally subsided, and I glanced up at him.

He held out his handkerchief, which I took graciously. I wiped my face and blew my nose.

'Everything I have told you is the truth I swear it on my life, I would never lie to you.'

He said nothing, he just stared at me and I had no idea if he had even heard me.

'Have you not heard a word I said?' I exclaimed.

'I have heard,' he said dryly.

'I suppose you think I'm mad as a March hare ?'

'Well, I have heard many a tale or two, but not quite as elaborate as this one.' The corners of his mouth lifted slightly.

'You think I'm making this up?' I pulled back slightly to look up at him.

'I don't quite know what to think, but I know some of what you say.'

'What to do mean?'

My spirit lifted and for the first time in weeks I felt hopeful.

'Two weeks ago, you say?' His eyes softened as he studied me.

'Yes.' Was that recognition I saw on his face?

'I had the strangest of dreams. I saw you, you were walking away from me, you had these strange pink things on your feet and your legs were on show, but I could not see your face. I remembered calling out your name, because it woke me from my sleep.'

'That's when I heard your voice! When I got hit the wind picked up, it seemed to have carried your voice to me, but 'it was just a whisper, but so clear.'

Confusion crinkled his brow as he looked deep into my eyes.

'Oh, Nicholas.'

My insides were bursting with joy, all this time hiding the truth, it never crossed my mind that my husband had experienced something similar.

'So, do you believe me then?'

'Yes, I believe you, love, and I have had the strangest feeling for days now that I have known you my whole life. I dream of you, it's like little pictures flash in my mind, but never the same image, different versions of you, but, like you, I don't understand it, Lina, but in time I think we will.' He brushed his hand across my face before he pulled me into his embrace.

We held each other tightly for some time, then I raised my head up so his lips could find mine, before I knew it we had stripped each other of our clothes and we were naked on the bed, kissing every inch of each other's bodies as if we had never tasted each other before. It was not like before in the woods, with urgency, it was somehow different, like finding ourselves all over again.

After, I lay in the warm curve of his shoulder, letting my tired mind drift without the worry and the uncertainty of why this had happened.

'I'm so glad you believe me,' I said sometime after.

'Yes, I believe you, but it would have been much simpler if you had been a traitor.'

'And, pray, what would you have done with me if I were?'

'Taken you back home, locked you in my bedroom and made love to you every day until I convinced you to fall in love with me and turn your beautiful, stubborn head to my beliefs. Well, the loving you would be the easy part, because I'm already there.'

'You love me?'

He smiled down at me. 'Did I say that?'

'Yes, I distinctly heard you say it would have been easier...' before I could finish, he kissed me with such passion. A single tear rolled down my cheek, and he kissed it away with his lips.

'Yes, I love you now, I loved you before and I will continue to love you even after death.'

My heart melted. 'I love you too.'

We lay still in each other's arms for some time, until Nicholas lifted his head and looked down towards me. 'What is this word you keep saying, *can't*, sometimes you say it so quickly I often mistake it for sailors' talk.'

I tipped my head up towards him and laughed, I laughed so hard my sides ached.

His brows drew together. 'It's no laughing matter, at times this word doth comes out of your mouth at the strangest of times and it takes me by surprise, it is most un-lady like, love,' he said, rather animated.

My laughter subsided. 'Can't is not the word you think it is. In my time words have been shortened, you say cannot, in my time we have shortened it to can't. Another example you would say, *is not*, but I would say *isn't*... get it?'

'Umm... I suppose, but if you say it, it must be true.' I could hear the mirth in his voice.

'So, in the future you all talk rather lazily?' he quipped.

I chuckled a little. 'No it is not, and we do not,' I empathized the way he spoke. 'Talk lazily. It's just that our speech has evolved over four hundred years.'

'Umm, it is strange in my mind, king's English is English, and should not be changed,' he said rather matter of factly. His eyes were more slanted than usual as he smiled at me, half lidded and a little drowsy. He rolled onto his back and lift his arm so I could cuddle up to him.

'Well, my love, shall we just agree to disagree?' he said.

'Mmph, Let's call it a truce then.'

The hollow of his throat lay just by my face. I set my lips there, he shivered. I smiled to myself as I pulled the heavy quilts up and snuggled down in the softness of the mattress, with my husband at my side.

'Goodnight, husband,' I said as Nicholas tightened his grip.

'Goodnight wife.' He gave a sigh of pure contentment, and I relaxed against him, feeling our cocoon of warmth surround us. We fitted perfectly.

I lay awake long after Nicholas had fallen asleep. The candle had guttered and gone out, the fire on the hearth burned low. The bright moonlight shone through the misted window, and, as dim as it was in the room, I could still pick out all the details of the room; the washstand with the China basin and jug, the dirty plates from our meal earlier, even our heap of discarded clothes, which had been thrown rather hastily onto the floor.

I turned my head to look at Nicholas. The covers had slipped down past his chest, which rose and fell softly with his breath. My fingers traced the powerful lines of his ribs that formed his chest, and I ran my hand down his belly towards his hip. I admired the long slant of his belly, where small sprays of dark hair spiraled across his olive skin.

145

The last traces of the light from the fire outlined his beautiful body. He stirred ever so slightly at my touch as I put my hand on his legs. I felt it flex under my touch.

'God, you're wonderful, I love you so much,' I whispered faintly, as I kissed his shoulder.

His warm hand still held me, and I felt his thumb brush my skin ever so slightly. Making me tingle at his touch.

'Wife, we have a few hours of night left, unless you want me to keep you awake for the remaining, I suggest you get some sleep.' His voice was husky with sleep.

'No, I guess not.' I smiled as I snuggled closer.

With a sleepy murmur of assent, he kissed me and then he rolled onto his side facing away from me and drew the quilts up to cover us. I curled up behind him, knees fitting perfectly behind his own.

The warm firelight was behind me now, gleaming over his broad smooth shoulder. I put my hand across his stomach and felt his hand close over my own.

The inn had become quiet, and I could feel my eyelids getting heavy. I was struggling to keep them open but I tried to resist falling asleep, because I knew my dreams would disturb me.

They were more frequent now, and somewhere buried deep within me I knew these were not dreams, they were little snippets of a life before, but not a life of this earth. I felt myself drift into the darkness of my mind.

I felt as if I were in the clouds, floating above the earth, looking down on everything. I was in a long line with other people, waiting, unaware what was happening. The line seemed to be getting shorter by the second. I saw what looked like an officer inject a white glowing substance into the sides of their necks with a small syringe, then they would disappear through a white light.

'Excuse me,' I said, catching the arm of the older man in front of me. 'What's happening?' A fear of mingled dread and confusion bubbled through my stomach.

His face screwed up in thought. He inhaled and exhaled rather deeply.

'We are having our memories wiped before we step through the portal,' he said, as he shuffled a few steps forward.

I felt the panic rise within me. 'Pardon? I don't know what you mean?'

'They don't want us to remember,' he said, as sadness clouded his features. He turned back around and shuffled along the decreasing line.

'Who doesn't want us to remember?' I touched his arm to get his attention again. He sighed and gave me a weak smile that didn't quite reach his eyes.

'Don't you see? It's a game for the angels. It's to see if soulmates can find each other once their soul has been placed.'

'Placed?' He started to walk away. 'Stop, please I don't understand!'

'Caroline, it's Claire, please wake up, you have been asleep for days now, and we need you to wake up. Please! We miss you.'

8

No friend of mine

I woke with a pounding headache. Every muscle and joint in my body ached. I had slept deeply, but the disturbing reality of my dreams kept my mind active, which made me mentally tired rather than physically, but then yesterday had been quite an ordeal.

I pushed my thoughts and fears to the back of my mind and sat up in bed. It must be late morning, because the sun streamed through the little obscure glass windows. The light sliced through the wooden floor, which made the room appear cozy. I could even see the tiny particles of dust floating haphazardly around the room.

The room was empty save for my discarded gown on the chair and a fresh tray of food, with a goblet of sweet wine on the table. It didn't worry me too much, as I knew Nicholas would be back at some point, he had probably gone into town to seek out Stefan and Gregor.

I climbed out of bed and pulled the blanket with me. I wrapped it around my naked body. Even though the room was filled with sunlight, it still wasn't enough to banish the late morning chill from the room. I knelt by the hearth and went about the task of re-kindling the fire, wishing I had a box of matches. Striking the sparks of the flint, I expected to it work first time, but no such luck; after the dozenth time, a small spark flew on the twisted tow that was used for kindling. It grew at once, and formed a tiny flame. I carefully placed it beneath the little pile of fresh logs that Nicholas had left for me. I picked

148

up one of the light peat bricks from the basket to feed the fire further.

I was rather pleased with myself as I stood back with delight, and marveled at the luxurious warmth the fire now radiated. I walked over to the table, and sat down to a breakfast of crusty bread, boiled eggs, and cheese. The bread was still slightly warm, so I knew Nicholas had only left a short while before I had woken.

*

The boredom was killing me, my mind wouldn't let me settle, too many thoughts about my situation were running around in my head. I had lost all sense of time, and no idea how long Nicholas was going to be, so I decided to get dressed and go outside for some fresh air.

Wandering around the small town, I came across a little square. In the centre there were makeshift stalls where market traders were selling their wares. As I walked past each stall, I stopped to admire all their goods on display.

Nicholas had left some coins on the table and I presumed he had left them for me. I bought myself a basket, a woollen shawl, and gloves for the chilly evenings. Much to my delight, I came across a stall selling herbs, mixtures of roots and homemade remedies for all types of aliments. I was totally in my element.

Everyone I spoke to was friendly and helpful, and I was starting to feel very much at ease in this time. The last stall I came to was filled with fruits and vegetables, and after purchasing some apples, I made my way back towards the inn, blissfully taking in the wonderful surroundings.

I was in my own little world, eating one of the delicious apples I had just bought and thinking about Nicholas, and wondering if he was back. Just then I felt something sharp press against my side, and dropping my basket, I watched the apples roll down the hill.

'Where is he?' Turning my head to see who had grabbed me, I came face to face with the man I had seen from Barnwell, with his pox marked face and thick-set body. He was holding me in such away I couldn't escape, yet to anyone looking on, it would seem as though we were acquainted. I felt the colour drain from my face.

'Sorry, I don't have the faintest idea as to whom you are talking about, and I would be thankful if you removed that knife from my side.' I tried to come across confident, but inside I was trembling with fear.

'My nephew Nicholas.' he sneered at me.

'Who? What?' I couldn't think straight, my mind spun in small circles around the central fact that the Earl of Essex had found us.

'Of course, you do, my dear, he is the one who took you from my sister's house.' His nostrils flared at me in contempt.

I tried to appear unfazed by this man, so I continued with the charade. 'Oh, that gentleman. I have no idea, I was visiting Elizbeth, and I woke to the sound of gunfire and we both fled.'

Water pooled in my eyes at the thought of Beth lying dead by his feet. I blinked the tears away hoping he didn't see.

'We made our way up here, he left me at the inn with some coin, and made off two days ago.' I jerked furiously as he dug the knife in deeper.

'You lie, I have spoken to the owner. Now, where is he?' He glared at me, eyes narrowed, and I suddenly realised that the calm he was displaying on the outside was not what was going on in the inside; he was extremely angry. I saw the muscle of his throat move as he swallowed, he was trying to keep himself in check. I continued with my lie.

'I've told you; I don't know. I woke up this morning and he was gone.'

He picked up my left hand. 'Well, Lady Trevilian. If I have you, then he won't be far behind.'

Crap he knows. 'How?' The horror of my situation hurtled full speed through my body. My mouth dried and my heart hammered fiercely in my chest.

The corners of his mouth lifted. 'It's amazing how much information you can get out of a tortured chamber maid.'

'No. Damn you. You ugly, poxed faced bastard, you will pay for that'

I flung my words at his face and he flinched slightly. The colour was rising in his face; the tips of his ears were red, and his skin was stretched over his cheekbones, a true sign of impending fury.

'Let go!' I kicked him sharply in the shin, hard enough to numb my toes, but instead of letting go he squeezed tighter, making me yelp. His eyes turned dark, menacing. I tried hard to break free, I swung at him and missed. I didn't see the closed fist that punched me so hard at the side of my head. I lost consciousness.

*

I woke to unfamiliar surroundings; it threw me for a moment then clarity set in. I had a terrible headache from when he knocked me unconscious. Sitting up from the four-poster bed I looked around the room; the bed was heavily draped in red and gold fabric that matched the curtains on the windows.

The room was quite large, with light oak wall panels that pictures and tapestries hung from. A large writing desk with gold handles stood at the far end of the room next to a large wardrobe and dresser. Under the window there was a small lounge chair that looked newly upholstered in gold velvet. The oak fireplace was beautiful, it was carved out with patterns of roses and birds, the embers had almost died down, which made the room chilly.

I walked over to the window and peered out, all I could see beyond the hill was farmland and a few estate cottages scattered around. I had no idea where I was, or even how long I had been away from Nicholas, but judging by the mist rolling along the fields it was just after dawn. The weather was cloudy with a small drizzle of rain, and I shivered as the cold seeped through the windows onto my face and neck.

I walked to the door and turned the handle, locked. My vision blurred, and I started to lose my balance. I was still reeling from the blow the Earl had given me. Very reluctantly I climbed back into bed to stop the spinning. I couldn't think straight, I needed a clear head to plan my escape, but deep down I knew this to be futile, and I was desperately hoping Nicholas would find me.

I buried myself under the covers, not sure if it was for the warmth or security.

My eyes started to feel heavy and it wasn't long after that I fell back to sleep.

It was late morning when I woke again. After cleaning myself up with the chilly water that had been left in the basin, I sat at the dressing table studying the swollen black eye that I had received from the earl. It must have been quite some hours since I got the blow, because the bruise was starting to turn a purplish colour. Food had been left on the table, bread, cheese and some slices of ham. I was ravenous and it was gone in seconds.

My stomach turned in dread as I heard the lock in the door turn, the earl sauntered in quite casually, as if I were a welcomed guest.

He gave me a once-over glance that took in my tattered appearance, and without saying a word, he pulled a chair up and sat opposite me, staring.

His was quite handsome to look at, he had the same family trait with the blue eyes, but his face was lined with age and pitted terribly, obviously having had smallpox at an early age. He stretched his legs out in front and crossed them at his ankle near to my feet, and this action reminded me so much of Nicholas.

'I must congratulate you, my dear, on your newly appointed vows to my nephew.' He gave me a half-smile that didn't reach his eyes.

'I'll be sure to relay your message as soon as he comes to free me,' I said coldly. I tried to keep my expression closed off as I didn't want to show my fear.

'Oh, I don't think that will be happening anytime soon,' he smirked.

My bravado waivered slightly 'What do you mean?' terror overtook me as I conjured up images of Nicholas lying dead somewhere.

'I thought I would leave one of my men in your lodgings, and when my nephew eventually decides to go back, instead of finding you, he will find my man with a knife to his throat.' He mimed a slash of the knife.

'You actually think your man will best Nicholas.'

I laughed at him, which he did not take to kindly and he repaid me with a sharp slap across the face, the force of which threw my head sideways. My teeth smashed against the side of my cheek, blood pooled at the bottom of my mouth, I raised my head up and forced a smile to my lips. I spat the blood in his face. He wiped it away with the back of his hand and it smeared across his cheekbone. His face hardened, without uttering a word.

'He is your nephew for god's sake! Why?' I said furiously.

'He is a traitor, and traitors must be dealt with.'

His hand flicked away a piece of imaginary fluff on his shoulder. He appeared nonchalant and unamused.

'Not to you he's not, just because he has different political views, it's pathetic. It's a silly war for silly men.' I knew all too well what I was doing, but I couldn't help myself, the more I looked at him the angrier I got.

'Where has he taken the King?' He forced a smile on his face as he leaned further forward. He placed his elbows on his knees and looked up towards me.

'We don't have the King, and if your informant had given you the correct information you should know he was being held at Holdenby House.'

154

'You lie.' A vein throbbed furiously in his neck, I knew he was about to lose control, but I cared not.

'No, sir I do not, you're the liar, and a traitor to your King.'

'Royalist bitch.' That earned me another slap around my face, my head snapped back.

That was it, I was not going to take this anymore, my self-defense classes kicked in. I was up in a flash, and I drew my right fist back so quickly he wasn't prepared. I punched him so hard on his nose it popped under my knuckles. He was up in an instant, he lunged at me as I tried to get to the door, and he grabbed me from behind. Managing to twist around him, I kicked his legs out from beneath him and he fell with a thump to the floor. After a swift kick to his face, I ran for the door.

Just as I threw the door open, he rugby-tackled me and I hit the floor with an almighty thud, the air was winded out of me. Breathing heavily, the earl grabbed my hair and twisted me around. He hit me hard in the face, but it didn't knock me out.

He settled his eyes on me and in that fleeting moment I could see the passion hidden in the depths' he liked this, his was getting off on it. I felt his excitement as he pressed himself against my stomach. He punched me again but this time in the ribs. One of my ribs broke with the force, and I screamed with the pain as I tried to bring my knee up to his groin, but I missed, the pain was unbearable as I struggled to fight him off.

I didn't feel the rip of my gown until I felt the warmth of his body on my bare breasts through the thin linen of his shirt. I tried to scream, but he covered my mouth with his own, hard enough to leave the iron taste of blood in my mouth. This man was determined to rape me, I knew then he was done talking.

'If you're good enough for my nephew, then you're good enough for me.' He moved in fast; scrabbling with one hand to raise my skirts, he thrust his knee between my thighs, I cried out as his weight pressed against my ribs.

'Go ahead, darling, scream.'

I got another punch to my face. Gone was my fear and in its place was anger and sheer survival.

He elbowed down onto my ribs and the burning pain spread throughout my body. The pain was unbearable. It almost felt like I had been stabbed, I screamed for help, he stiffened more. I fought him with boundless fury and the more I screamed the harder he got. He was extremely aroused. *Sick bastard.* He was loving every minute of this.

I realised if I needed to take charge of this situation, I need to humiliate him. So, I laughed and laughed, I felt him soften, which earned me another punch to my face. My lip split. I spat the blood from my mouth onto his face and laughed hysterically. I could taste the blood between my teeth.

'Shut your mouth, bitch!' he screamed at me, as his face came within an inch of mine.

I slapped him hard across the face, my fingers curved as I raked my nails down his cheek. He jerked back and grabbed both my hands; they were pinned to either side of my head. Without any thought I flung back my head I brought it back so fast my forehead connected with his already broken nose, he screamed in pain and relaxed his grip. I took the opportunity to roll away.

Bleeding and in pain I ran through the door and down the stairs with the Earl close at my heels.

Some of the servants came out, and he screamed at them to get back to their duties and to stay away. I ran through the nearest doorway and headed towards the fireplace and grabbed the first thing my hand touched: a coal shovel. Turning back, I ran full speed at him, I don't think he expected that, as I caught him off guard. Swinging with all my might I hit my target. I hit him so hard on the forehead he collapsed, out cold on the floor. Dropping the shovel, I ran through the house screaming for help, but no one came except a young boy.

'This way miss,' he said, with a frightened look about his face.

I was so grateful, I followed him through the house, luckily encountering no one on the way. I think they were too afraid to come out.

My lip was swollen, my jaw felt like it had been broken and I had a terrible burning pain in my side, so all I could manage was a weak 'I need a horse.' The boy took me to the stables and gave me a blanket to wrap around me. 'Where am I?' I whispered weakly.

'York, milady,'

'Can you point me to the main road?'

He pointed towards the cottages I had seen out of the window this morning. 'Go past those cottages over yonder and you won't miss it.'

'Thank you so much.' Words couldn't describe my gratitude to the boy.

'You're welcome.'

'Will you get into trouble?' I asked pensively.

'Nah, master's out cold and us servants all stick together,' the boy said as he helped me mount the horse.

After ten minutes or so, true to his word I came across the main road, but I was in a dilemma, which way should I go? I couldn't see any signposts, but I knew I needed to go North, so I turned left and followed the sun.

9

Safe and found

I was hoping to get some ground covered before the earl woke as I feared he would relentlessly purse me. Having bested him it would not go unpunished, so I rode the horse as fast as I could, not stopping for anything not even the pain. I rode most of the day, without really noticing where I was going, taking heed only of the general direction of the sun.

I stopped when the light began to fade and when I was satisfied I had not been followed. I struggled to get down from the saddle because of my battered body, but once down I managed quite successfully to tie the horse to a tree. I heard water running and after a few minutes of searching I found a fresh spring of cool crisp water. *What a bit of luck.* I thought as I drank greedily from it ignoring the pain from my jaw, only stopping when my stomach felt full. Then I laid down, hidden from sight. I wrapped the blanket around me and I dropped straight to sleep, unwilling to stay awake for fear I might think and remember. Numbness was my only shelter.

It was pain and hunger that brought me unwillingly back to life the next morning. I drank once more from the spring before I set off again. By noon, my stomach protested loudly, but I was nowhere near a village. I forced myself to carry on, and prayed I would eventually find the main road. My heart sank as I approached a dense forest. Somewhere, I must have lost the road.

It was past mid-afternoon; the rising wind came whooshing past me. *Could it get any worse?* I thought to myself. The cold wind whipped my skirts tightly around my legs and it stung my face with its icy coldness. I looked up at the thick black clouds choking the sky. I pulled the blanket closer for warmth.

The storm that had been threatening all day suddenly whipped itself into a frenzy, lightening split the sky, followed by the primitive boom of thunder. Within minutes the rolling storm was upon me, I bowed my head as I leaned into the wind and rain. I had to stop somewhere for shelter.

I dismounted and tethered the horse, and took cover under an old oak tree. I pulled the blanket higher over my head, to keep the increasing downpour out of my face. I sat for some time, the rain eased up a little, but I was wasting precious time. What was the point in sitting here getting wet, when I might as well get wet on the horse? I re-mounted my steed, and braced myself against the hard English storm. Cold rivulets of rain ran down my torn gown on to my bare chest, and the blanket was now soaked through and offered no protection.

It was near dark; the storm had abated and the blood on my face had now been washed away, but my skin felt tight, stretched as thought ready to split. I knew my face was swollen terribly. My vision was becoming exceeding difficult as the swelling increased around my eyes. I tentatively touched the area. I winced with the discomfort.

The cold and wet had now penetrated though to my bones and I couldn't control the shaking. I pulled the wet blanket tighter around myself, however, it gave me little comfort or warmth.

My pace was much slower now as I struggled to hold onto the reins. My eyes were getting heavy and all I wanted to do was sleep. The pain in my side was more of a dull ache now, and I was fighting hard to stay seated in the saddle. I had covered quite a bit of distance, and wondered why I hadn't come across a village yet. I was completely unaware of the time, the minutes like hours and the hours like days. I had no idea how long I had been travelling for. The hardest thing was trying to stay focused and keep myself balanced, because I knew that if I fell I would not be able to get up again.

In my delirious state I thought I heard horse's hooves heading towards me. I tried to focus, but my eyes rolled, I started to sway in the saddle, my head felt heavy and I could no longer see. Please don't let it be the Earls men. Could I hear my name being called in the distance, or was it my muddled brain playing tricks on me? My horse stopped, and before I knew it I was being pulled from my saddle onto someone's lap.

'Lina, thank god I found you!'

'Nicholas…you—'

'We need to find a doctor now!'

He has found me, I'm safe.

Closing my eyes, I succumbed to the darkness.

*

Too many voices, I can't focus straight. 'Nicholas?'

'Caroline, can you hear me it's Mum.'

'Mum' I tried to speak but nothing was coming out.

'Get the doctor quick, my daughter spoke!'

'Lina, can you hear me?' It was a man voice now.

'Nicholas,' I managed to whisper, 'turn the light out, it's too bright.'

'Caroline, can you hear me, it's Dr Lewis, if you can hear me squeeze my hand.' More light shone in my eyes, and I tried to pull away.

'She is coming to. Stefan, pass me a cold cloth.'

Was that Nicholas's voice I could hear?

'Mrs. Curtis, are you sure you heard something?'

'Yes, doctor she called out, 'Nicholas.'

'Who is Nicholas?'

'I have no idea.' I heard my Mum talking to the doctor, my spirits lifted. *Am I home?* The light was back. It hurt my eyes and I flinched away.

'Mum, please switch the light off.'

'What is she saying, Nicholas?'

Was that Stefan in the background?

'I don't know, she is delirious with the fever, she has been like this off and on for a while.'

'Water,' I whispered

'Pass me the chamomile water, Stefan.'

'Lina, drink this.'

Somewhere in the fog of my brain I heard Nicholas talking to me. 'Drink, love.'

Ever so slowly, I sipped the drink offered, coughing a little as Nicholas laid my head back on the pillow.

I drifted in and out of consciousness over the next three days. I could hear my parents and Claire, but when I managed to speak it was Nicholas who answered me.

By the fourth day my fever had broken. I opened my eyes and looked around. Nicholas was asleep, his head rested by my side. Lifting my hand, I placed it on his head.

He was awake in seconds.

'Lina? How are you feeling, love?' A small smile hid in the corners of his mouth.

Tears stung my eyes; he raised his hand and stroked my face.

'I didn't think I would ever see you again, I thought he was going to kill me.' I cried softly in his hand.

He gently sat on the side of the bed, then lifted his arms and drew me close. He held me in such a way, more of possession, like I was his alone. He kissed the top of my head. 'Well love, he nearly did, and twas only by chance we took a wrong turn and found you when we did,' he said rather solemnly.

'I was on the main road,' I said softly.

'No, love, we found you riding off the beaten track, heading further into the forest and if we had not found you when we did…' His voice trailed off; I could hear the hitch in his voice.

'…but you did.'

He kissed my forehead and clasped his hand over mine.

'He was going to have you killed,' I said.

'He tried, but failed, the inn keeper tipped me off.'

I breathed in a heavy sigh.

'Ouch.' The pain in my jaw and in my side was apparent. 'Everywhere hurts like hell.' I said, as I managed a weak smile.

'He broke a couple of ribs and bruised your jaw,' Nicholas said as I tried to look up at him. I could see the sadness on his face as he nodded, not looking at me, just staring ahead.

We were quiet for a few minutes, the peat hissed on the fire in front of us, it smelt of the earth, we watched the fire dance and flicker up towards the chimney; I seemed to be drawing strength and peace from Nicholas as he stroked my shoulder ever so gently. Closing my eyes, I breathed him in, he spoke and broke the silence.

'When I found out you had been taken…I was like a wild animal, I could not think clearly, my mind was raging, I imagined all sorts of things, but most of all it was the feeling of total helplessness that I fought with. I wanted to kill someone. God, I wanted to kill the inn-keepers wife, for giving my uncle the information he wanted.

'She wasn't to blame, Nicholas,' I interrupted him.

'I know, but I was so thankful when we found you, for two days nigh we searched, and it was Stefan that suggested we ride through the forest away from the main road. When we found you, you were in a terrible state. I wanted to hold you so close and never let you go.'

'Was I that bad?'

'Words cannot describe how you looked; I hope one day it will fade from my memory. Once you were taken care of and I knew you were safe, my worry turned to rage, I wanted to kill the bastard, it took Stefan and Gregor to hold me back. How did you manage to get away?' he asked curiously.

'I hit him on his head with a coal shovel,' I managed a week smile.

'Coal shovel, ingenious.' He looked down at me and chuckled, I chuckled with him, which helped relieve some of the anger and tension that still radiated from him.

'Oh, god, Nicholas, don't make me laugh, my ribs hurt too much,'

'No seriously, how did you escape?'

'I took a self-defence class when I was the other me, and my training kicked in. If you think I look a mess, you should see your uncle,'

'Did he touch you?'

'He tried, but failed miserably,'

'Thank god, I don't think I have lived with myself if he had,'

'But why?'

'Because I didn't protect you, I should not have left you on your own for that length of time,'

'I should not have left the room, so I'm to blame in this mess too.' I felt him kiss the top of my head. 'I'm so sorry, Nicholas, I should have stayed at the inn.' Silent tears once again ran down my face.

'You have nothing to apologise for. We were not far from Sommerhill, a few miles maybe.'

'Just as well really, I would never had lived with myself if anything would had happened to any of you.'

Nicholas gave a heavy sigh. 'And I was so looking forward to killing my uncle and rescuing my damsel.'

'Well, this damsel can look after herself,' I smiled up at him.

'And, don't I know it.' He kissed me again.

'Do you feel hungry, love.'

'No, but I'm thirsty.'

He nodded and reached for the tumbler of water, he put it to my lips rather awkwardly, I took a few slips and put my head back on the pillow.

'You boiled up chamomile water?'

'No, it was Stefan, I was near useless when we brought you back.'

'Who nursed me?' I questioned.

'Myself, with the help of Stefan and young Alec.' My frown creased my brow as I looked at Nicholas.

'A doctor could not be found,' he said.

'I must thank them when I see them next,' I yawned and closed my eyes.

'Sleep, love, you will feel better on the morrow.'

'You won't leave me?' I said with concern.

'Never…hush now and sleep.'

10

A plan takes flight

Everyday my strength improved and by the fifteenth day I was up and mobile.

'Take it easy, love,' Nicholas looked up from the letter he was writing, and a frown flickered across his brow.

'I'm fine, just sore and bruised, plus I need to get moving before my legs seize up.'

Walking over to the table where Nicholas sat, I put my arms around his neck and leaned my chin on top of his head. 'What are you doing?'

'Making plans,'

'What plans?' I asked in curiosity.

'If what you say is true about the Scots receiving four hundred thousand pounds. I have a source in Whitehall, and he says the money is yet to be dispatched,'

'And?'

'I'm going to steal it *en route,* before it even gets to the Scots.'

'Firstly, it's not four hundred,'

'But you said.' He half turned towards me; the look of exasperation filtered through his face.

'No, listen.' I let go of him and took a seat opposite.

'Fairfax and Essex promised the Scots four hundred thousand pounds...but they can't raise that amount, they only send them one hundred thousand, with a promise of more.'

'Then what happens?' His smile held a bitter edge, his right hand unconsciously went up to massage his muscle between his neck and shoulder, you could almost feel the tension radiating from him.

'They never receive it, even after the death of your uncle,'

'What?' His eyes widened in shock.

'I didn't want to say anything, but he dies soon, sometime in September if I remember correctly,'

'How?' Nicholas frowned, looking troubled.

'A stroke,'

'What is a stroke?'

'It's where the blood supply to your brain is cut off.' I could tell Nicholas really didn't understand.

Then it dawned on me, could the wallop I had given him cause the blood clot, or was it just a coincidence? Had the capture of Carolina been destined, was this how it was supposed to play out? History foretold of The Earl of Essex's stoke, so had I been the cause all along? Nicholas's voice broke me from my thoughts.

'Whatever caused my uncle to die gives me some sort of satisfaction.'

'Well he gets his comeuppance in the end, what goes around comes around,' I said.

'I could not agree with you more, love. Anyway enough talk about him, what more can you tell me about the Scots.'

'They lose patience with Charles, because he will not agree to Parliament's terms. They are bitterly unpopular, and this damages your uncle; because they still don't receive the money as promised they want to hand Charles back to the royalists, and withdraw their army back to Scotland. They rely on your uncle to continue to look after their interests in Parliament, but before any funds can be sent your uncle dies,'

'I was so hoping to run him through myself.'

'Shush, let me finish, so with Essex dead, the Scots were more anxious than ever about handing Charles over to an unstable Parliament.'

Nicholas interrupts me again. 'I suppose the best thing I can do is wait until the bastard dies, and then ride to Holdenby and somehow convince the Scots to hand Charles over to me.'

'Don't you see, Nicholas, no matter what we do to try and change the future, history will always push back.'

'I don't know what you mean.'

'History will always fight back, all I can do is try to save *you*. If you know what's coming, you can prevent it yourself, but we cannot stop the wheel of time, it's got to play out with Charles, otherwise the future I know might not exist.'

'So, you're telling me I have to accept Cromwell, and watch him ruin our country.'

'Yes, that's exactly what you have to do, you're part of the problem too, the rich get richer and the poor get poorer – the king and the land-owners tax the life out of them, and they have no say, no vote, no voice. This changes the future for the better, both men and women, poor, middle-class and the upper-class, we are all equal, and by letting this play out it will work to the good of this country. I know you cannot see this now, but trust me, please.'

'I cannot do that. While I have breath in my body, I will see Charles back on the throne, what you're saying is treason.'

'No, it's called progression.'

'No, it's idiocy, Caroline, this is not just about taxation and not knowing his subjects, this all started over the king's religion and a war overseas. Parliament and the people want to remain Presbyterian, and the king is a devout catholic, but this is what they don't understand. Yes, he says he is the divine right and he can do whatever he wants, but he will never force his religion on his people. It's propaganda by Cromwell and his lackeys, they were angry because Charles kept abolishing parliament when he could not get what he wanted, then when he opened it up again he had the audacity to walk into the house of commons and demand. They took this as an affront to their rights.'

'I don't understand, what do you mean?'

'House of Lords do not enter the House of Commons, and vice versa, it is forbidden but Charles, being Charles, stormed down the corridor, entered the House of Commons and demanded, instead of petitioning the house. It's all to do with funding; he wanted money and they refused, this is what started it. People have forgotten the reform Charles has done for this country, it has improved so much under his leadership.' Nicholas sighed and ran his hands through his tousled hair, he leaned back and closed his eyes for a second.

I wished I could take away his worry, but all I could do now was advise him on the next best course of action.

'The biggest problem we have now is what history has foretold, you will raise an army with the Prince of Wales, but you fail and in the process of helping the prince escape, you are caught and, on the 30th of January 1649 you are beheaded along with your king.'

His face dulled, and drained of all colour. I waited for him to say something, anything. That all-too familiar muscle twitched in his jaw as he sat and stared out of the window. He turned his attention back to me.

'Now I know my fate, and the king's, I can put in motion a different plan, will you help me?' How could I refuse him? How could I help? I didn't know everything, only what we had learned in school or read in books.

Nicholas took hold of my hands, his eyes burned with hope and passion.

'You have knowledge of the future love and that's a start.'

I ran my hands through my hair and leaned back in my chair. The situation weighed heavily upon my small shoulders. He really didn't get it. If I couldn't change his mind, then maybe I could change his future.

'I will write to the Queen, tell her everything that I have learned,' he said.

'You cannot tell her everything!'

'I'm not that silly, love, I can just tell her about my fears with the Scots, and ask her to raise funds for Charles's escape,'

'He will never be back on the throne, and I won't help you put him back.'

'Very well, but at least we can try to save him and get him to Holland or France, to live in exile.'

'All right, then,' I conceded. 'But if it doesn't work, we save you.' Nicholas went to speak but I put up my hand to silence him. 'No, only you!'

In my head I knew it would fail, but my heart was telling me it could work, but would the outcome of this new predicament alter history as I knew it? Was it a risk I cared to take? The knowledge that something was going to happen to him should be some defence, but somehow it didn't feel like it. I looked down at Nicholas and saw hope in his eyes, and my stomach lurched with dread.

*

Over the next several months, Nicholas wrote letters to Queen Henrietta, and to the King's eldest son Charles, the prince of Wales. With the help of Stefan, none of the letters had been intercepted at the docks. The queen was to raise funds that were needed, and when the time was right the Prince of Wales would make his way back to England.

'But we don't want him to come back, tell him to stay in Holland with his sister.' I said one afternoon, as we sat reading the letters he had received from the Queen and the Prince of Wales.

'I have asked him to stay, but he insists on coming.'

'Don't you see? History is pushing back!'

'We can change that, love.'

I sighed in exasperation. 'I'm telling you it won't work.' I was becoming anxious. I clenched my hands into fist and my nails dug into my palms.

'With the funds we get from the queen, I can raise a small army, and the day the king gets moved from Holdenby to Whitehall we will intercept. I will have a ship waiting at the docks to take him to Holland before the Prince of Wales even sails for England.

'The money the Queen raises gets stolen.' I felt awful, every good idea he had, I quashed it.

'Stolen. How?'

'I don't know, all I know is when the queen's loyal troops take possession of the funds, the money gets stolen *en-route* by bandits,'

'That's too much of a coincidence.' I could tell from his face he felt angry and frustrated. He twisted the stem of his cup in his fingers as his brow furrowed in thought. 'Unless there is a traitor in the ranks…do you know who, love?'

'I have no idea.'

'That doesn't bode well for us.' He closed his eyes and inhaled deeply, nostrils flaring.

'What shall we do, Nicholas?'

He opened his eyes back to me, one of his curls fell over his brow, he flicked it back unconsciously. 'I will go to France with Stefan, and we will bring it back safely,'

'And what about me?'

'You will go back home.'

I was shocked. I couldn't quite believe what he had said. I looked fiercely into his eyes. 'I will not.'

'Yes, you will.' I could hear the slight command in his voice as he eyes bored into me, but this did not deter me.

'We are not having this conversation, Nicholas, I know more than you, and I can help, so I'm coming with you.' I crossed my arms over my chest and set my mouth in a hard line. Nicholas sighed in exasperation; he knew it was futile to argue with me.

'I have another idea.' I said. 'Instead of going to France, why don't we go to Holland and get the funds from Mary? Surely her husband William of Orange, will give it to her, and while we are there, you can persuade the Prince of Wales to stay with his sister while you arrange the escape of his father. The attack on the Queens funds can still take place, and no one will be aware of our plans. It makes more sense.'

The certainty I had of Nicholas's fate started to change, I felt hopeful.

His eyebrows rose high and he nodded. 'That sounds like a better plan...no one would expect William of Orange to help...well, that's if he can.'

'What makes you say that?' The slight quiver of my voice as I spoke gave me away. Nicholas put down his cup of ale and came towards me. Stooping low, he picked me up and cradled me against his chest. I could smell the clean scent of the soap he had used, through the folds of his clean white shirt.

'His father, Frederick Henry, still reigns, and most of their funds were used to fight the Spanish.'

My brows drew together in wonder. 'Is Holland at war?'

'Not Holland, the Netherlands. They had been engaged in a war against Spain for its independence, but now it's finally come to an end, they are negotiating terms for a peace treaty as we speak.'

'Do you think they will help?'

'We can only try.' I felt him kiss the top of my head. 'Come and lay your head, love, he said quietly. 'It's been a long day for us both.'

Nicholas fell asleep quickly, and the stress of the day had already fled his face, leaving it peaceful and smooth by the time I blew out the candle beside me.

I found sleep hard, my mind was restless, I replayed our conversation over in my head, thinking and wondering if this was the correct way to go. I turned on my side to look at his dark hair, and his highbrow, his strong stubbled jaw. My heart was struck with both anguish and joy. It was bliss to lie still next to him, especially with his warmth growing about my cold limbs. The small ache of tension from my back and neck soon started to fade into the soft layers of sleep.

It was my sister's face I saw, as I sank further into my dreams. We were in an old house somewhere, with an ancient timber ceiling, and old, worn, parquet flooring, with highly varnished weathered oak-panelled walls.

Display cabinets with objects of antiquity were lined up along the outer edges of the room for the visitors to see. Old, scented perfume bottles, a ladies toilette brush and porcelain backed hand mirror that had faded to yellow, with small hairline cracks in the varnish. A gilt inkstand with a feather quill, silver spoons that were speckled brown with age, and an ivory clock that had yellowed over time. Behind the row of objects was a row of painted miniatures, laid flat on a long, dark, velvet, thin cushion. Faces slightly hidden by the light reflecting off the display glass. Claire's blond head bent, absorbed, over the objects.

'Caroline look at these miniatures, most are alike except these two.' Most of the tiny paintings were alike, cherub faced and pale. 'Look at this lady, she looks like you.' She turned towards me in excitement.

I cupped my hands over the picture to stop the sunlight bouncing off the glass, and when I peered closer, there I was, with blonde curly hair flowing over one shoulder, and wearing a necklace of diamonds and a large center sapphire, it was my *something borrowed* from Beth, for my wedding. It was a mirror, not a painting.

My cheeks flushed and my lips trembled as I looked at the miniature portrait next to mine. Nicholas's blue eyes blazed out; his dark curls were combed back neatly. His handsome features bold above his white jabot and dark navy doublet. His mouth half-curled at the corner as if he were about to speak. Our wedding day? But I didn't remember these being painted.

The small white label above, said the Lord and Lady of Debden Manor, Nicholas and Carolina Trevilian, The fourth earl and countess of Essex. I was real, of course I was bloody real, I was living a past life. I was both Carolina and Caroline. Was I dreaming? Why was I looking at us. Had Nicholas survived? Had we managed to change his fate after all? But why was I not with him, had I gone back to my own time? I was having trouble breathing, the velvet cushion the miniatures sat on was smothering my face. The soft material was pressing on my nose and mouth.

Claire pulled the cushion off my face. 'You will never be together; they won't allow it.' She turned away from me.

'Why would you say that?' I screamed at her.
She turned her head slightly. 'You broke the rules.' Her face twisted with hate. She walked away towards the light.

'How can I make amends? I shouted at her, but there was no reply.

I woke up, the sheets were twisted around my body and my cheeks were wet with tears.

Nicholas's hand was on my cheek, gently stroking it. 'Shush, love, you're only dreaming, I'm here.'

I turned my face into his naked shoulder. I clung tightly to his body, frightened to let go. The small sounds of the night and the low noise of the inn brought me back to this life.

'Sorry I woke you,' I whispered. 'I was dreaming about...about...'

He drew me under his arm, and I laid my head on his warm chest. He reached for his handkerchief and dried my tears away. 'I know, you were calling out Claire's name.' He sounded resigned. I snuggled in closer. He smelled warm with his own sleepy scent, which blended in with the clean smell of the freshly washed sheets.

'I'm sorry,' I said again.

He snorted briefly, not quite a laugh. 'You don't have to apologise, love, I'm just sorry I cannot help you with them. I cannot even make sense of my own dreams.' His finger gently caressed my cheek.

'I miss them terribly, my other family, especially my sister Claire, though the guilty part of me would rather be with you, here and now. But the dream was strange, and made no sense no matter how hard I try to piece them together.' I reached up to smooth the rumpled curls off his face.

'Then don't try, but there may come a time, love, that you will feel the loss.'

I pressed my face into his chest and closed my eyes tight, trying to block out the imagine he had created.

'I won't mourn you, because I won't have to. I won't lose you, and you will not lose me. They cannot tear us apart.' Then the thought struck me, and I looked up at his stubbled face. 'Are you afraid I might go back?'

'No,' he replied quickly, as I felt the strength of his arms around me. 'No,' he said again more softly. 'We have a special connection, be it in this life or the next and nothing on this earth or heaven is going to part us.' His large hand stroked down the curve of my back. 'You're mine, Caroline, you always will be and I will never let you go, you are my soul and my spirit, 'til our lives shall be over, and as god is my witness, I will fight Heaven and Earth to keep you here with me.' He closed his eyes briefly.

'You promise?'

'Go back to sleep, love.'

He didn't speak further but relaxed a bit when he felt my arms go around him.

11

Farewell, England.

We had spent the rest of the year in Durham, hidden from the roundheads. During that time we heard that after a sixty-five day siege Oxford had surrendered and it seemed, after that, other Royalist strongholds fell and Charles was now a political prisoner.

It was 1647 and we had seen the new year in. The winter had been harsh, so we waited until the weather warmed before we journeyed across to Hull. Stefan delivered news that the last Royalist post, Harlech Castle in Wales held out a little longer, but surrendered on the thirteenth of March, ten days ago.

We took up lodgings near the port. Letters were written, and sent home with Stefan to explain, travel arrangements made, provisions obtained, and by early May we were walking up the gang plank, and following in our wake were Gregor and young Alec, carrying our trunks. We boarded the Jozua, a Dutch ship that was heading back to the Netherlands after dropping off their cargo of Baltic timber.

'What's so important about the timber the Dutch deliver?' I questioned after I noticed a lot of merchants where arguing over the price.

'Well, love, the Dutch move most of the timber, and we as a nation depend on the Baltic timber because it's the best for ship building and the Dutch know it. So whenever they come into port the price goes up.'

'Only timber?'

'No, they are also the major carriers of grain that comes from the plains of Poland. They are so advanced in agricultural revolution we cannot quite match up.'

This piqued my interest, maybe I could learn a few things once we arrived in Holland.

We were welcomed onboard ship by Captain Bram Van den Berg and his first officer, Mr. Luuk Visser. The captain was a small, portly man, with hair that was greying around his temples. He was red with exertion, and the colour crept up his forehead and into his receding hairline. His face was shiny with perspiration and small beads of moisture sat in the hollow crevasses of his eye sockets.

'Welcome aboard,' he said with excitement, as he shook my husband's hand.

'Thank you for taking us, I know you don't normally take passengers,' said Nicholas.

'Well, the price was too good to refuse, my lord and the truth be told, I welcome the company.'

He shook Nicholas's hand so fast I thought his arm was going to come away from his shoulder.

'May I introduce my wife, Caroline.'

The captain took my hand and placed a kiss on the top of my knuckles. 'It is a pleasure to meet you, my lady.'

'The pleasure is all mine.'

'I have given you my captain's quarters for the duration of our journey,' he said, finally letting go of my hand. I wanted to wipe it down my dress, but I was too polite to draw attention to the fact that his hands where clammy and damp.

'Thank you so much,' I said, as I looked into his kind eyes.

'Think nothing of it, but as a thank you, I request the pleasure of both you and your husband's company for dinner tonight.' He tried to take my hand again.

'That would be wonderful.' I quickly placed my hand on my husband's arm, well out of reach. 'We would be happy to join you, wouldn't we, Nicholas?' I turned to Nicholas for approval.

'Of course, we shall look forward to it.'

'Right, I'll let you two settle in. Dinner will be served seven o'clock sharp. SEM!' He shouted. We were temporarily forgotten, when a skinny young boy with blonde hair and blue eyes, no more than thirteen, ran over.

'If you follow Sem, he will take you down to your cabin, and from there he will show your men where to bunk down,' the captain said kindly.

We nodded our gratitude, and followed young Sem down the gloomy corridor into the bowels of the ship, I could hear the wooden hull creaking as the waves moved along the moored vessel. Breathing in I could smell a mixture of un-washed bodies, the damp, and the salty sea air.

'It doesn't smell particularly healthy down here.' I held my hand over my nose to block out the smell.

'You will get used to it, love, once we set sail the fresh sea air clears the smells away,' Nicholas said, as he held out his hand and helped me down the narrow wooden steps.

We walked along the narrow corridor to the very end. To the left of us, another narrow staircase descended to the bowels of the ship, and to the right lay the captains quarters. Sem opened the door and held out his hand.

'Thank you, Sem,' Nicholas placed a coin in his palm.

'Thank you,' Sem replied in broken English, as he took his cap off and bowed.

'The Captain, will sup at seven.'

Then Sem pointed down the staircase to Gregor and Alec. 'You shall bunk down there, with the rest of the crew,' the young lad said as his R's rolled off his tongue.

Gregor grunted and muttered under his breath whilst Alec followed.

'Gregor doesn't appear to be happy. Where will they be sleeping?' I asked Nicholas, as he closed and locked the door.

'They will string hammocks up, and bunk down in the crew's mess.'

'Will they be comfortable?'

'They will be fine. Stop worrying about my men.'

'Sorry, I cannot help it, we have the nice comforts of a bed, and a fairly decent room, and they have nothing. Was that why Gregor grunted?' I asked curiously.

'They are used to it Lina anyway, Gregor hates confined spaces, it makes him a little grumpy. Now come here and let me kiss you,' he said with a one-sided grin.

'Well it has been a few hours.' I raised a delicate eyebrow, and smirked at him.

'We have some time to kill, my love, so we might as well make the most of it.' Nicholas wiggled his eyebrows at me as I walked into his arms.

'Pervert,'

'Pervert? What is this word?'

'Never mind,' I pulled his head down to kiss my waiting lips.

We took our time which each other, and whenever we lay together it brought flashes of other memories, but not the one I'm living now or even the life before, of Caroline Curtis.

They were clips of our previous lives, always together, but mostly they carried with them the overwhelming loss of losing Nicholas. It almost felt as though I wasn't allowed to keep him. The vision was always only fleeting, and would fade away as my passion burst through every core of my being.

Maybe this is what Claire meant in my dream. My punishment for not following the rules. But how do I make amends, if I have no clue what I had done wrong? And why am I re-living a past life? Or perhaps I haven't lived all my lives yet? Maybe time is irrelevant, and doesn't follow in a linear line as I had always known.

I glanced up at Nicholas. He had his eyes closed; his long thick black lashes moved ever so slightly.

'I can hear you watching me.' he never opened his eyes, he just smiled, and I leaned up on my elbow and kissed him softly on his nose.

'I love you so much it hurts. I know that sounds silly but if I lost you again, I think I would die.' I knew I was being over dramatic, but I couldn't help myself.

'Lost me again? You have never lost me.' Confusion creased his forehead as he absentmindedly stroked my shoulder.

'I have, somewhere in another time maybe, all I know is I have this strangest feeling that I have lost you before, many times, I think.'

'What makes you say that?' he shifted slightly away from me so he could look down at me.

'Because the emotion I have inside fills me with terrible grief, I cannot explain it, it's just a feeling that is buried deep down. The memories are murky, and I cannot piece them together.'

'Like I said before Caroline, don't try, we are here together, now, and nothing is going to tear us apart, I promise.'

'Don't make promises you cannot keep.' I tried to hide the sadness from my voice, but I wasn't doing a particularly good job of it.

He pulled me closer to his side, and I felt his chest rise as he sighed heavily. 'Now I know my fate, I have the power to change it and we will not be parted, ever.' He raised my hand and kissed it.

I said no more as I laid my head on his chest knowing full well the powers that be will not let us change a thing.

My previous life seemed like a distant memory now, almost forgotten. A future without Nicholas, and the thought of going back to my old life without him, still filled me with fear. How could one man consume me? I hardly recognised the girl I had become, even the dreams had subsided for a time, and I no longer woke in the night screaming out for him.

The sound of Nicholas's breathing changed, it was deeper, so I knew he had fallen asleep. I leaned across and picked up his pocket watch, three o'clock, and by the sound of the waves against the creaking ship we had only been out to sea for a short while.

Sleep was almost impossible; my mind wouldn't let me settle, so I climbed out of bed and picked up Nicholas's discarded shirt from the floor. I slipped it over my head as I made my way to the captains bookcase where I browsed through the books that were on display, hoping to find one in English.

The Twelfth Night, written by William Shakespeare, caught my eye. With the book in my hand I made my way to the bay window. I sat and stretched my legs out in front of me, pulled the discarded blanket that had been left at the end of the seat over my legs to take the chill away, and opened the book. I started to read a wonderful tale of unrequited love, hilarious heartbreak, and twins that had been separated in a shipwreck and forced to fend for themselves in a strange land.

As I read further into the story, I felt I had a close affinity with Viola, although I wasn't in a strange land, I was in a strange time. My mind was full of unexplained questions that I couldn't find answers to. Which life and century was I really supposed to be in? Unable to concentrate I closed the book and looked out at the vastness of the ocean. The water was choppy, the horizon dipped in and out of sight as the ship plowed through the waves.

*

We got ready in a comfortable silence, every so often Nicholas would walk over and help me with either lacing up or fastening buttons. All that was left to do was my hair, which I tied into a bun at the nape of my neck and pulled a few lose curls out so they framed my face.

'That will just have to do,' I said as I gave myself a once over in the mirror.

Warm arms circled my waist and I felt soft lips on the side of my neck.

'You can wear a sack and you would still look beautiful,' he exclaimed.

We walked back down the corridor to the front of the ship, the rocking of the vessel made it a little difficult to walk, and at times I would lose my footing. Having never been on a ship I found the experience a little strange.

'I feel a little off balance and peculiar,' I said as Nicholas placed his hand on my back to help steady me.

'You will get used to it love.' he chuckled.

The ship took a dip, bile rose in my throat, I swallowed it down. 'I hope so,' I smiled weakly at Nicholas. He opened the door to the captains dining room.

'Come, come, sit.' Captain Bram stood and gestured wide with his hands. To my considerable surprise the dining cabin was warm and cosy, with warm shades of green, reds and golds. The dining furniture was dark mahogany, and the table was laid with silver, from the candlestick holders to the plates. Even the knives, forks, and spoons were silver.

'You remember my first mate, Luuk Visser. He shook Nicholas's hand and then turned to me.

'My lady.' The second in command took my hand, and kissed the back of it. Mr. Visser was a very slim man with nondescript mousy brown hair. He had a sickly pallor and his eyes held a faint look of dryness which was rimmed dark around his hollowed sockets. Bad diet and lack of sleep was the common cause, but overall he was a pleasant young man, and easy on the eyes.

'It is a pleasure to have such beautiful company.'

He seemed to hold onto my hand a little longer than necessary. Nicholas cleared his throat and frowned at the young seaman, and a little embarrassed, he dropped my hand and stood by the chair opposite me.

Nicholas held out my chair, the men waited until I was seated before they sat.

'Lord Trevilian, how do you find my cabin?' The captain poured the wine and passed one to me and then to Nicholas.

'Please, just Nicholas. Yes we find it most comfortable, thank you.' He raised his glass towards the captain.

The ship took another dip.

'Oh my.' All eyes turned to me. 'My apologies, gentleman, this is the first time I have travelled by sea, and the experience is quite new and a little unsettling on my stomach.'

'First time is always the hardest, but over the next few days you will become accustomed to it,' The captain said with concern.

'Few days? I thought by morning we would be in Holland,' I said, somewhat miffed that I would be longer on the ship than I anticipated.

'No, my lady,' he chuckled slightly.

'Captain, please call me Caroline.'

'Well, Caroline as I was about to say, it may take us a few days to cross and that's if we have the wind behind us.' He picked up the wine decanter and pour himself some more wine. He went to pour more into my glass, I put my hand over the rim.

'No more, thank you Captain.' I grimaced and rolled my eyes at Nicholas. 'I don't think my stomach will take a few days,' I protested. He took my hand and gave it a gentle squeeze.

'I shall make sure Sem keeps a bowl of apples in your room.' The captain paused for a moment.

'Apples, Captain?' I asked curiously.

'Yes, we found that eating apples helps battle the symptoms of sea sicknesses.'

'Which is a diet all your men could partake in. Apples have a huge amount of vitamin c and would reduce the scurvy on board, and would generally improve the wellbeing of your crew, Captain, notwithstanding the fact that apples could be an expense you do not wish to lay out. However, pickled cabbage is a good source of vitamins, as well as fresh vegetables.'

I got a swift kicked to the shins by Nicholas, much to say, shut up, Caroline.

The captain and his first officer looked alarmed at me. After a few moments of awkward silence, the captain raised his glass.

'To my most honorable guests, I hope you find the voyage amenable.'

We raised our glass and clinked, and the captain took a sip of his wine. 'Umm, Marvelous Bordeaux, sixteen-eighteen excellent vintage.

'And here's to the apples,' I smiled, but I knew it didn't quite reach my eyes; the thought of three days at sea filled me with dread. Nicholas narrowed his eyes at me, insofar as to say, *shut the hell up about the bloody apples.* I mentally kicked myself, I must remember to be seen and not heard in public.

I must agree with the captain, the wine was wonderful. I sipped it slowly as I listened to men talk about the journey across.

'What's the route we will be sailing?' Nicholas asked the captain.

'We shall be sailing straight across to the Hook of Holland, then through the waterway canal to the little harbour of Berghaven,' he said cheerfully.

'How long will it take to reach The Hague once we disembark?' Nicholas asked with interest.

'Not too long, about an hour's carriage ride.' The first officer interrupted.

Nicholas nodded his head in acknowledgement.

'That's not too bad, can we take lodgings by the harbour?' His attention was back on the captain.

The captain crinkled his nose. 'Yes, Berghaven has wonderful little cottages for hire or you can stay in one of the inns by the waterfront, although it does tend to get a little rowdy at night, but my best advice is to take a carriage at the harbour and travel straight across to the Hague.

I leaned into Nicholas. 'I would rather go straight there,'

'As you wish, love,' he said, as he took hold of my hand and brought it up to his lips and kissed the back, in a public display of affection which I found rather odd. Thinking this may be more for Mr. Visser's benefit than mine, I inwardly chuckled to myself at this new side of jealousy that Nicholas was displaying.

'Have you any idea what sort of lodgings you will require?' The captain asked Nicholas.

'We are hoping to rent a house in town, near The Binnenhof.'

'May I offer you my humble town house? It's not much, but it overlooks the Hofvijer lake and resides on the outskirts of the Binnenhof homestead.'

'We wouldn't be putting you out, captain?' I enquired.

'On the contrary I shall not be there, this time of year I'm rarely there as my business at sea keeps me away for prolonged periods of time, but I'm more than happy to rent it to you for as long as you both require it.'

We were interrupted by Sem placing our food on the table. The food looked wonderful, but my stomach protested it. The ship lurched over a wave and then dipped back down. I felt the sickness wash over me. I swallowed, feeling a bit queasy.

'Please can you excuse me, gentlemen? I'm feeling a little under the weather and the thought of food just turns my stomach,' I said weakly as I rose from my chair; Nicholas went to stand. I placed my hand on his arm.

'It's fine, Nicholas, stay here, have some dinner and finish your conversation, all I want to do is lie down and sleep.'

'I'll walk you back.' His smile slipped and his eyes narrowed, I could tell he was concerned.

The three men were in good spirits, and the conversation was flowing nicely around the table and it was the first time in months I has seen Nicholas relaxed and carefree.

'No, please stay, I'm sure young Sem will walk me back down the corridor.' With goodbyes said, I made my way back to my room escorted by Sem.

'Thank you, Sem,' I said. He took his hat off and bowed.

'You're welcome, my lady.'

'Goodnight.' I nodded at him and closed the door behind me.

I had high hopes of sleeping through my sickness, and made my way towards the bed.

The ship dipped through a verve and I staggered forward. Before I knew it my head was down a bucket throwing up the wine that I had drunk at dinner along with the bile from my empty stomach. I needed to take the edge off my symptoms, so I searched through my basket of herbs for the ginger root I had purchased just before we sailed. Ginger was one of the healthiest spices on the planet and can treat many forms of nausea, including sea sickness. I cut off a good amount of ginger and I chewed it until it was a fine pulp, then I washed it down with the warm ale that had been left on the table before dinner. Not very pleasant, but it should take the edge off the sickness.

After cleaning myself up and undressing, I climbed into bed and lay on my side as I waited for the effects of the ginger to kick in, bringing my knees up, I curled into a ball and clutched my aching stomach.

I laid there quietly and all I could hear were the sounds of the sea hitting the hull of the ship and the creaking of the wood. The rocking motion of the ship soon put me into a deep sleep, so much so that I didn't even hear Nicholas coming back to the cabin.

'Caroline can you hear me? It's Dad. Please, baby, wake up, we miss you terribly, we can't seem to function as a family without you, so whatever is keeping you away from us, let it go and find your way back to the light.'

191

I could hear my dad's voice, he was crying, he missed me, then the image faded. Then another image floated through my dream. I stood looking at Nicholas, it was as if I was waiting for him to walk towards me, then he was set upon by a group of angry Viking men. I screamed for him.

I woke with a start and sat up, it took a few seconds to get my bearings, I had no idea how many hours I had slept. I felt much better in myself, my sensory system became normal and my stomach pains had subsided, but my head pounded with images of past and present.

I was surprised to hear the rich baritone of Nicholas's voice as he spoke. 'How are you feeling?'

A small scream escaped my mouth, and my hands flew to my chest.

'Sod you, you made me jump, you're back early.' I giggled, half in fright and half in silliness.

'Sorry, love, it's not that early, I have been back for some time.' He placed the book on the table next to him, and walked over to give me a kiss.'

'What is the time?' I enquired as I sat up very reluctantly waiting for the sickness to wash over me. Nope, all good. My symptoms had passed for the time being.

'It's an hour past midnight,' he said as he undid his breeches.

'Oh, I've been asleep for more than a few hours then.'

'Has the sickness passed?'

I watched him as he pulled off his woollen socks. 'I think I'm over the worst. It's still lingering, but if I keep up with the ginger and the apples, I should be much better.'

'Good, can you move across, so I can get into bed?'

'Why didn't you push me over?' He shrugged his shoulders. 'Didn't want to disturb you.'

I moved over onto the other side of the bed. He blew out the candles and climbed in next to me.

'How come I get the cold side?' I said, a little miffed. He laughed at me as he lifted his left arm.

'Because I have sat freezing my balls off waiting for you to wake up and one more thing, love, try to remember you're in the seventeenth century.'

'Sorry about that, I thought they would find my comments useful?'

'These are men of the sea, Caroline and unfortunately women's views are irrelevant.'

I said no more on the matter as I snuggled in closer to my husband.

*

The ship plunged into a deep channel and with its chunky bow, blew twin flumes of spray aloft where they were seized by a force of wind that whipped across the deck with a vengeful verve. I gasped as the stiff, water-laden gusts hit my face. The coldness penetrated to the very marrow of my bones and I clung carefully to the rail, as I struggled up to the quarterdeck where Nicholas and the captain were conversing.

The captain favoured me with a nod and he turned back to watch the binnacle over the shoulder of his helmsman. Nicholas was shocked that I had ventured out of the cabin.

'Caroline, you feel well enough to be out?'

193

'Yes, I'm fine, I just can't spend any more time in that cabin, I feel like a prisoner. At least up on deck I have a small sense of freedom, plus it helps with the sickness.'

Nicholas chuckled and pulled me into his embrace. We stood near the stern, slightly out of sight, so we would be out of the way of the crew going about their daily routine. Nicholas held me from behind as he gave me the warmth and comfort of his body. At times I would avert my face from the wind and the salty spray as I refused to yield to the elements of the sea.

We stood in silence as we watched the captain work. Captain Bram Van de Berg scanned the straining masts and the billowing sails high over our heads, he stepped away from the helmsman. Carefully inspecting every line and spar of his ship, he strolled the reeling deck quite comfortably as if he were quite at home on the high seas. Huddling in my woollen cloak for warmth, with the feel of my husband's arms around my waist, I had another vison. This memory was of us standing in almost the same position, but we stood looking out from a Viking long boat.

'We have done this before,' I said as I turned around to face him.

'I know.'

'Do you see the visions too?' I looked at him, he frowned and puffed out a breath of air.

'Everyday, love, but I haven't said anything, because I thought I was going out of my mind.'

'Well, we can go out of our minds together.' I turned to face him, put my arms inside his cloak. We held each other tight and braced the strong winds together.

*

The ship sailed along its halting course. The land was fast approaching, and the lookouts watched for shallow waters. I stood on the deck with Nicholas, anxious to see what I could of this land, wherein we would be staying for some time I imagined. We saw mostly lowlands until banks of buildings and houses began to rise on the southwest corner of Holland. The ship turned at the mouth of the shipping canal as we left the North Sea.

We pulled into the small harbour called Berghaven, and along the water's edge I could see other merchant ships. I had to shield my eyes from the glare of the afternoon sun as it shone out and made the light bounce off the water, from this distance it looked like shards of diamonds twinkling in the light.

Finally, the ship approached the harbour's edge, and the seamen rushed aloft to reef the ships sails and secure the lines. Our trunks were brought up by Gregor and Alec. We stood waiting for the signal to disembark.

The order was given, Gregor and Alec went down first with our provisions. Nicholas shook the captain's hand.

'Thank you for the use of your house, it is much appreciated.'

'The pleasure is all mine.' The captain returned his handshake, then drew his attention towards me.

'Lady Trevilian, I have very much enjoyed your company on this voyage,' he said as he took my hand.

'Thank you, you have made our journey most comfortable.'

'Lady Trevilian 'it was an honour.' A tiny smile appeared on his lips, and he inclined his head briefly as he kissed the back of my hand.

'Give this address to your coachman, and upon arriving please give this letter to Mrs Janssen my housekeeper.' The captain handed me a sealed letter and the address for the coachman.

'Thank you again for your generous hospitality.' I passed the note and letter to Nicholas.

'Think nothing of it, the house is empty for most of the year, it will be good to have a little life inside of it.'

'Maybe we might have the pleasure of your company?' I paused invitingly.

'Unfortunately, Caroline, I'm far too busy this time of year, but I will be more than happy to return you both to England when your husband's business concludes here.'

'We might just take you up on your offer, if our business does not go as planned,' Nicholas interrupted. 'Come we must make good time before it gets too late,' he said. I took his offered hand, and we said our goodbyes, and I followed Nicholas down the gangplank. He stepped off first and held out his hand for me. My foot touched down in Amsterdam. I had a sense of both relief and foreboding with what lies ahead of us.

12

Oranges and princes

The captain's townhouse was by no means modest. It stood magnificently overlooking the Hofvijer lake, and almost next door to the Hague where Princess Mary and William of Orange resided. The Binnenhof was a wealthy homestead which had expanded from a small town to a large bustling city. On the outskirts of the lake stood the palace, and next to or surrounding it there were stone-faced terraced houses, apartments and residential rooms, all set over various floors and as Nicholas stated, 'The Binnenhof was the oldest houses of Parliament.'

'Almost like our English inner court,' I said, as he took my hand to help me down from the carriage.

'Exactly. It's a meeting place for both houses of general affairs and the Stadtholder,'

'Stadtholder?' I asked curiously.

'The Stadholder is like a ruler of the country,'

'A king?'

'No, love, more like a prime minister, but that should all change once they get their independence from Spain.

'What is that building.' I pointed towards a large building with a gable roof and two pepper pot turrets.

'That, my love, is the Ridderzaal or the Knight's Hall, this is a meeting place for the newly formed State General of the Dutch Republic.'

There was a large courtyard in front of the Ridderzaal and a smaller square behind, where there was a hive of activity, not only the wealthy but the middle class and lower class as well.

My interest was piqued. 'Why so many people?' I questioned.

'This was initially a public space and is still used by traders, stallholders and booksellers, why do you ask?'

'No particular reason, I was just interested that's all.'

'Come, let's not keep the house waiting.' I linked my arm through his and we ascended the stone steps.

Nicholas pulled the iron bell handle and we waited patiently for the door to open. We heard a shout from the other side. 'Ik kom even!' The door opened.

'Kan ik je helpen?' The housekeeper said as she looked suspiciously at us.

'Ik heb een brief van kapitein Bram Van den Berg, ben jij Ms. Janssen de huishouster? Nicholas said, as she looked at us with a puzzled frown.

'Yes, I'm Ms. Janssen, the housekeeper,' she replied in English with a heavy Dutch accent. I was pleased she spoke our tongue. Nicholas handed her the letter from the captain. She read the short letter from her employer; she blushed a little and then folded it back up and placed it into her apron pocket.

'Please come inside, if you follow me to the parlour, I will bring in some refreshments, then I shall introduce you to the rest of the household.

She was very pleasant, easy on the eyes with her curly brown hair peeking through the sides of her cap with a splattering of greying hair here and there.

She rang a bell, and a young lad, roughly the same age as Alec appeared.

'Yes, Ma?' He peeked his head around the door to look at the new guests.

'Wilhelm, please show these gentleman where to take all the belongings and please escort them to the kitchen after, so they can take refreshment before you show them to our staff's rooms.'

Sir Gregor and Alec graciously took their hats off and nodded their thanks, then they followed in Wilhelm's wake.

Inside, the house was elegantly furnished, but comfortable, a little bare in places, but this house represented the unmarried status of the captain. No wife to come home to, so he furnished this house for himself only.

'Well, I imagine he has a mistress, of course,' Nicholas said when I speculated about the captain's private life.

'And I think she resides under the same roof.' Nicholas looked puzzled.

'Ms. Janssen?' I said. He raised an eyebrow at me.

'Well, didn't you notice the flush in her cheeks when she read his letter?'

'Men don't notice such things as you women.' The corners of his mouth lifted as we were shown into the parlour.

'I suppose so,' I agreed.

*

Over the course of the next few months I got to know the staff, although at first, they were a little wary of me, especially Ms. Janssen. However, she soon realised that I had no intention of interfering with her work, or taking over the daily running of the household. In fact, there were six servants, counting the groom and stable boy, housemaid and valet.

Nicholas was out most days, he made his connection with The Prince of Wales almost immediately upon arriving, which surprised me greatly as I was totally unaware that they were already acquainted with each other. Together they would make their rounds amongst the genteel of the Danish court hoping to find allies to help his father's cause, once they got enough funds from the nobility, they would then present to Prince Frederick that they had the money, but not the means.

I was of little consequence, a meager female in a male dominant world, what help could I be to Nicholas? So my days were long and sometimes boring, Ms. Janssen made it quite clear she oversaw the household and would come every morning into the salon just to consult me on our menu for the day. After that, my time was my own.

*

It was dark outside. I had once again eaten alone in my room waiting for Nicholas to come home, which was most evenings. I lay on the bed thinking of my life before this strange twist of fate. Pleased with the distraction of Nicholas's appearance, I sat up as he came in the room. He staggered over to the large armoire and rather pathetically tried to hang up his cloak. He smiled at me, but didn't say anything. He staggered a little towards me with a silly grin on his face.

'Jenever,' he slurred.

'And by the looks of it you have had far too much of it.' I frowned.

'Never.' He shook his head slowly from side to side and stepped a little closer. I'm sure I heard the alcohol sloshing around in there somewhere. His eyes where glassy from the gin, and his nose pink from the cold outside. He lurched forward, then took a few steps to the side and tried to straighten himself. Unsuccessfully.

'Come to me, my wife, my lover, my beautiful green-eyed goddess, and let me take you to bed and ravish every inch of your body,' he said as he gestured with his arms wide open.

'You're drunk as a skunk, come and let me help you undress, and get you into bed.' I put his arm over my shoulder as I guided him towards the bed. He didn't argue when I sat him down and started to undress him.

'I don't need help, love,' he said, pushing my hand away as I tried to unbutton his jerkin. 'I'm not drunk.'

'No, course you're not, you're completely pissed.'

He looked down to his breeches and put his hand on his groin. 'No, I'm still dry.' He gave me a quizzical look.

Nicholas tried to un-button his shirt without much luck. I pushed his hands aside and finished the task for him. I looked at his naked chest, showing the hollow dip in the center where I often rested my chin. He saw me looking at him, he reached for my hand and placed it over his heart, moving closer his other arm swept around me. He pulled me down and we both laid back on the bed with me on top of him.

Then he stilled. Then came the snore. I chuckled to myself as I pulled away. I looked down at his face, so handsome with his soft kissable lips, which was set in a dreamy smile. I pulled off his boots, tights and pantaloons, he hated the court dress, but he needed to blend in. I picked up his feet, and swung them around into the bed, then I gently pulled the covers over him. I climbed back into bed and snuggled into his warmth, but after a time I had to turn my back to him because the smell of the Jenever and the spicy food he had eaten was keeping me awake.

*

The rattling of carriage wheels, and general noise below, woke me just after dawn the next morning. I left Nicholas asleep as I quietly left the room and made my way down to the kitchen for breakfast as I did most mornings; I preferred to eat with company than alone in the large dining room, unless Nicholas joined me. As I approached the kitchen, I could smell the aroma of eggs and ham cooking and the jovial noise of morning chatter.

Upon entering everyone stood. 'Please sit,' I said, 'you do not have to stand whenever I walk into the room. Good morning everyone, did you all sleep well?'

'I heard Lord Trevilian coming in late last night,' said Ms. Jannsen as she dished up my breakfast.

'Do you mean staggered in?' I rolled my eyes towards the ceiling.

'Took me a while to get him into the coach, he's a bloody 'lump' when his drunk.' Gregor looked aghast and cleared his throat, 'Sorry, my lady I forgot my manners.'

'Do not worry, Gregor, as you know I'm a bit partial to the odd swear word.'

'Hear you go, my lady.' Mrs. Janssen put my plate of food down in front of me.

'Mmm, looks lovely thank you, Ms. Jannsen.' I picked up my knife and fork and tucked into my breakfast.

Once breakfast was finished, Alec and Wilhelm excused themselves quite solemnly, which left the three of us sitting quietly round the table drink our tea. Tea was made different here, Ms. Jannsen would brew it with oranges, until I asked her if she would do it without, so I could add milk. She was rather taken back, but once she tried it, after weeks or persuading, she loved it just as much. Even Gregor had become accustomed to it, Nicholas not so much, he preferred black.

'So, what's on everyone's agenda today?' I asked.

Gregor spoke first. 'The boys are in trouble, so I will have to find them extra duties today.'

'Why are they in trouble?' This peeked my interest.

'Making mischief in town last night,' he said gruffly.

'Oh, what were they doing?' I hid my smile behind the rim of my cup.

'Usual boys' stuff, drinking a little too much ale and being rowdy with friends,' Gregor huffed, as he leaned back in his chair and placed his hands on top of his head.

'And I told them they had to be home by ten, and they rolled in at twelve this morning. More tea, my lady?' Ms. Janssen said, as she picked up the teapot.

'No, thank you, Ms. Janssen, I did wonder why the boys were quiet at breakfast, and hardly touched their food.'

'I do not mind them going out, but they need to be more responsible, because it reflects on this household,' she said.

'I do not think so, most people understand, we were all young once, and did silly things like that.'

203

Two alarmed faces looked at me.

'Not that I did anything like that.' Little did they know. I smiled to myself as I took another sip of tea.

*

The morning slowly slipped into the afternoon, and Nicholas had yet to rise. If I didn't go wake him up now, he would never sleep tonight. Walking into the room, I made my way to the heavy brocade curtains and pulled them back.

His eyes were tightly shut to block out the sunlight, his hair was a mess of tangles, and his face was all but drained of colour. I leaned over him and prized an eyelid open.

'Good afternoon, handsome.'

'That, my love, is a matter of opinion.' And with that he closed his eye again and placed his arm across his brow.

'I have no sympathy for you, totally self-inflicted.'
The corner of his mouth lifted slightly in a reluctant smile. 'How did you get me undressed and into bed?' he grumbled beneath his arm.

'You managed to stagger, with my help, to the bed. I undressed you and then you fell asleep, then all I had to do was lift your feet and pull the covers.'

'Was I sick?'

'No, thankfully.'

'I didn't piss myself?'

'Why would you say that?' I laughed.

'Well, at times when I have been so in my cups, I have pissed myself, or pissed somewhere in the room.

'Well, that surprises me Nicholas, a man of your standing, and no you did not piss in the room either.'

'Thank the lord for small blessings,' He groaned.

I settled myself quite comfortably next to him and placed my chin on his chest and he lifted his arm to accommodate me.

'Although, you did tell me I was your green-eyed goddess and the love of your life.' I could feel the chuckle vibrate though his chest.

'Oh, well, might had been worse,' he laughed, and drew me close.

'God you stink. How did you get so drunk?' I asked curiously.

'Prince Frederick's hospitality.'

'Really, so you finally got to meet him then?' I looked up at him with excitement.

'Yes, both Charles and I were invited to his private rooms to sample his fine collection of jenever, and it would had been extremely rude of me to refuse his generous hospitality.'

'Yes I quite agree with you.' I smirked and raised an eyebrow towards his general direction. Nicholas tried very gingerly to sit up. I plumped some pillows behind his head to make him more comfortable.

'How much did you sample?' I questioned.

'Lost count after the second bottle.' He put a hand on his forehead and leaned into it. I knew he held his head tightly, because his knuckles had turned white with the pressure.

'Caroline, I feel positively awful.'

'I can only imagine,' I said cheerfully.

He opened one eye and looked at me. 'My head feels like it has been split with an axe.' He sighed heavily and leaned back into the pillow and closed his eyes. 'What's the time, love?'

'Ten o'clock, why?'

'We have an engagement at the Hague tonight.'

'I'm finally going with you. How wonderful,' I said sarcastically.

He opened one eye again. 'There is a ball, and we have both been invited.'

I jumped up in excitement and straddled his legs.

'So that requires a quick dash to Madam Groot's she has finally finished my dress orders, at least I'll have something to do this afternoon.' I clapped my hands in excitement. What the hell had come over me? I don't feel like me anymore.

'Stop! Don't move the bed,' he barked and took in a deep breath, fixing his eyes resolutely on my face.

''Twas not such a clever idea Caroline.' He eased me off his lap and laid back down, he placed both hands to the side of his head.

'Hair of the dog is what you need!'

'Dog's hair, what has that got to do with the state I'm in?'

I left the bed, and walked over to the fireplace to ring the servants bell.

*

I walked out of the front door and took a deep breath. Nicholas was waiting for me by our coach, and he looked up as I walk towards him. His eyes narrowed.

'Good god, Caroline, it's a bit revealing!' he said and fell silent.

Madam Groot said it was the latest fashion from France.' I smiled sweetly up at him.

'But you, I can see your bosoms almost and where…' he cleared his throat. '…your collar and kerchief should be.' He absently stroked his finger across my bare chest.

'Where is your corset.' He frowned.

'Didn't want one, anyway stop being absurd, I'm not going to be dressed differently to other courtier ladies.'

'Well, I'm, not concerned with other ladies, plus other ladies wear corsets.' His tone was suddenly bitter. 'Good god, Caroline the Prince of Wales will be trying to get under your skirts, you know what sort of reputation he has, let alone the other men at court.'

'Don't worry, if little fingers wander, I'm sure you'll break them.' I said cheerfully as I descended the stone steps into the courtyard.

'Little fingers won't be wandering under your skirts madam, they'll be trying to grab your bosoms. I cannot believe you are going to go out in society looking like that! If I look down…' He said as his face took on an expression of disbelief. 'I can almost see your bosom buds' His voice trailed off in a whisper as he peered down my cleavage.

'Don't be bloody absurd,' I was totally miffed by this point, and I thought I looked wonderful. I was especially nervous, and he was not helping things.

'And who wears a dress that is almost the colour of skin, you look positively naked under that gown.'

'Don't be daft, you can't see through it, just the outline of my breast. You told me we needed to make a really good impression, and I thought this is what you had in mind?'

'Hmm, I thought you would do something with your hair?' he said looking as displeased as possible.

'So is my hair not up to standard any other time then?' I gave him a sideways grin.

He puffed out his lips. 'You know I didn't mean that, it came out wrong.'

'Hmm, anyway, you must know what the ladies are wearing at court as you spend nearly every waking hour there,' I said a little piqued. 'So, it shouldn't come as such a shock.'

'But you are for my eyes only and no one else's…anyway they wear bright colours, thick materials and bloody corsets that do not show the true shape of their breasts, *your* dress is too thin.' His eyes blazed with passion, and my face softened towards him.

'Then, my handsome husband, it should be more in your favour to know that I'm going home on your arm and nobody else's.' I raised my head towards him, and gave him a cheeky wink. He harrumphed under his breath and rolled his eyes skyward. I laughed as I placed my hand into his.

'Have you any idea what you look like in that gown?' he whispered in my ear. 'You must be careful, Caroline, trust no one. Can you not at least cover the top with something?'

I flicked open my fan that matched the material from my dress and fluttered it over my cleavage.

'That's not what I had in mind,' he said through gritted teeth.

'I know.'

'Gregor close your mouth,' Nicholas said as we passed him. A little too churlish for my taste. Poor Gregor blushed so deep he didn't know quite where to look as he closed the door behind us.

'Don't mind him, Gregor.' I gave him a wink through the window as the carriage pulled out of the courtyard.

*

From what I could tell we seemed to be making quite a good impression, I wasn't quite sure if the success was down to my witty banter or the unusual look of my gown. However, regardless we were two new faces in a court of intrigue and scandal. The court ladies either looked on me with admiration, or frowned at me through jealousy.

Most of the flamboyant and very colourful dresses where made of a similar cut, but none was quite as daring. My gown wasn't colourful, it was a very pale blush that outlined the top part of my body to perfection. However, the effect I was having on staring eyes was playing havoc with Nicholas's temper. He stuck to me like glue, and glared at any male who would have the audacity to ask for an audience.

'If you continue glaring at all the guest you will never make any good connections, so you need to stop it now,' I whispered behind my fan.

'Bloody damn tulip munchers! I hate court life, and all the sex and scandal that goes with it, you should have worn a more suitable gown.'

'You will just have to calm down and go with it, you know why we are here and you're making far too much fuss over my gown!'

'My blood is boiling so much, maybe in your time gowns like this are acceptable,' he said, still surly, 'but not here and now.'

'Don't be such a prude, everyone is wearing a similar cut.'

He turned his head suddenly to face me, eyes troubled in the flickering light of the ball room.

'Yes, but their damned dresses are not that low and not bloody see-through!' The muscles in his jaw were twitching ten to the dozen.

I leaned close to his ear. 'It's not see through! Calm, yourself down, Nicholas.'

He groaned and squeezed my hand. From across the room Charles, the prince of Wales had spotted us. He made his way through the crowd along with a young couple. I knew this was Mary, Charles' sister, and her husband William of Orange.

The young princess must have been no more than fifteen, very elegantly dressed. She was beautiful, charming, and exquisitely tiny, with a fine boned but nicely rounded figure, with unpowdered dark glossy hair, and the most extraordinary white skin, with a slight flush of pink that adorned her young cheeks. Her colouring and complexion reminded me very much of her father Charles. Her husband William, who was no more than a few years older was dressed just as finely with silks and jewels. He too was dark and not much taller.

'Nicholas old chap.' Nicholas took Charles hand and bowed his head.

'Your Highness,' he said.

'Come now, you know better than that, Nicholas...' said the prince. He then turned his attention to me.

'…and who is this lovely creature.' His eyes roamed up and down my body in a possessive way.

'May I present my wife, Caroline, Lady Trevilian,' I watched my husband closely as he introduced me, and the tic in his jaw was apparent as the future king of England took my hand; he almost looked as if he wanted to devour me there and then, but behind his foppish façade you could see an astute young man.

'What an exquisite beauty you are, no wonder Nicholas has kept you away from court for so long.' He turned to my husband. 'Tsk, Tsk, Nicholas for keeping her all to yourself.' He wagged his forefinger at my husband.

Nicholas grinned through clenched teeth; I squeezed his hand for reassurance. He checked himself and was back to his charming self. The prince, not stupid, realised this and played well on Nicholas's jealousy, but all in good humour.

'I must spirit your wife away shortly, Nicholas, but before I do may I introduce you both to my dear sister Mary, and her husband William. I dipped automatically, with my eyes down towards the floor. 'Your Majesties,' I said.

'Welcome to court, Lady Trevilian, how do you find it?' said the young princess.

'Colourful, to say the least.' We both smiled at each other, like two co-conspirators.

'Come, follow me, let's leave the men to talk, I'm in need of an English ally, in such an unfriendly court.'

'Yes, I to am finding it difficult in a strange country.'

I followed her through the French doors that opened out onto a terrace, and we stood side by side overlooking the beautiful gardens.

'Oh, my, what wonderful gardens you have here.' I said, once my eyes adjusted to the darkness.

The garden had torches burning around it, and from my vantage point I could just see a few of the guests disappearing into large hedgerows, beyond the parterres.

'You love garden then, Lady Trevilian?'

'Please, call me Caroline and yes, I love gardens and I love to garden too.'

The princess looked surprised by my admission. 'You labour?'

I smiled at her and nodded. 'Yes, I find working in the gardens relaxing and satisfying, the pleasure I get when a plant or flower has grown beautifully by my hands fills me with such satisfaction and pride.' The princess looked on at me with interest in her eyes. 'Have you ever tried to grow anything, your majesty?'

'No, we would not be allowed,' she rolled her eyes and sighed.

'Why?' I asked with interest.

'Royals do not get their hands dirty,' she looked down at her hands.

'Bet it gets frightfully dull around here if you're not allowed to do anything,' I snorted. 'Would you like to learn?'

Her young eyes lit up. 'Do you think I can?' She said with a hint of excitement.

'Why not? You're a princess, and if you want to do something then you should, and without question.' I said quietly, so my comment could not be overheard.

'I would love to learn,' she said. 'You would teach me?'

'It would be my pleasure, when would you like to start?'

'As soon as possible. I will speak to my husband first and then if he allows it he could speak to the palace gardeners and ask them to allocate me a plot. Maybe we can start the day after the morrow?'

'You need to ask permission from your husband?' I said in mock outrage. She looked a little startled.

'Don't you?' A look of perplexity washed over her face.

'No, if I want to do something, then I will, then I would tell Nicholas, but I would never ask his permission.'

'That's very forward of you, but my husband would not approve of that sort of behavior from me.'

'I suppose we have vastly different roles…'

'There you both are,' Charles interrupted me, he frowned at his sister. 'Your husband has been looking for you, your presence has been gone too long,' he said. 'You know the protocol.'

Mary's eyes twinkled at me as I lifted my lips in a slight smile, it was almost like a secret pact we had made together. I shook my head. I will never understand men, especially those of this time.

'Yes, sorry, Charles,' Mary said. She turned her attention back to me. 'Caroline, 'twas a pleasure to meet you, see you soon.'

I curtsied and looked up, and with the nod of her head she was escorted away from the terrace by her brother.

I go in search of my husband. No longer deterred by Nicholas, the gentleman of the court surrounded me like a flock of seagulls, readily waiting for a crumb of food.

My hand was kissed repeatedly and held far too long in my opinion, and glasses of wine were brought in abundance. *Were these men deliberately trying to get me intoxicated?* After an hour of their unwanted attentions, my face ached through smiling and my hand hurt with all the swishing of the fan, I was also feeling rather tipsy.

'I must take my leave gentleman; my husband will be wondering where I have gotten to.' I politely tried to excuse myself from these pompous men.

'Nonsense,' said the Marquis von Holsten. 'Your husband is probably finding his own entertainment.' He gave me a sly wink.

'All the same, sir, I would like to find him.' I was starting to feel uncomfortable in their presence, their attentions were becoming far too familiar for my liking.

'Well, Lady Trevilian, said the Marquis as he held out his arm. 'I shall escort you to find your husband.'

I was rather grateful that there was someone here in this group of men who was being chivalrous. He steered me to one of the alcoves, and I hesitated.

'Come, do not be alarmed, my dear…' He lifted the curtain for me to enter. 'I am sure I saw your husband come this way.'

The alcove was empty, I turned to say as much, but before I knew it, he was on me.

'Madame. At last.'

'I beg your pardon,' I pushed his lean frame away from me. 'I do not wish to be alone with you, sir.'

'Come now, don't play coy with me.' He pinned me against the wall of the alcove. 'You swished your fan to indicate differently.' He proceeded to lick the top of my cleavage. 'How dare you, you ghastly man.' My temper flared as I walloped him hard on the top of his head with my closed fan. He staggered back slightly, and hit something solid behind him.

*

'What did I tell you?' Nicholas's eyes blazed with fury.

'I know what you told me. I was careful. I went looking for you, but I was surrounded by the court gentlemen and I could not get away from them. Anyway, you attracted quite a lot of attention, more than me.' I sighed heavily as I hung my gown in the wardrobe. 'He won't forget this Nicholas, you dragged him out by his ear and threw him over the balcony, you're bloody lucky 'twas only two feet above the ground,' I exclaimed.

'He's lucky I didn't rip his head off,' he said, as he stripped away his jabot. 'Anyway, he didn't break anything, it's only his pride that was injured.'

'I suppose he should be thankful you showed some self-control,' I said sarcastically. I sat down on our bed to remove one of my stockings. 'Apart from defending my honor or your marital rights, did you make any more useful contacts?' I asked in interest.

'The Stadholders minister of finance and Admiral of the Dutch fleet,' he said, as he pull his shirt off over his head. His shoulder blades parted and the muscles on his back flexed. He threw the rest of his discarded clothing on the chair by the armoire.

'And?' My eyebrow arched. He turned back round to face me.

'And, we are to meet the day after the morrow with Charles and Frederick to discuss plans on sending a fleet of war ships to England.' He stood completely naked before me and I felt my pleasure start to build.

'Without the prince?' I questioned. My eyes pursued his body from top to toe. I was more interested in looking at his body at this moment.

'That will be the hardest part, trying to convince the Prince of Wales to stay in Holland.' Desire lurked behind Nicholas's eyes.

'That works fine with my plans, I said as I removed my other stocking, 'at least I won't be on my own anymore!'

He walked towards me and crouched down in front of my bare legs. 'Plans?' He took my foot and slowly caressed behind the back of my knee.

'I'm to meet with the young Princess Mary' My eyes closed as he slowly continued up my leg. 'She is keen to start a little garden of her own and I have offered to teach her.'

'Well done, my love. Infiltrate from the other side.'

'Yes, that's what I thought. If I could get Mary on side it might make it easier to convince Frederik. Although I think she needs a friend, she seems lost and alone. Especially in a court that mistrusts her and has no time for her.' I sighed in pure bliss as his hand reached the soft triangle between my legs.

'You got all that within meeting her for half an hour.'

I opened my eyes and glanced at him. His pupils were large and burned with passion.

'Umm, I could just tell.' I moaned as he inserted his fingers into me. 'Are you trying to distract me my lord?'

My breath quickened, my head tilted back and I closed my eyes, savoring the pleasure he was giving me.

'Getting back to my first question, what did I tell you?'

'Umm, to be mindful of the men.' My mind became foggy with passion.

'And?'

I tried to answer him with a clear mind; but my pleasure was almost to the surface. 'Umm…' I moaned as he continued with his pursuit. 'Don't trust anyone,' I said, as he drew his fingers in and out. I was just about to come when he took his hand away and stood up. Breathlessly I looked up at him. 'What are you doing?' I was puzzled.

'That's how you make me feel when I'm unable find you…' his eyes narrowed at me. '…and when you do not do as you are told.' He walked round to the other side of the bed. 'You promise me something, then you do the opposite.'

'You are being cruel and unfair.'

'Life at court *Caroline*, is scandalous and dangerous and you need to be more on your guard.'

He brushed his hand through his hair and puffed out a large breath of air.

'Never let a man you don't know escort you anywhere and whilst you're with the princess, maybe she can find someone to give you etiquette lessons on how to use a bloody fan. Is that understood?'

I pulled my nightgown back over my knees, stood then walked around the bed. I threw back the covers in anger and flopped sulkily down on the mattress and drew the covers over me. 'What has a bloody fan got to do with it?' I said.

He glared at me through angry eyes and blew out the candle.

13

Friends and enemies

As I walked down the connecting pathways through the parterres, I admired the symmetrical patterns of the plant and flower beds. The green and pungent smell of the garden surrounded me, it calmed me. Nicholas and I hadn't spoken for a couple of days; every morning when I woke, he was gone, and wouldn't return home until sometime in the early hours of the next morning. Anger still came between us, I couldn't forget what he had done, my pride was wounded and neither of us would apologise to the other.

It had been months since I thought of my other life, it almost felt like a distant memory, and over time it had faded from my mind. That was until today. Walking among the palace gardens filled me with a longing for home, sitting with my Mum in the hammock watching my dad tend his garden. My sister Claire handing me a chilled glass of wine, whilst my niece and nephew played on the lawn.

The grounds of the Hague were open to the public, and all diverse groups of people were mingling together, from the merchants to the nobility, mostly there to meet family and friends or to just enjoy the warm weather of early summer.

The sudden opening of a nearby door in the far corner of the garden distracted my thoughts, and Princess Mary was presently making her way towards me. I smiled to myself, as I saw she was still dressed in her good silks, whereas I had donned a brown woolen dress, with a white apron, and to anyone looking on I would be mistaken for a house maid.

'Caroline, I'm so glad you came,' she fidgeted with her hands, unsure what to do or say next.

'I would not have missed this day for the world,' I assured her as I shifted my basket of garden tools from one arm to the other.

'Can I help.' She offered her arm.

'No it's fine, honestly. Did your gardeners find you a little plot where we can start?'

'Yes they did.' Her eyes twinkled with excitement. 'Please follow me.' She gestured with her hands.

We made our way through the gardens, and approached a little doorway, surrounded by a thick privet hedge. With a small silver key, Mary opened the door and we stepped inside.

We were surrounded completely by a circle of high laurels and the most amazing but overgrown little garden. In the center was a bench with a pathway leading from the door. This was once a garden that had held love and attention, but it seemed over the years to have been forgotten, then lost to the outside world.

'Oh, your highness what a wonderful little garden,' I said with excitement.

'Yes, it is marvelous. I spoke to William about having our own little retreat away from court life and I told him you were going to teach me to garden. He was most pleased, this was his grandmothers little secret, which she shared only with him, but when she died the garden became neglected,' she said as she shrugged her delicate shoulders.

'So, he was fine about you getting your hands dirty then?'

Mary smiled brightly at me. 'Yes, he said he was glad that I had found an interest, but I must take it easy not to lift anything heavy.' She put her hand onto her tummy.

I looked at her in surprise. 'You're not, are you?'

Her little face beamed at me. 'Yes, I'm going to be a mother.'

I tried to hide my disgust; fifteen years old and with child? But I must remember I was in a different time, and young mothers of this age were not uncommon.

'Oh your highness, I'm so pleased,' I lied. 'How far gone are you?'

She rubbed her belly affectionally. 'About five months, the baby is due in November.'

After a moment's consideration Mary came nearer to me. She spoke in hushed tones, and her eyes darted around to make sure no one was listening.

'We have decided to keep it quiet for now, because I have been so unlucky in the past.'

'Well, young Princess, we must take care of you. I'll let you into a little secret, everything we will grow in this garden will make you healthy, strong and help battle any illnesses.'

Her small face creased with curiosity.

'How is that possible, Caroline?'

'I know which plants and flowers can help cure most common illnesses, everything grown from the soil can be made into medicines. I was taught by an incredibly wise man.'

'Was he a warlock?' she said. Her face resolved itself from a look of shock to wonder.

I laughed at her naivety. 'No, let's just say he had the knowledge of certain plants that could help heal and battle certain illnesses.'

'So, like you then, Caroline?'

'Hmm, yes I suppose so. Anyway, enough talk for now.' I pulled out one of my kerchiefs and tied it around my head like a large headband, I pulled on the loop hard and tied it with a tight knot. Mary looked on with curiosity.

'This stops my hair coming out of my bun.' I gave her a wink. 'Right, first things first, we have to clear the garden. It's going to be messy, so you will need some old clothes.'

Mary glanced down at her dress 'These are old clothes.' Then her dainty slippered foot peeked out from under her petticoat '...and these are quite old now.' She giggled.

'No, your highness, *these* are old clothes,' My hands air swept down my body. I lifted my dress just above my ankle. 'And these are gardening boots.' I stuck out my foot to show her what she needed on her feet. 'So, today you sit, watch and keep me company, and tomorrow you will start properly.'

*

I was up early the next morning, keen to make a start on the little garden. Noticing Nicholas had again left just before dawn. I was starting to feel the loss of his company, but I was by no means going to back down and apologise for my behavior, when I had nothing to be sorry about.

Ms. Janssen kindly left me a basket of food and wine, as I told her I wasn't sure what time I would be home. Not overly concerned about coming home for a solitary dinner, as I knew Nicholas wouldn't be home till the early hours. I planned to stay as late as I could in our secret little garden.

Mary proved to be an apt student,. She did as she was told and wasn't afraid to get her hands dirty, and I think for the first time since arriving in Holland she felt useful.

I had cleared all the dead plants and overgrown bushes yesterday, and the gardeners had come to take the rubbish away early this morning. So, today we could concentrate on turning over the borders and flowerbeds.

'This is so nice to be outside away from the palace,' said Mary.

Stopping what I was doing I sat back on my heels and wiped the sweat from my brow with my apron.

'Do you not like it here?' I questioned.

Mary looked up from her task. She rolled her shoulders and stretched her neck out. You could tell she wasn't used to manual labour.

'It is fine now, better than when I first got here.

'How long have you been in Holland?'

I've been here since I was nine. However, I miss my mother terribly and now I fear I shall never see them again. Especially my father.' Her eyes held so much sorrow. My heart went out for her.

'Oh, your highness I'm so sorry. It must have been terrible for you to leave your parents.'

This was something I could never imagine or comprehend. To lose ones child and then a child to lose her mother at such a young, impressionable age.

'Please Caroline, call me Mary whilst we are away from the palace and yes it was.' Mary sighed heavily. 'For one entire year I would cry myself to sleep every night.' She looked upwards to the sky. She blinked a few times to clear her tears. Her sadness was apparent.

I changed the subject from her parents. 'How do you find being married? Do you have affection? Love?'

Mary turned her attention back to me, she smiled. The smile did not quite reach her eyes.

'Not at first. William was a bully, and last year he bullied his way into my bedroom, but all is well, he is much kinder to me now.'

My heart tore in my chest upon hearing that because no matter the century she was still only a child.

'Come, let us have a break, we shall sit and have a picnic with the basket of food and drink I brought with me.'

'What about our hands?' she looked down at them and then back up to me. Her brows drew together.

'Wipe them on your apron. A bit of dirt doesn't hurt anyone.' I smiled reassuringly at her.

'What about the babe?'

'He or she will be fine.' I placed the food and drink onto the blanket.

'Come, let's eat.'

Mary sat down next to me and we tucked into our much needed fare.

*

It was well past dusk by the time I arrive back at the town house; Ms. Janssen met me at the back door. I handed her my empty basket with my dirty apron and kicked my boots off.

'Leave them there, I'll put the boots away for you.'

'Thank you. Oh, by the way the food was wonderful today, Ms. Janssen, even Princess Mary remarked on what a wonderful cook you were.'

She gave me a smile from ear to ear. I had finally cracked that frosty exterior.

'The Princess of Orange?' her face whole face lit up.

'Yes, the very one.' I said and smiled.

She puffed her chest out with pride and clasped my hands, her voice dropped to almost a whisper as she leaned in towards me.

'Mistress Caroline, your husband arrived home three hours ago to have supper with you.' Her eyes darted back and forth, as if looking for any eavesdroppers. 'You must go up at once, he has been pacing back and forth…he even sent Willheim and Alec out to look for you, but they were unable to find you.' A worried frown creased her forehead.

I inhaled in and placed my hand on my head and shook it gently. I exhaled out with a puff of my lips and looked kindly up at her.

'No, it's a secret garden that's not for public use. They would never have found it, but thank you, Ms. Janssen, for the warning.

My nerves were heightened as I climbed the stairs to the sitting room. The room was dark, save the flames from the flickering fire. There I found Nicholas, sitting in the wing backed chair with a brandy in his hand staring at the fire.

When he spoke, his voice was low and curt.

'Where in god's name have you been.' Not even bothering to look at me as he continued to swirl the contents of the brandy around the glass he was holding. The golden amber liquid danced in the crystal as the fire glinted through the cut glass.

'Well, for your information I have been with Princess Mary in the gardens.' I swallowed down the urge to say *what's it to do with you.*

'The gardens were checked; you were not in them.' I could hear the underlying anger in his voice.

Walking towards him I stood in front of the fire, facing him. 'I *was* in them, but in a private garden for royal use only, and if you had been here over the last few days you would have known, instead of bloody sulking like a baby over the incident with the Marquis.'

He stood and leaned down to me, we were almost nose to nose. I could feel his breath on my face.

'Sulking,' he said 'Sulking, am I? I'm this close to taking you over my knee and giving you a hiding, you won't forget.' His expression hardened.

'What in god's name is the matter with you, you chose to stay away from me for two days, as far as I knew *you* were sulking.' I sighed with exasperation.

'Do you honestly think I want to be away from you? I've had to entertain the minister of finance, and the admiral of the Dutch navy, along with Charles. We need their money and their ships.' He took another step closer.

'So, believe me, Caroline 'twas not by choice.'

He grabbed my shoulders and his fingers bit into my arms.

'I came home to spend some time with *my* wife, and not one person in this household could find you,' he barked.

'Are you trying to tell me this is my fault?' I pushed on his chest, 'You haven't been around! If you had left a note... I would have made sure to have been home.' I felt the rage build inside me.

'You should have been home long before dusk...walking the streets of the Binnenhof on your own is not done...it is dangerous, Caroline. I imagined all sorts of things. In future you stay put, and you do not leave unless you have an escort and I have agreed to let you go, is that clear?' he shouted into my face.

I pushed his hands off my shoulders, and tried to push his bulk away from me.

'You do not tell me what to do. I'm my own person. What do you think would happen? You know I can bloody well take care of myself, I proved that when your bastard uncle took me and as I recall I bloody well rescued myself.' My cheeks flush hot with anger.

I must have hit a raw nerve, and pushed him a little bit too far. His face went bright red and a vein popped out on the middle of his forehead. I have never seen him this angry. I took a slight step back, he followed.

'You take it into your head to do as you damn well bloody please, and damn the consequences. This is not your time *Caroline*. I don't know about your time, whether you can walk about on your own after dark. But here and now it is not done. Is that understood?' He sighed with frustration and ran his hand though his unruly curls.

'No I don't suppose it is with you, because I'm just your bloody husband. Your job is to take care of, and see to the organisation of this household.'

'So, I'm only your wife, is that it! Am I not to have my own mind, my own interests save but you? And as far as the household is concerned, Ms. Janssen oversees that and a bloody fine job she does too. More than I could ever do.'

We were shouting into each other's faces, both red with anger, and neither one of us backing down.

He grabbed me again. This time his fingers dug harder.

I couldn't feel the pain. I was so angry I was unable to stop myself.

'Am I only allowed to do as you say? Follow your orders? Sit around and wait for you like a good little wife. Lay on my back when you feel the need to stick your dick into me as and when the mood takes you. My god Nicholas, marriage is a partnership *not* a fucking prison sentence,' I screamed.

'The words that come out of your mouth are no better than those from a filthy whore! Say those words again and I will slap your arse so hard you won't be able to sit down for a month.' His face twisted with rage.

'Don't you dare. You're a fool and a bully.' The silent tears started to flow down my cheeks as I struggled to get out of his grip. 'Let go of me.'

He dropped his hands down and turned away from me. He placed his hands on the mantel of the fireplace, and dropped his head in defeat.

'You're turning my insides out with worry, Caroline. I've made an enemy of the Marquis von Holsten.' Nicholas inhaled deeply and slowly blew out a measured breath. 'No one could find you in the gardens, and I had terrible visons of what might be happening, you seem to have forgotten what we are here for. We have to tread carefully, there are spies everywhere even in the Danish court. You must also remember these are unsettling times, and you cannot go about and do as you please.'

He took another heavy sigh and closed his eyes. I could see the anguish on his face.

Cautiously I came up behind him and put my arms around his waist. I put my left cheek on his back. I stared towards the door. I could hear his heartbeat, it was rapid and steady. I closed my eyes.

'I'm sorry, I should have considered everyone in the household, especially you. I was hurt and angry with what you did to me, and I suppose I was punishing you in a way.'

'I'm sorry too, love.' He turned around and crushed me to him.

'I should never have done that to you. I should have woken you to tell you that I was sorry, and that I love you. I promise I will never do that again.' His expression softened as he held me.

'I'm sorry I made you worry. Please forgive me, Nicholas.'

'Do you forgive me too? I was angry and said more than I intended.'

'Forgiven always.'

He drew me slightly away and glanced down at me.

'But, Caroline, you must remember this is not your time. You have to be mindful of your actions, not only does it reflect on you, but me too.' He gave me half a smile and pulled me back into his embrace.

We held each other for some time. Our hurtful words stayed in my mind, forgiven but not yet forgotten.

*

Lost in my own thoughts thinking about the events of last night, I was inattentive for most of the afternoon, and not much company for Mary.

'You're quiet today, Caroline,' she called over from the flowerbed opposite mine.

'Hmm, sorry, Mary,' I said as I became aware Mary was talking to me.

She stopped tending the garden and sat back on her heels. 'I said you are quiet today?' she repeated.

'Sorry, I was in a world of my own, I struggled to sleep last night.' Finally abandoning my work, I stood and stretched out my aching back. 'Come, let us take a break.' I said as we made our way towards the bench. I opened the basket of food Ms. Janssen packed for me.

'It's so unlike you to be this quiet, what is troubling you?' Mary took the chunk of bread and cheese that I had offered her.

Husband?' I sighed.

Mary placed her hand on my arm. 'Well, yes I have one like that too.' We both laughed.

'Nicholas was most displeased when I didn't come home for supper, and annoyed that I didn't have an escort to walk home with me.'

Her brows drew together sharply as she looked at me. 'Do you mean to tell me that every day you leave here you walk home alone?'

Looking at Mary's face, I could see she shared the same views as Nicholas. 'I thought it would be safe,' I said.

'Caroline nowhere is safe, especially for a woman alone after dusk. If I had known I would have insisted on you taking an escort. No wonder your husband was angry.'

Realising I'd get no support on this matter I said no more.

We sat in comfortable silence whilst we finished our lunch and drank the warm buttermilk.

'Come, let us finish planting our Irises and tulip bulbs.' I stood and brushed the crumbs from my apron.

We worked in companionable silence until Mary spoke. 'How is Nicholas's and Charles's campaign going?'

My eyes grew wide with astonishment. 'You know about that?'

'Of course, nothing is secret in court you know.' She never looked up, just continued to dig a hole, and plant a bulb.

'I'm not too sure, I think it's going well.' I said.

'Be careful of Marquis Holsten, he is trying to turn the nobles against funding a hopeless cause. Can you pass me some more bulbs please?'

I passed her some more bulbs, and continued to dig. 'The Marquis Holsten, but why?'

Mary was silent for a time, so I stopped and looked up at her. Mary pursed her mouth into a tiny circle, portending the telling of some scandalous gossip, she leaned in closer towards me.

'Marquis Holsten, Von Holsteinborg is an evil man.' She glanced around as though we had company in the garden, or those that might overhear who could be lurking in the laurels.

'He is a cruel man and it is known he takes a keen interest in affairs of the state and likes to whip up uncertainty amongst the nobility.'

'Simply great, we managed to pick a fine example of a man for an enemy.'

'But, despite all of this, women are mad for the man, he has a different woman on his arm every night.'

'What of his wife?'

'She is just as bad as him, so please be mindful of them both.'

'I will, promise, hand on heart.'

*

A few weeks later, Nicholas and I were taking a much-needed day off from court, and we sat quietly in the captain's study, occasionally talking over the day's business or discussing the most recent letters from France. Queen Henrietta had apparently been told of her son the Prince of Wales's plan, and approved wholeheartedly.

'...as a very sound scheme,' Nicholas read aloud, 'which I cannot but feel will go a great way in providing you the necessary funds for your father's position in England, and hopes that it will secure his throne back.'

'So, she thinks the money is intended to establish Charles back on the throne?' I said.

'Looks that way, but I have told the prince that it's to secure his father's escape until England wants a king back on the throne.' Nicholas looked grim at the thought.

'Hm,' I said. 'Well, all things taken together, it seems a good bet that the prince isn't taking your advice.

'If I were a wagering man, I'd lay my last garter on it,' Nicholas said. 'The question now is, how do we stop him coming?'

'Well, that is going to be the hard part, especially if you do manage to procure the funds and the ships.'

The answer came with a knock at the door sometime later.

'Enter.' Nicholas's rich baritone voice broke my concentration and I glanced up from my book to see Alec walking into the room.

'Sorry to disturb you, my Lord, this has just arrived for you.' Alec handed a letter to Nicholas.

'That will be all thank you Alec. Alec bowed his head and departed the study. My head peeked from around the corner of the book. 'What is it?' I watched Nicolas break the wax seal.

'Looks to be an invitation.'

I groaned inwardly. 'Not another one?'

Slowly, the frown left his face and the vertical crease between his eyes disappeared. A deep, thoughtful look came over him, and he lay back in his chair, hands linked behind his neck. The hint of a smile twitched his mouth sideways. I stood and walked over to the desk and picked up the letter.

'Oh, the Admiral of the Dutch fleet Cornelis Tromp is hosting a dinner party for the Prince of Wales, and we have been invited.' I looked up at Nicholas, he was still smiling.

'That's wonderful news, you have been wanting to get close to him and now is your opportunity. Let's keep our fingers crossed that this will be the start of getting those ships and funds.'

'Let's hope so, love.'

*

Cornelis Tromp lived by the Rizerdaal, in a large four bed apartment which was modest and very tastefully decorated. He lived with his sister Genovita, both were unwed and had no intention of changing it. We were the first to arrive, and it gave us time to get acquainted before their other guests descended upon us.

'How are you finding Holland?' Genovita asked as a servant handed me a glass of wine.

'I love it here; it is peaceful and safe.' I took a sip of the wine.

'Well most of the time, but like all towns it can have problems,' she said.

'Yes, I know. But it is nice to be away from the conflict and the uneasiness of England now. I just wish we could stay.'

'Are you not then?' Curiosity overtook her face.

'No.' I sighed. 'We have to go back home at some point. Nicholas is hell bent on saving the Prince of Wales's father.'

'Yes, it must be such a burden upon you both.' She placed her glass on the table in front of her and absentmindedly smoothed the creases from her skirt.

'I have not really thought about it like that, we just get on with it and try to live as normally as we can.'

Genovita took my hands. 'Very well put, my dear, such wise words.' She patted them affectionately.

The butler walked into the drawing room, and announced the other guests.

Baron and Baroness Van Asbeck, Duke and Duchess Van Hoensbroech and the Marquis and Marchioness Von Holtsen Holsteinborg. I glanced towards Nicholas; my stomach turned over in dread.

'Kees it's so wonderful of you to invite us.' The Marquis Holsteinborg extended his hand as he walked towards the Admiral. I turned my attention back to Genovita.

'Kees is my brother's nickname, only his friends can use it,' she said as she looked at the Holsteinborgs in contempt. 'However did those awful people get an invite?'

'I gather you're not a fan of them?'

'A fan?' she looked confused.

I laughed despite my blunder. 'Where I come from a fan could be two things, the fan we hold and a fan meaning an admirer or a devotee of sorts.'

'Oh, I get it. Very modern of you and no I'm not a *fan*,' she emphasised the word and giggled. 'I detest them, as do most of the genteel.'

'Why are they here then?'

She made a small sound of dismissal, deep in her throat.

'Knowing them as I do, they probably wrangled an invite from my brother and knowing Kees he was unable to refuse.' The smile had vanished from her eyes.

235

'Well, let's just say they have ruined my evening?' I shook my head with disapproval.

'Do not be disheartened, dear Caroline. We shall stick together and take no notice of their spite.' She picked up her wine and we clink our glasses together. She gave me a wink as we took a sip to seal our pact.

That was easier said than done, every question we answered was commented on with a sarcastic remark or a rebuff. I had to hold my temper in check, so God knows how Nicholas felt. The Prince of Wales sent a messenger on ahead to tell our host he would be late and to start dinner without him, and I'd been so hoping the prince's no-care attitude would give us some relief over the dinner.

The conversation around the table was more civil, until the Marquis mentioned the King.

'I understand things are not going too well for your Monarch. We have heard it will not be long before he is tried as a traitor, and sent to the block.' He gave a low, sneering chuckle.

The muscle in Nicholas's cheek moved. I knew he was at breaking point; I was praying he would keep himself in check. The Marquis knew this, and he kept goading him, then the bloody Marchioness piped up.

'It must be awfully dreadful to be married to a man that is deemed a traitor, why, you cannot possibly go anywhere.'

I glanced towards Nicholas and he shook his head at me.

'Oh how your parents must be thrilled, and we heard through our friends in England that you were mistaken for a harlot, and your husband and his men had their way with you, but that once the mistake was discovered…' she giggle with malice. '…that you were a lady, your husband was forced to marry you. Oh, the scandal.' Her hands flew to her chest in mock horror. Then both she and her companion sniggered behind their hands.

'How embarrassing to know that the marriage came about because she was thought of as a whore,' the marchioness replied under her hand. Discreetly, but loud enough so I could hear. Genovita squeezed my hand under the table. My clenched fist was itching to punch the woman in the face.

'She is not worth it,' Genovita whispered into my ear.

'Well let's face it ladies, it was an easy assumption to make.'

The Marquis allowed his eyes to drift over me with a hint of contemptuous amusement.

He was seated opposite me, and Nicholas was at the far end of the table with Cornelis. Nicholas heard the exchange, within seconds he pulled the Marquis from his chair.

The ladies screamed as he punched him on the nose, it popped underneath his knuckles. Hell had been unleashed in the small dining room. The tablecloth was pulled from the table, plates of food and the centre candelabra were lying all over the floor, the men were frantically trying to pull Nicholas off the Marquis. The Marchioness went to jump onto my husband's back.

'Big mistake, lady,' I grabbed her by the hair to stop her.

'What the...' her wig came flying off in my hands, and she screamed, and we all looked on in horror. She was bald as a coot, with the odd hair springing out here and there. Her scalp was full of psoriasis, and it looked as though it had never been treated.

'You will pay for that, you bitch!' She grabbed the wig, and left the apartment with as much dignity as she could muster. This seemed to have stop the men fighting. Nicholas shoved the hideous man away.

The Marquis straightened his waistcoat and jabot, picked up his jewel encrusted walking stick and started to leave the room, then stopped and turned.

'You will have no idea when your fate will find you, but when you do, you'll know it was by my hands.'

What had Nicholas done?

*

Sir Gregor and Alec took it in turns to watch the comings and goings of the Marquis, but apart from the entertaining and the remarkable number of visitors they received, they detected nothing out of the ordinary. Although we were surprised to discover that the Prince of Wales was a regular visitor, and always stayed more than an hour. The dinner party at Admiral Tromp's proved to be disastrous for our cause and because of this the nobles were reluctant to entertain us, for fear Nicholas would start another fight; we had become pariahs.

The Prince of Wales began to require more of Nicholas's assistance, and would sometimes keep him well into the night, so I became accustomed to eating dinner and going to bed on my own, waking only when I felt the bed dip with his weight.

A few weeks later I woke just before dawn to find the other side of the bed empty. I knew he hadn't come to bed, because the pillow had no indentation on it and his side of the covers were still intact.

I leaned over the banister in just my nightgown and gave young Alec a shock. 'Is lord Trevilian in the study?'

'My lady please cover yourself!' He put his hands over his eyes.

'Never mind about that, Alec, I'm looking for my husband. Have you seen him?'

'No, miss, I'll go find Sir Gregor for you.' He didn't uncover his eyes until he reached the last step.

'Mind you do not fall, Alec, and thank you.' I chuckled to myself as he disappeared out of sight.

After dressing in a hurry, I made my way downstairs and met Sir Gregor halfway.

'My lady, My Lord did not come home last night.'

'What do you mean? 'I said bluntly.

'The kitchen door was still unbolted when Ms. Janssen went down to start breakfast. Lord Trevilian always bolts the door after himself when he comes in late, so we know he did not come home.' His dark brows shot upward, and he smiled awkwardly showing small, white, even teeth.

'Would you mind sending Alec and Willheim to the Hague, to see if he stayed with the prince.'

'Yes, of course, my lady.

'Sir Gregor,'

'Yes, my lady?'

'Please find him.'

'Yes, my lady, all will be well I'm sure.' He gave me a nod and went to find the boys.

My mind raged with worry, was he safe or was he lying bleeding face down in an alley with his throat cut?

The sun was past midway in the sky, as it was nearing the afternoon, and we still had no idea where Nicholas was; my stomach was in knots and I felt sick with worry. Had the Marquis done something to him? Had he been tied up and sent on a ship back to England?'

Sir Gregor, Alec and Wilhelm had been searching for him all morning and now they were back without any news.

'My lady, there is no sign of the Prince of Wales either.'

'Good god, you don't think both have been kidnapped, do you?' If it were personal, then just Nicholas would have been taken, so it must be political.' The terror I felt inside was intangible.

There was so much kerfuffle going on in the house we didn't notice the spare bedroom door open.

'What the devil is going on?' Nicholas stood there dumfounded, rubbing the sleep from his eyes.

'Nicholas!' I ran up the stairs straight into his arm, where have you been, we have all been worried sick, you didn't come home last night.'

'I did, but I didn't get home till about four this morning and I did not want to disturb you, so I slept in the spare room.'

I looked closely at him and I could see his eyes where bloodshot and he smelt of cigar smoke, gin, and cheap perfume. I was not amused.

'Pray tell, where have you been all night?'

'Entertaining the Prince of Wales and the nobles trying to restore my reputation,'

'And where were you entertaining those nobles? I said dryly.

'Hmm, well that's the thing. they wanted to go to Madam Fleur de Elisa's.' The smile slipped from his face.

'The bloody brothel house. Christ…Nicholas!'

'Well I could not refuse them, after all I had to try and make amends for the mess I created at Admiral Tromp's dinner party.' He gave me a lopsided grin.

I crossed my arms over my chest and pressed my lips together. My foot tapped on the wooden floor with impatience. I was miffed.

'I did warn you Nicholas that you cannot go punching nobles in the face no matter what they say, I just hope you have repaired some of the damage.'

'I hope so too love.'

I looked around to see if anyone had witnessing our trade off, but somewhere between Nicholas coming out of the bedroom and the bloody brothel comment, Sir Gregor, Alec, and Wilhelm had made a quiet escape.

'Come, I'm in need of a good bath and you my wonderful, stubborn and annoying wife can scrub my back,' he said rather too cheerfully for my liking.

'Scrub it yourself.' I walked away in a huff as I heard him chuckling behind me.

14

The best laid schemes

Every new contact made with the promise of funds was quickly quashed by the interference of the Marquis von Holsteinborg and his wife, so, between that, and life at court, Nicholas and I had truly little time together. I said as much one morning at breakfast.

'I know you have a duty to Charles, but do you think you can have at least one or two nights off?'

Nicholas looked up from his breakfast.

'I'm tired, and I need a break from all the intrigue and scandal at court and the eternal visits we have to attend at the houses of the nobility.' My shoulders slumped, and I sighed. 'I see so little of you now.' I said.

Nicholas put down his knife and fork, and sat back in his chair and patted his legs.

'Come here.' I stood and made my way towards him. 'I must confess, I'm getting tired of it too.' He slid his chair back ever so slightly from the table to make room for me. 'So, my love…what do you have in mind?'

Nicholas placed his arm around my shoulder and pulled me towards his chest. I snuggled close and leaned my head on his shoulder.

'Can we go on a little holiday away from this place?'

He raised his eyebrows suspiciously at me.

'And I can tell from your face that you have already decided.' The corner of his mouth lifted.

'Well, I was thinking we could go to Haarlem. It's just a stone's throw from Amsterdam, and it's the biggest tulip growing region,' I answered sweetly, provoking a sudden look of speculation, followed by a lopsided grin.

'Ah, I wondered when the catch would come into it.' Nicholas laughed, as I planted loads of kisses over his face.

'Please?'

'Very well,' he said, resigned. 'We will also take Alec and Willheim with us this will give Gregor and Ms. Janssen a break.

'Why?'

'Well, between those two boys they have been running around the city causing havoc, and they are at the end of their tether.'

'I didn't know the boys were still making mischief.'

He chuckled. 'Well, you do spend your days lost in your little garden, and by the time you're home, the trouble has been dealt with.'

I pushed back a loose curl that had escaped midway through me kissing his face. 'Oh dear, I do hope it hasn't been that bad.'

'No, love.' He made a noise deep in his throat, one of humorous disgust. 'Just stupid boys misbehaving.'

I laughed at the thought. 'Are you sure it's wise to take them, especially with the huge quantities of beer that's available there.'

'They will have a responsibility to me, so they will behave themselves,' he said with half a smile. I smirked to myself at the naivety of Nicholas's response, but said no more on the matter.

*

We travelled at an easy pace, and made a few stops along the way, so I could purchase my bulbs and the extra herbs that I was unable buy in the city. The Dutch countryside was beautiful. The fields beyond the eye could see were full of rainbow coloured tulips, laid out in balanced patterns. This was the rich agricultural heart of the Netherlands with prosperous farms that spread over the flat lands with the wonderful colours of their native tulips.

Nicholas and I sat side by side, on the narrow-padded wooden seat of the coach. Our hands were clasped together as I sat looking out the window, and as always, his presence gave me a sense of confidence and certainty that this is all I wanted from my life now, and all I hoped was that it would last forever. But deep down I knew it wouldn't.

The coach continued to bump and sway over a particularly bad stretch of road, which had been potholed by Holland's harsh winter and from the ever increasing traffic of carts, carriages, and horses. The air in the coach was warm, and dust came through the windows in small spurts, whenever we hit a patch of dry dirt that had formed around the small potholes as the carriage wheels plunged though them.

I might have slept, too, soothed by the coach's pace and the warmth of my husband beside me, but the constant changing of the road's surface was making my neck ache from all the jolting.

Nicholas leaned towards me and I felt his warm breath on my neck. 'You're lost in thought,' he said.

I frowned slightly and adjusted my position yet again on the hard seat. 'I was thinking of home,' I said with a smile.

His expression dulled. 'Home? Does that mean you'd like to go back to your own time?

'Go back? No, I miss my other parents, and my sister, but I cannot imagine my life without you.'

He kissed the hand that he was holding.

Notwithstanding the dust, I breathed in the fresh air of the countryside, it was rich and intoxicating after the close, horrid smells of the city and the un-washed bodies at court.

'Was your life much different to now?' he ventured.

I was shocked; this was the first time he had asked me about my other life. 'Oh my god. You have no idea. It was so much…'

'Lina, please.'

'Sorry, *don't take the lords name in vain*…I forget how religious you all are.' I smiled at his frown.

'Do you not practice your faith in your time?'

'No, not really.'

He glared at me and dropped my hand. This stopped me for a moment, then I continued.

'Times have changed so much, how do I start? I don't think you would understand if I tried to tell you.'

His eyes darkened, and his wide generous mouth clamped in a straight line. Shoulders wide and back stiff as a board with his arms folded across his chest like a cast-iron statue, 'uninviting' was precisely the word I would use to describe his demeanor at this very moment.

His jaw twitched in irritation. 'You think me that stupid?'

'I didn't mean to upset you. What I meant was, that me trying to explain things like equality, women's right to vote—'

'whoa…that last statement, I don't think I heard correctly.'

'Don't be obnoxious.'

He puffed out his lips in exasperation. 'I'm not, Lina. I'm just interested that's all.'

'Alright then, after the great war ended in 1918.'

'Another war?' A look of surprise and perplexity washed over his face.

'See what I mean? I start to explain then you ask another question and it throws us off the first subject, I cannot cram four hundred years in one carriage ride. Women fought hard for their rights, it's not just a man's world anymore and women have a voice too… and they fought hard to use it.

'Why? When men can provide and do their thinking for them, all they need to worry about is running a household and look after children.' He lifted one eyebrow.

'This is why we had a suffragette movement, because of thinking like this! What women need and want is more freedom, and a simplification of many the institutions of Government. In my time, girls are educated, women go to work, I had a job…I lived on my own…I drove a car, and basically a woman can do a man's job. Well, within reason.'

I was starting to get frustrated and I could tell by Nicholas's face he didn't quite get it and no amount of persuasion would make him accept this forward way of thinking.

He waved his hand up to stop me. 'But the philosophy of education, women would not be able to grasp abstract truths and axioms…therefore their education should drastically differ to men, women should be educated to be gentle, while men should be educated to reason.'

I could not quite believe what had just come out of his mouth.

'What utter nonsense! the ability to reason is not for the purpose of women gaining power over men, but to gain power for themselves, and to give only men rights would not be enough. Women also require the opportunity to fully develop their own reason. The tyranny of husbands means that women live in an oppressed state, just like the woman absolutist France and England right now. A revolution in manners and customs is required to free ourselves and over the years this changes the expectations of what women should be – not just chaste, but virtuous in the fullest sense of the term.'

'In my mind this sort of thing now would not work, and would cause no end of problems. I can see your point of view, and yes, I do agree on some things but not all and that's why I love you. You're different. Independent…but a little too much for my liking, and your mouth doth tend to speak before your head has thought it through.' His mouth curved into a smile, which helped calm me.

'Oi you!' I slapped his arm. He laughed at me and pulled me closer, he was trying to defuse the conversation, because he could tell by the tone of my voice I was getting miffed.'

'My wife from the future doth surprise me greatly, and my life would be very dull without you.'

My face split with a smile from ear to ear. I squeezed his hands tightly with appreciation.

'Nice of you to say so.' I kissed him soundly, and he pulled away from me.

'What is a car?' He screwed up his face in puzzlement.

'Kind of like a carriage without a horse...it runs with an engine.'

'How is that possible?

'Not only do we travel by horseless carriages, but we also fly from one country to another.'

He shook his head 'Now I know you are jesting,' he said, as I laughed with him.

'Let's change the subject please, you're having trouble trying to understand equal rights, so I'm not going to try and explain a car or even an airplane. These subjects can be saved for another time. I just want to enjoy our time together away from everything and not think about anything else.'

'Mm, that sounds good to me. He nodded in agreement.

I shifted my position once more, wriggling my toes as I kicked off my leather shoes.

'Aww, that's better.' I sigh in contentment. Shoes were so uncomfortable, no left or right, cobblers made every shoe exactly the same way, which I found extremely odd, all that was different was the length.

Nicholas smiled suddenly at me and stretched out his hand. 'Give me your feet love.'

I offered no protest as I swung them up onto his lap. His hands were big and strong, but gentle fingers worked wonders. His thumbs rubbed down the arch of my foot and I lean my head back as a soft moan of pleasure escaped my lips.

We travelled silently for some time, while I relaxed into a state of mindless bliss. Head bent over my white silk stockinged feet. 'Does this feel better?' he remarked casually.

'Mm, yes,' Relaxed as I was by the warm sun and the foot massage, I could just make out a few coherent words. His hands stilled at my feet as I felt them move up to my ankles.

'I'm sorry for being boorish, I'm so short tempered and a bit touchy at the moment.'

'You have been working awfully hard,' I said soothingly.

'It's not that.' His hands stilled and he shook his head. 'I feel like I'm fighting a losing battle. A real battle I can handle, but not all this sneaking around trying to win favours at court, and playing one noble against the other.'

'Nicholas,' I said softly, 'we can only try our best.'

He smiled warmly as his hands started their leisurely perusal of my legs. 'I'm pleased you said we, love, because sometimes I feel so much alone with it all.'

'You know I wouldn't let you do this on your own. Let's face it I was my idea in the first place.' I laid the side of my head on the cushion back part of the seat and took pleasure as Nicholas' hands moved up behind my knees.

'Is the Prince of Wales much help?'

He scoffed and one brow sharply arched. 'In some respects yes, he is bright and articulate, but his young years are often a hindrance. He gets quite easily distracted. Woman and Brandy!' he said hopelessly. 'I could talk to hundreds of nobles, drink with Charles 'til I'm near flat on my arse, and never know if I'm getting anywhere.

The nail in the coffin was the fiasco at Cornelis Tromp's house, I feel even further away than we did weeks ago.'

I cast my eyes to his and put my hand on his cheek.

'I hope it hasn't caused too much damage.'

'Agh, pay it no mind, love, they deserved it. Anyway, enough about all this bother, come here, wife and let me ravish you.' He pulled me across his lap, kissed me deeply and lifted my skirt. I lost all train of thought.

*

We spent our days idly, rising late in the mornings, and in the evenings after supper we would retire early. It was as if our bodies needed to re-charge after months of entertaining and late nights. The week, which I had expected would pass slowly, seemed to pick up speed as it went, and the precious minutes and hours rushed along, slipping out of my hands as I tried to catch them and drag them back. Soon our little holiday would be over, and we would have to go back to life at court.

Haarlem was the most charming little city, the architecture of their monumental buildings were amazing, a true inspiration for the artists who were selling their work along the busy cobbled streets.

Nicholas's arms were laden with our purchases as we walked towards the Grote market where we were instantly hit with the aroma of coffee.

'Smell that, isn't it wonderful? Let's stop and have a coffee,' I said as I pulled him towards the direction of the smell.

'You like coffee?' Nicholas looked on in disdain.

'Don't you?'

He crinkled his nose in disgust. 'Cannot stand the stuff, too thick and too bitter.' He shook his head and grimaced.

'You will like this coffee, trust me,' I said steering him towards a neat row of shops across from the market square.

This reminded me instantly of home, not the old buildings or richly clad customers browsing in the shops, but the collection of the businesses side by side; a baker's shop selling food to eat now or to take home, a little chocolate shop, and even a florist. I pulled him towards the quaint little coffee house with a scattering of tables and chairs outside, with long planters adorning the front and sides, spewing forth a range of wonderful colours and smells that mixed with the aroma of the coffee beans. I was totally amazed how progressive this little country was compared to England.

I sat down at one of the little bistro-style tables and Nicholas looked at me rather oddly.

'We are sitting outside to drink.' He said as I patted the chair next to me.

Nicholas put our purchases down and we waited for our waitress.

'Is this normal for your time?' He stuck his nose in the air and glanced around him.

'Yes, my Mum and I would often stroll around our local shops, and once we finished our shopping, we would have lunch out.'

'You would sit in the street and eat, like local peasants?' he looked alarmed.

'Don't be such a snob, Nicholas, and yes this is quite common in my time especially when it is a warm sunny day like today. We call this *al fresco* dining.'

'Well, this is not your time, and we do not do things like this,' he screwed up his face.

'Here we go again,' I said dryly and rolled my eyes skyward.

'What's that supposed to mean?' he sighed and changed the subject, clearly knowing only too well this would lead to another argument about equality.

'Where are those bloody boys?' he said, as he looked about the market square.

'I told you it wasn't a clever idea to bring them both, even Gregor said as much, but you didn't listen *and* being two sixteen-year-old boys having the freedom of no mother or guardian breathing down their necks they were bound to get into trouble.'

'You're right, probably both quite comfortable in the brothel at the edge of the town.' Nicholas snorted as I gave him a look of I told you so.

I was quite surprised at the several types of coffee, I felt as if I were sitting outside a Costa Coffee, minus the paper cups and plastic lids. The waitress arrived at our table.

'Can I take your order please?' She was a pleasant looking thing, with bright copper hair that was plaited and entwined with ribbon. She wore the tradition Dutch dress and pinafore and had wooden clogs on her feet.

'Can we have two medium strength coffees, a little pot of warm milk and some sugar, please.'

'Anything to eat, My Lady?'

'Yes, and two pieces of your stollen cake, please.'

'Apple or Almond?'

'Apple please.'

'Good choice, My Lady.' She nodded and walked away with our order.

Our coffee arrived; Nicholas watched me closely as I mixed in the warm milk with a lump of sugar. I passed him the mug. 'Now, try this.' He smelt it. 'Don't sniff it, just drink it.'

He took a delicate sip, and waited a little for the flavour to hit, then his eyes widened.

'Mmm, this is good.'

'See, I told you so.'

'Although not quite as good as a proper English cup of tea,' he said with a smirk.

We sat in a comfortable ease savoring our coffee and eating our cake talking casually about the cities architecture.

'My Lord! My lady!' We both looked in the direction of the shouting. Willheim was running towards us. 'I have been looking everywhere for you, My Lord,' he said alarmed.

'Whatever is the matter, Willheim?' I said, and from the look of his face I could tell the news would not be good.

'Alec has been arrested.' he said through large gulps of air, as he rested his hands on his knees to catch his breath.

Nicholas rose quickly. 'Bloody hell, now what has that boy done?'

'He has got into trouble with the inn-keeper, something to do with his daughter.'

Nicholas glanced at me and hesitated.

'Go,' I said, feeling somewhat alarmed at this new predicament. 'I'll be fine, I'll meet you back in our rooms.'

'Willheim, escort my wife back to our rooms, and then meet me at the magistrates.'

'Yes, My Lord.'

So much for our nice quiet day I thought to myself as I slumped back into my chair.

*

It seemed hours since Nicholas left, and, sick with worry, I waited for him to return with news. I kept myself busy sorting all our purchases and packing them away, but this didn't take long to do so I wrapped all my tulip bulbs and herbs into linen cloths, and tied them securely with burlap ribbon, which took me no more than thirty minutes.

I sat for a time, picturing the encounter with Alec and the inn-keeper's daughter, and wondering how it was going. Was Nicholas able to sort it out? I was so concerned, I had almost bitten my nails down to the quick.

The boredom, and the not knowing, were driving me insane, and I started to pace our room backwards and forwards. After an hour or so I couldn't take it any longer, and walked out of the room in search of something to do.

I could hear cries coming from the back of the inn. The closer I got to the kitchen the louder the cries became. Pushing open the heavy oak door I noticed spatters of blood over the kitchen countertop, and a young girl out cold on the floor with the landlady trying desperately to wake her up.

'Whatever has happened?' I rushed over to the landlady.

'Oh, Mistress, young Brigit has cut herself with the kitchen knife, and with all the blood she passed out! And my husband is in town on business.'

I pulled the fraught landlady away and tried to calm her down. 'Mrs...?' I smiled reassuringly as I waited for her to tell me her name.

'Sorry, I'm Mrs. Hoyt.'

I took her hand and guide her to the stool behind the kitchen countertop. 'Mrs. Hoyt, please sit down. I will see to the young lady.'

'Her name is Brigit.' She paled as her eyes darted between the blood and the young girl, who was still out cold on the kitchen floor. I knelt to survey the damage; she had a deep wound between her thumb and forefinger, and a slight gash on the side of her forehead.

'Mrs. Hoyt, please go upstairs to my chamber, and bring down my wicker basket. You'll find it on the dresser. And some clean linen, please.'

She nodded and left to do my bidding.

Brigit was only a slight little thing and with the help of a frightened girl huddled in the corner I managed to lift her onto the tabletop. 'What's your name?' I asked the chambermaid.

'Freya, Mistress.' She was white as a ghost, with unshed tears in her eyes.

'Brigit will be fine, Freya. Would you do me a favour, and boil me a saucepan of water please.'

'Yes, Mistress.' She seemed grateful for the job; it kept her mind busy.

In no time at all everything I had requested was done, efficiently and with speed.

Brigit had yet to awaken, which made my job at little easier. On proper inspection, the cut was not as deep as we'd thought, and there was only a small cut on her forehead; the amount of blood made it look worse than it was.

After the wounds were cleaned and bandaged, the young girl started to regain consciousness. She was much calmer when she realised she had been cleaned up and all traces of blood from the counter tops had been cleaned. She looked at my apron, her face went grey.

'Brigit.' Distracted from my apron she looked up at me. 'Don't worry about what's on the apron.' I took it off and passed it to Mrs. Hoyt.

'You will be sore for a few days, but this tea will help take the discomfort away. I hand her the mug of the warm golden liquid.

'What is this?' she sipped the drink rather cautiously.

'Its fine, it won't hurt you, it's made from willow bark. You need to drink this every few hours, it will take the soreness away, and the pain from your head.'

She nodded silently at me and drank her tea. Mrs. Hoyt approached me and took my hands.

'I cannot thank you enough. Please, if there is anything I can do for you, do not hesitate to ask.'

'A nice hot bath wouldn't go amiss.'

'That will be my honour, My Lady and if you need anything else, please do not hesitate, nothing will give me more pleasure.'

'A bath and some food is all the thanks I need.'

*

After the events of the last few hours, I struggled to keep my eyes open despite the crackling sounds coming from the open fire. I felt warm and cosy after my much-needed bath, and I must have drifted off to sleep waiting for Nicholas to return.

I woke when I heard the key turning in the lock, and Nicholas entered, frowning.

He took his coat off and threw it over the back of the chair.

'What happened?'

Atoms of dust puffed out of the chair as Nicholas slumped heavily into it. He took a large breath in and exhaled. 'That boy, I could wring his bloody neck sometimes,' he said.

'That bad?' I asked.

'He was caught in the stables with the inn-keeper's daughter.'

My hands flew to my mouth, trying to hide my smile.

'Nothing to smile about, love, this sort of thing is not done, especially with a virgin of fifteen.' He smiled dryly at me, sidelong.

'Is she still a virgin?' I asked as he kicked off his shoes one at a time.

'Yes, the mother caught them before he got his breeches down.' With one hand he pulled off his stockings and tossed them on the floor next to his shoes, whilst his other hand loosened his collar.

'So, what's all the bother then?'

'The mother said she caught him finishing the act and was pulling his breeches up. Alec swears on his honor that the girl kissed him after he had finished peeing, he said he pushed her away to do himself up.'

'Do you believe him?'

'Alec is many things, but a liar…no.'

'So, what's the outcome?'

'He either marries her, or I pay a hefty fine.' Nicholas entwined his fingers, and placed them on top of his head and leaned back, closing his eyes.

'Let me guess, you paid the coin?' I mused. 'How much?' He opened his eyes and gave a hearty yawn.

'Fifty Krone,' He muttered under his breath.

'How much is that in sterling?'

'Twenty-five pounds.'

'My god, Nicholas that's extortion!' I exclaimed.

''Yes, it is…I also think the inn-keeper and his daughter knew the boy had a master with a fair coin on him, and tried to take advantage of him. The mother got there first, then it blew up into a big drama, she demanded a marriage…the girl cried with a fit of hysterics, then the father demand payment instead of marriage.'

'So, basically it was a mess?'

'Yes, so then the magistrate summoned a doctor to examine the girl—'

'Her maidenhood was intact?' I interrupted.

'Yes, Alec was telling the truth, but unable to prove that he didn't lure her outside to the stables.'

'How is Alec?'

'To be fair he handled it with maturity, but deep down he was scared witless.'

'I bet he was.' Standing, I made my way towards Nicholas. I placed my hand between his neck and shoulders and started to massage the knot of tension.

'Mm, you don't know how good that feels.' He closed his eyes as I continued to rub away the worries of the day.

'Come, let's get to bed,' I whispered into his ear.

'Love, that's the best offer I have had all day.'

We climbed into bed, Nicholas stretched, shifting the weight of the mattress under me and I took the opportunity to snuggle into his side. He placed a possessive arm around me. I felt his chest rise with a yawn. I followed shortly with my own. It was contagious. We fell asleep almost instantly.

*

The morning church bells rang in the nearby square, it woke me from my sleep. I glanced over at the window; the day was going to be bright and clear.

I stretched the last remaining sleep from my body and turned towards Nicholas, who was still asleep. Even by my movement there was no response from the large, warm body next to me, apart from the faint sound of his breathing. The bed creaked as I climbed out.

'Where do you think you're going, madam?' The low rumble of Nicholas's voice startled me.

259

I glanced down at him and was met with a reluctant smile that curved his mouth.

'Surely not now?'

'Oh, well…if you're not up to it, love.' He closed his eyes again.

'I am game if you are.' Totally unable to resist him as always.

He grabbed my wrist and pulled me towards him, the bed creaked beneath us as he shifted his weight above me. He tugged at the ribbon on my nightdress as he bent his head to kiss each breast, touching the nipple ever so softly with his tongue.

'God you're beautiful,' he whispered as he cupped both breasts. My hands drifted down the contours of his back to his bare buttocks and I tried to pull him towards me, he pulled back gently and pushed me back down onto the pillows as he kissed my neck with his tongue. His head dipped lower, and his hands spread my thighs apart.

The chilly air hit my skin as he ripped the rest of the nightgown off. The coldness was soon forgotten as the warm demands from his mouth started to spread from my naval to my face. I felt his loose hair tickling my thighs as he administered more kisses. I didn't mind the heaviness of his weight between my legs, he seemed to fit me perfectly as though we were made for each other.

His large hands cupped the roundness of my hips as he lifted me further up towards his mouth, I gasped in pure bliss as his tongue darted in and out of me, whilst his nose rubbed my soft mound of pleasure. Arching my hips in response to the exquisite pleasure that was building up, until the tiny shudder exploded into a million pieces through my body, and left me limp and out of breath.

Nicholas waited a moment for me to recover, then he rose to his knees as I pulled him closer, he rested his elbows either side of me to take his weight, but comfortably so not to crush me. Groin to groin, lips to lips he moaned softly as he entered me. He took his time, slow and gentle and pausing now and then to kiss me. I felt his thigh muscles trembling against mine as he drew in and out.

He seemed to hold back slightly, taking his time so my passion would build up again. Sighing with deep satisfaction as my climax came to the peak, I moved my hips faster, higher, and higher until he met my rhythm with every thrust until our world shattered into tiny stars.

We lay quiet for a time, huddle together under the quilt, sealing us in our own little cocoon of love. We could hear the faint sounds of the inn stirring to life, and the noise of the streets below, the occasional clatter of the pots and pans in the kitchen, and the clip clop of the horses and carts outside on the cobbled streets of Haarlem.

I turned on my side and placed my hand on my head. I glanced down at my dozing husband. 'So, what's the plan for today?'

'Home.' My face must have betrayed me, 'don't look so disappointed. I know you're upset, love. But one, I cannot trust those boys.' He sighed heavily, 'And two, we have been away long enough. I told the Prince of Wales we would only be gone for a few days, and it's been a lot longer. His expression became vacant as he absentmindedly stroked my side, and I flopped back down and sighed as he leaned over to kiss me.

'Go and get yourself ready, and take the morning to do as you please. By the time those boys get the carriage packed up and ready to go, it will be a good hour past midday… and don't forget to take an escort with you. I rolled my eyes as I climbed out of bed. I gave him a lopsided grin and went to get myself ready. I wondered wildly if he wanted to stay here as much as I did. The thought of going back saddened me because I finally got a glimpse of what domestic life would be for us both. The worry would return and once again play heavy on our shoulders and my heart.

Mrs Hoyt kindly offered Freya as my escort for which I was grateful. We spent the time I had left in the town until it was time to leave. Nicholas found us having fun haggling over the price of some valerian root and rosemary.

'There you are.'

Price agreed, I paid the coin and placed my purchases into my basket. I turned towards him. 'Is that the time already?'

'Yes, love, we have got to go.'

I took his offered arm and we walked back to the inn where the boys were waiting patiently to leave. Alec appeared, a little sheepishly.

'Are you well now, Alec?'

'Yes, my lady.' He blushed slightly and nodded.

'Good, I'm glad to hear that.'

I took my husband's hand and he helped me into the carriage. Once we were both settled, he banged on the top to let Willheim and Alec know that we were ready to leave.

Not long into the journey, I started to feel my eyes growing heavy.

'Come here, love.' Nicholas lifted his arm and I lay my head down on his lap and tucked my legs into my side.

'It was bad enough we didn't get to bed until past twilight, but you did insist on spending most of the morning ravishing my body,' he remarked with some asperity.

'I beg your pardon?' I looked up, and found him smiling down at me. 'You are such a joker.' I felt the vibration of his chuckle under my cheek. 'Sleep for as long as you can, love.' Nicholas gently stroked my neck and it was not long before I fell asleep.

We arrived home in a gale of good humour and high spirits. Ms. Janssen was waiting to greet us as we stepped into the entrance hall, and I passed her my basket as Nicholas walked past me; he planted a kiss on my cheek on his way towards the study.

We have only just got back.' I said with a pouty frown.

'…and it's back to business I'm afraid, love.' He kissed the top of my forehead and disappeared behind the door.

'Did you have a pleasant trip, My Lady?' Mrs. Janssen asked as I handed her my cloak.

'Please, Ms. Hanssen, call me Caroline, we are well past the formalities now. I consider you a friend.' I placed my hand on her arm.

'Very well, Caroline, then you must call me Deanna.'

'Deanna, what a lovely name.'

'Thank you, I was named after my grandmother. Now you are back would you like to go over the menu for dinner?'

'No, leave it for the moment, just see to the rest of the household as I don't know what Nicholas's plans are for the moment.'

'How did Willheim fare? Did the boys behave themselves?' she asked.

'Oh, yes they were exceptionally good, and behaved impeccably, you would be enormously proud of Willheim.' Her face lit up and her chest puffed with pride. Deanna didn't need to know the details of their escapades with brothels, beer, and tavern girls. Things like this were best left unsaid.

'The boys will no doubt be hungry, would you like something to eat?'

'Yes I would, thank you.' We both made our way towards the kitchen.

15

Joy and sorrow

Summer and Autumn had been and gone, and Nicholas was no nearer to getting the funds to support the king. It was late October, nearing Princess Mary's confinement, and not long before I found myself pregnant, but I had to be sure before I told Nicholas.

My doubts and fears set in; would he be pleased? I knew this was not the right time to have a baby, but when was there ever an appropriate time? I got careless. I lost count of my days after my monthly flow. How could I have a baby? I'm not even in the right time, the right me, and if I go back what will happen? Will I remember my baby? Will I be heartbroken? will the other Carolina love it... What silly nonsense, of course she would, because she is me. I had such a mixture of emotions running through me. I was joyous one moment, then scared then next.

I had loads of questions that I couldn't answer rolling around my head, and to be quite honest I didn't even want to think about it.

I became a regular visitor to the Hague. The weather was cold and miserable, so our little garden had been closed for the winter months and Mary and I spent our time together reading. She also taught me how to play chess, and I taught her boxes and hangman, which she loved. Mary wanted me near her, and she appointed me lady of the bedchamber, which didn't sit well with the other ladies at court, especially the dreadful wife of the Marquis von Holsten.

'Mary, I'm incredibly grateful for the position you have given me,' I said to her one afternoon, 'but why do I have to take up residence in the palace? It doesn't take long for me to get here, and I cannot be parted from Nicholas.'

'Please, Caroline, this is only temporary, until the baby is born.' She took hold of my arm, and we made our way out into the corridor towards a door opposite her own.

'This is where you will stay,' she said as she unlocked the door.

The suite consisted of six rooms, three on each floor, strung out straight along the water's edge.

'My god, Mary this is huge.' I walked over to the windows and looked out over the Hofvijer lake. 'What an amazing view.'

Mary's face beamed at me. 'Do you think Nicholas would like it here too?'

'But that's not normally done, do husband's not stay at home?' I asked rather tentatively.

'Yes, but Frederick and William have made an exception. Anyway your marriage is not like other marriages, most wives wish to be away from their husbands.'

'Before I say yes, please let me go home to discuss this with Nicholas.'

Mary linked her arm through mine as we left the apartment. 'I'm sure he will be pleased, plus it keeps him closer to Frederick.'

'Why, you clever little girl.'

We giggled like co-conspirators as we made our way back to Mary's rooms.

*

It was just before supper that I decided to ask Nicholas about the new sleeping arrangements, and to tell him about my pregnancy. I waited until he was nicely settled in the bathtub before I broached the subject. Nicholas was relaxed into the tub, a high slipper bath that rose at the back to allow for lounging. Times do not change, I supposed, especially having the trouble to get the bath filled, one might as well enjoy it, no matter what century we reside in.

Nicholas was unaware I watched him, for a time. His stubbled face assumed an expression of pure relaxation as he sank even lower into the hot water. He had a pink flush to his skin and his eyes were closed, and a faint mist of moisture gleamed across his brow and shone in the hollow ravines of his eye sockets and on his broad cheekbones.

He picked up the cake of soap and diligently scrubbed himself, dipping the cloth and soap occasionally into the water to re-lather it up again.

'Nicholas,' I said at last.

'Bloody hell Caroline…you startled me.'

'Sorry, I didn't mean to.' I pulled a chair up towards the bathtub, facing him.

'I don't want to quarrel with you, but there is going to be a change in our living accommodation, and other expectations.' He stopped washing and was watching me intently.

'The thing is…Mm…' To my slight irritation, I was a little lost for words and I started to flush slightly. However, I wasn't sure if it was the heat from the water that rose to my face or I was feeling embarrassed about telling him.'

His hand rose from the water and rested on my hand.

'What is it, love?' he said, 'out with it.'

'Er, well, Mary has appointed me lady of the bedchamber, and we have to move into the palace until she reaches her time. Before you say no, it might be in our best interest, especially being closer to Frederick,' I added, as he sat for a time contemplating.

'You are a genius, love.' Nicholas grabbed me laughing and pulled me into the tub. Water sloshed over the sides. I laughed as he planted loads of kisses on my face and neck.

'So, you don't mind, then?'

'Mind? This is the best news ever, I can push our cause more without any outside interference.'

'Thank god! I was ever so worried, because I can't say no to Mary, and the thought of being away from you—'

'Well, my love, it's all falling into place nicely.'

I withdrew slightly. 'I have something else to tell you.' I wavered for a second, and Nicholas narrowed his eyes at me and seemed about to reply, but before he could I blurted out. 'I'm with child!'

Nicholas's face transformed from relaxed and playful, to thoughtful. He drew in a breath.

'How long?'

'About four months,' I said hesitantly.

'Why didn't you tell me sooner?' He smiled down at me; I felt the relief flood through my veins.

'I had to be one hundred percent sure.'

'Caroline, that's wonderful news, although the timing could have been better.' He put his arms around me. 'I'm so happy, love.'

'I was worried you would be disappointed with me, especially with everything that's going on at the moment.'

'My god, woman, nothing you can do or say would ever disappoint me, my life is you, and now our babe too.' I felt the soap bubbles around his neck and shoulders, as I put my arms around him.

'How about you take this gown off, and get into the tub properly,' he said, as his eyes blazed with passion.

I peeled the gown off, and sat in between his legs facing him. 'Will you help me wash my hair?' he said as he held out the misshaped ball of soap.

I lathered the contents in my hand and dropped the soap back into the water. I could feel the solid curve of his skull under his thick, soapy hair. I dug my fingers firmly into his head and massaged away the grim and tension of his day.

With his eyes still closed, my hands travelled down to his chest following the straggle of soap bubbles. My fingers seemed to glide on the smooth surface of his skin, and I picked up the jug that sat on the stool opposite and filled it with the hot water. I poured it leisurely over his head to rinse the soap away, and touched the small scar on his left cheekbone, which he had acquired some time ago in battle. He had such a brave heart, and I was so moved by my tenderness for him that I brushed my lips across it. I straightened and placed the jug back on the stool. He opened his eyes.

'Well, I must say that was the most memorable experience I have ever had whilst having a bath.' I felt his pleasure brush against my thighs.' He stood up, the hot water flowed in rivulets down his body and the steam from the heat rose off his skin.

He towered over me as I looked up at him. 'Come, wife.' He picked me up and cradled me against his chest as his long legs stepped out of the tub.

*

By mid-November we had settled into our rooms next to Mary's, our life was quite different now, but I found it fascinating.

Mary's last four weeks had taken a toll on her, so I made it my duty to keep her comfortable. Rumors swept through the palace corridors; her majesty was ill and would lose another child. Nasty evil court women. I had no time for either.

Late one night I was summoned, Mary needed me urgently. She lay flat on her back in bed, surrounded by her maids and waiting-women. Her eyes were closed tightly to keep back the tears, for she was in pain and afraid.

Mary heard one of her closest maids turn and tell one of the others to get William, and cried out.

'No! Don't do that, don't send for him. It's nothing, it's just the labour,' she said, as I rushed over to her.

'Mary, I'm here.'

'Oh, Caroline the pain...' She held my hand tightly.

Penava one of the ladies maids spoke to me.

'The baby has not yet turned.'

I let go of Mary's hand and pulled Penava to one side, so we are out of ear shot.

'She is in early labour, so we need to get her up out of that bed and get her moving.' I said to Penava as she looked at me as if I'd gone mad. 'Walking can sometimes help the baby turn on its own. If not, then we must manipulate the baby, so the head is down. Where is the midwife? Has she been called for?' *How do I know this? I seem to have a deep knowledge of these things.* I had no time to think about this now. I shook the thoughts away and set about seeing to Mary.

'Yes, she has, we are expecting her anytime soon.'

A piercing scream escaped Mary's mouth. 'Caroline, please help me.'

Rushing over, my feet slid on something, and, looking down I was shocked to see quite a lot of blood on the floor. Why had I not seen this first?'

Calmly I turned to the ladies in the room.

'Send for a doctor, now!' I said in hushed tones. 'And clear the room, save for Penava.'

I removed the covers and pulled up Mary's night gown, the blood was everywhere.

'We have got to get this baby out, otherwise we are going to lose her.' By this time, my instincts just kicked in. 'Get me a bowl of water and some lavender oil.' William rushed in with his mother, Amalia of Solms.

'What's happening?' he asked. His features were etched with worry.

'Mary will die if we don't get the baby out.'

'What of the baby?' I heard Amalia ask Panava.

I interrupted them. 'I don't know if I can save them both but I will try, and where is that bloody doctor?'

Amalia approached me. 'Save the child.'

My horror must had been apparent, because before I could speak, William stepped in.

'No, save Mary, we can have other children.'

I nodded at him as he took his mother's arm to pull her away. 'Please leave, let me do what I can, and have someone find that doctor?'

The midwife had arrived some time ago, but the doctor refused to come, as he deemed it women's work. Silly man.

The hours passed quickly and during that time we managed to turn the baby and get him out, unfortunately it was too late. The little baby boy was already dead. The midwife cleaned and swaddled the little one, and then gave him to William.

My job now was to help Mary but the midwife pulled me to one side. 'There is nothing you can do, she has lost too much blood.'

'Nonsense!' I said in fury.

I heard a soft sound escape Mary's lips. 'Let me die...' William looked on in pity, he was by her side.

'I'm sorry. I'm so sorry Mary. You cannot die, my sweet, what would I do without you?'

His face looked tired and as haggard as mine, for above all things on earth he wanted a son, but I knew then Mary was much more important to him.

'William, I will stay with her and tend her, and I promise I will get her through this.'

He rose and took my hands, 'Please, if you can save her, then anything you want is yours.'

*

For five days and nights I tended Mary. I had little interruption, apart from William and his parents, and I didn't see Nicholas, but every so often food and drink were sent up to me. I knew he was looking after me.

I forced liquids down Mary's throat that were rich in irons. I even introduced smoothies to the palace cooks. Spinach, beans, lentils, that were crushed into pulp and made into drinks. Having no true medical knowledge, I thought the best way to build up her blood was through large quantities of iron, and a strong will from Mary. I prayed this would work, because the thought of losing Mary filled me with utter despair. I had come to love this young lady. I suppose losing my sister through time has made me lean more towards Mary. I wanted to protect her and give her the love she so missed when she first got to Holland and if truth be told, I missed that sibling connection.

By the sixth day the sickly paleness of Mary's complexion had almost gone, her lips regained their pinkness, and I knew then that she was well on the way to recovery. At last her eyes slowly opened and she saw William.

For a moment there was scarcely even recognition on her face, and then the tears came, and she turned her head away with an agonizing sob. My heart broke for her.

'Is it the pain Mary?' William looked at her with concern.

'There is no more pain, I so wanted to give you a son.'

'You did…and he was beautiful, but he was obviously needed for a higher purpose. Don't fret my little

273

dove…you will someday, and he will be great. Don't think about anything, just get well.'

I busied myself with tidying up my herb basket at the far end of the room, but I couldn't help but overhear.

'I don't want to get well. What good am I on this earth if I cannot do the one thing I was put here for?' The cry of anguish from Mary was heart wrenching. Her eyes flood with self-reproach. 'What if what they say is true…that I'm barren?'

'Oh, my little dove…' William's breath caught sharply and sadness clouded his features.

We had hoped she hadn't heard the horrible gossip.

I walked towards the bed. I'm sorry for eavesdropping your highness, but that is total bullshit…if you were barren then you wouldn't have fallen pregnant. Complications arose, and there was nothing we could have done. You are both so very young, and you still have plenty of time, but you must be incredibly careful. No intimacy for three months, you both need to wait a good year before you try again. You need to let your body heal, do you both understand?'

They both nodded. 'Mary, my darling.' I watched as William's long fingers stroked her hair and caressed her pale moist cheeks. 'You must rest now and grow well and strong…for my sake.' William smiled tenderly; he bent his head to kiss her.

'For your sake?' she looked at him trustingly, and at last she gave him a grateful smile. 'You are so kind…you're so good to me. This won't happen next time. I promise.'

'Of course, it won't. Now go to sleep, my little dove, and rest, and presently you'll be well again with Carolina's help.'

William remained kneeling beside her until her breathing became deep and regular, and when the little frown of pain had left her forehead, he got up. William walked towards me and took my hands. 'Words cannot express how grateful I am, please, my lady, what can I do to repay you?'

'No words are needed your highness and I need nothing. However, my husband and the prince of Wales need your help. They require funds and a fleet of war ships to rescue Mary's father.'

He leaned down and kissed both my cheeks. 'You will have both.' Then without another word he walked from the room and back to his own apartments.

The next day Mary was feeling much better, so I took the liberty of some fresh air and to go in search of my husband. The fresh air was invigorating, but my husband was nowhere to be seen.

Upon returning to Mary's room, I was horrified to find the doctor and priests in her bed chambers. My back had been turned for just a moment and I came back to this circus. The bloody idiots had cut fresh pigeons in half and tied them to her feet, they had given her purgatives and sneezing powders, pearls, and chloride of gold. The priests were groaning and wailing and praying and the room was filled with people. Royalty can neither be born nor die in peace or privacy. They were all convinced Mary was going to die and I suspected most of them hoped she would, and the talk was not so much of the dying princess as of the new one. Who would take her place?'

I was mad as hell; I slammed the door with such force they all jumped out of their skins. 'Everybody out!' I yelled at the top of my voice. 'You bloody idiots, Mary is not dying, she is recovering and whatever possessed you to put pigeons on her feet? I've just cleaned everywhere, then you do something idiotic like this. Everyone out, and if you grace this door again you all will be sorry...do you hear me?'

I heard a small chuckle from Mary, and her eyes glinted with mischief as they all scurried out.

'Thank the lord they have gone,' she whispered,

'And they will not be coming back either.' I exclaimed. 'I won't leave you until you are back on your feet.'

'Thank you, Caroline, I owe you my life.'

'That's what friends are for.' I walked over to her bed and untied the pigeons.

'You're more like my sister than a friend,' she said.

I leaned down and gave her a hug.

'I miss my Mother.' She cried in my arms.

'Shush...all over now,' I said as I stroked the back of her head. My heart broke a little more that day.

16

To ready the fleet

The docks were busy, ships with their gilded hulls gleamed, their tall masts bare as skeletons. The fleet lay on the quiet water in great numbers, in the process of a complete overhaul. Cleaning, seams being mended with boiling pitch, the ropes bound with oilcloths. Sailors, deckhands, officers, and porters everywhere, loading and preparing the ships to sail in the next few weeks.

Mary was recovering well, although not fully. Christmas was fast approaching and I knew we didn't have much time left in Holland.

I hadn't the heart to tell Mary of my pregnancy, and luckily, I only had a slight bump, which was hidden well beneath my clothes. I was exhausted and I missed Nicholas terribly.

'Go spend the day with your husband.' She said one evening, so without any refusal from myself I decided to surprise him at the docks. Alex and Willheim provided me with the escort I needed and we headed out early the next morning.

I got out of the coach and walked along the wharf between the two boys, shading my eyes against the cold December sun. A beggar tried to touch me, and some of the sailors whistled as I passed. I'd been too busy looking for Nicholas to take notice, although the boys had a few choice words in my favour.

'There he is, Nicholas.'

Nicholas turned as I shouted down to him. I started to run towards him. I was smiling eagerly, out of breath, and thoroughly expecting to be picked up and kissed.

However, instead he looked down at me with a scowl. His face was tired, his skin wet with sweat and he had lost weight. 'Love, what the devil are you doing down here?'

'We haven't seen each other properly for weeks and I wanted to spend the day with you.' I remarked.

We had become like ships passing in the night. I was asleep when he came back to the rooms at the palace and when I woke in the mornings he was gone. As the days passed into weeks I felt the loss of him more and more. Although most of my time was taken up with Mary making sure she was recovering well and to keep the nasty woman at court away.

'The docks are no place for a lady.' His expression hardened.

'I missed you, so I thought I would surprise you,' I said softly. 'Aren't you glad?' The smile slipped from my face. I thought he would be pleased to see me. Self-pity washed over me.

But his look of exhaustion was real, my eyes roamed over him with concern. I had never seen him this tired, and I so wanted to kiss away his frown and weariness.

Nicholas smiled at me faintly as though he was ashamed of his ill temper. He ran the back of his hand across his forehead to remove the sweat.

'Of course, I am, but it's not safe down here, love. There is sickness on one of the ships that docked in for repairs, unbeknownst to us it carried a disease…you have got to get away from here as fast as you can. Some of the men are saying it's the black death.'

I gasped in horror. 'You might catch it too, you have no idea how contagious it is, in six years' time it's going to wipe out half the population in Europe and England.'

'Don't panic, there have only been two sailors, but they are now dead, and, as far as we know there haven't been any new cases. Don't fret love because as soon as I saw the sickness I ordered the vessel to be sunk. I was only on board for a short while.'

'That's all it takes. Did any of the crew enter that room apart from you?' My fear was starting to build up.

'No, thankfully, it was only me. I wouldn't even let the doctor enter.'

'That was quick thinking on your part but you must leave with me now.' My self-pity had left, it was now replaced with fear. I knew deep down Nicholas had caught it. I needed to prepare because the next seventy-two hour I knew were going to be critical. Would I have the knowledge to save Nicholas? Only time would tell.

Nicholas gave me a look of exasperation. 'I cannot leave now, not until everything has been loaded on.'

'I won't go without you.' I stood my ground in anger.

'Christ, Caroline, don't be a fool, I'll meet you at the lodgings just outside the wharf, I reserved a room for tonight because I didn't want to go back to the palace just in case. Only go there and stay put. Keep off the streets, and don't talk to anyone, do you hear me?' He kissed me goodbye, and then walked down the docks and disappeared amongst the sailors.

I didn't do as I was first told, I needed to be prepared. Taking the carriage back to the Hague, making sure I encountered no one, I let myself into Mary's private garden. With my basket full to the brim: lavender, lemon balm, rosemary, thyme, sweet cicely, valerian, woodworm, turmeric, and yarrow, I made my way back to the carriage. I had to be sure I had everything, just in case Nicholas succumbed to the disease. I sent the boys home, and drove the carriage back myself.

Three hours passed, and I was beginning to grow impatient and worried. What could be keeping him all this time? I walked over to the window and opened it. The sun had set dark red over the water and the cold wind blew in. Shivering, I closed the window and paced the room in agitation.

At last the door opened and Nicholas walked in.

'What took you so long? I was worried.' A cold chill went over me as I watched him drop wearily into a chair, his eyes bloodshot, his face flushed with fever.

'You're sick, I knew it when I saw you earlier.' Rushing over I helped him stand. 'Let's get you on the bed.' Helping him to lie down I started to take off his clothes, starting with his neck cloth, down to his breeches and boots.

'I'm fine, truly, tired and overworked,' he whispered softly in my ear.

'No, you're wrong, you have the plague, you were exposed for too long in that ship.'

'I was only on there no more than ten minutes.'

'Ten minutes too long. Do you have a headache? Nausea? Dizziness?' My hands touched his forehead, he was burning up. My mouth went dry and my heart thudded hard against my chest.

'Yes, all.'

'And what about your body? Do you ache all over?' My hands ran down the full length of his arms and then back up to his face. He nodded.

'Bloody hell, Nicholas, you're a stubborn idiot, you should have left with me sooner, at least I might have helped with your symptoms much earlier.'

'You need to leave, love.'

'I'm not going anywhere. I'm staying to look after you.'

'Oh, Caroline, I won't let you, I might be dead by—' He took my hands from his cheeks and held me at a distance.

'Don't you dare say that! I have the means, and the knowledge, I will take care of you and that's final.'

'You might catch it too…and what of the baby?' His eyes drifted down to my stomach and the muscles in his jaw twitched. I knew he was worried about us.

'The baby and I will be fine, if I do the right thing.' He tried to move, but his muscles seemed useless.

He drifted in and out of sleep and shivered with the cold fever. I left him for several minutes, and returned with my arms laden with quilts and blankets.

I wrapped him in them tightly, and then stoked the fire, burning the mixture of herbs so the room stayed fresh.

Nicholas was lying flat on his back, but the quilts and blankets had fallen off and he was moving around restlessly. As I bent to tuck him in again his hand grabbed my wrist, giving it a savage jerk.

'What the devil are you doing?' His voice was thick and hoarse, and his words slurred over one another.

'I told you to get out of here. Now go, get out!' He shouted the last words as he flung my arm away from him furiously.

'I'm going to give you something for the fever and pain, it will be ready soon, but until then you lie still and be quiet, do you understand?' I put his arms back into the blankets and tucked it securely under the mattress and prayed this will keep him still.

Nicholas seemed to regain some sort of rationality. 'Please love, go, the thought of you and the babe getting ill fills me with dread. I'll be dead on the morrow, so please leave. If you won't, then I will.'

He started to sit up, the blankets all but came away from under the mattress. I pushed him back down, he was no match for me, at least for the time being, I knew I was much stronger than Nicholas at this moment. I hung over him anxiously, until he stilled, and it wasn't long before his breathing slowed.

I tip-toed swiftly over to the fireplace to stoke the fire hotter. I was nervous and scared, my hands shook with fear. I scooped up the tea I had made with all the necessary ingredients, when I heard a noise behind me. I found him standing in the middle of the floor, looking about in confusion.

I ran towards him. 'Nicholas, what do you think you are doing?'

His eyes blazed with fever, he was glaring at me but it held no recognition. I went to take his hand but he gave me a shove so hard that it nearly knocked me off my feet. I staggered backwards and grabbed hold of him to steady myself, we both ended up crashing to the floor. I was trapped beneath him.

He was still, his eyes and mouth open, but he was unconscious. Winded and stunned, I laid there with his heavy weight upon me. I managed to crawl out from under him. My skirt hindered my movement so I ripped it off. Then I paced my hands under his armpits and heaved back trying with all my strength to move him but he was too heavy to move. I sat back on the floor, legs ten to two with his head in my lap. I stroked his forehead and caressed his cheek. How was I ever going to get him back into bed?

I must had been on the floor no more than five minutes when all off a sudden he sat up, and then stood, his legs wide apart to steady himself, he swayed back and forth like a drunken man. He was so weak, any minute now he was going to collapse, I took this opportunity to guide him back into bed.

Nicholas lay quietly on his back now, and from time to time he muttered something unintelligible under his breath. Then the vomiting started, and the germ was now airborne, so every time he was sick, I cleaned everything. I kept my mouth and nose covered with a clean linen cloth, and made sure my hands were always washed. I burned our clothes in the open fire, and boiled our undergarments in the yarrow, to kill the germ.

It was now almost eleven, and the street had grown quiet, apart from the odd rumble of a passing carriage.

'Privy...' I heard him whisper. He tried to get out of bed, but I forced him back and brought over the chamber pot. My last hope died quietly as I saw the beginning of a plague boil, it looked tender and swollen, in his left groin.

The night passed slowly, I cleaned the room again with my herb mixture and fresh water. I washed the germs always from Nicholas's body, and my own with the lemon balm. I scrubbed my teeth and washed my hair in lavender soap and fresh water. Then I wrapped my hair in a clean linen cloth, which I secured tightly so it would not fall away. I put on my clean undergarments and apron from my basket. I got a quick glance of myself in the mirror... I looked like a world war one nurse, all that was missing was the red cross on my pinny.

Nicholas had an intense thirst, but I would only allow him to sip water with a mixture of turmeric, and I forced bone broth down his throat, prepared with chicken bone that I insisted on being brought up every two hours. The cook in the kitchen grumbled, but when he saw the pouch of coins he soon changed his mind.

I wrapped the soles of Nicholas's feet in washcloths soaked in cider vinegar, hoping to pull any impurities out. Why I chose to do this I do not know, but a memory of Carolina's mother doing this made me do the same.

'Lina…'

Nicholas tried to speak, but his tongue was swollen and covered in a thick white fur, although around the edges it was smooth and red raw. His eyes were dull, but he looked up at me with recognition for the first time in many hours.

'Lina…why…are…you…still…here?'

'Shush…be still my darling. I will get you through this, I promise.'

With quick resolution I went back to the task of caring for him, washing his face, arms, and body. The lump in Nicholas's groin was bigger, it had stretched so tight over his skin and if memory served me this indicated the last stages of the plague. The swollen mass must be lanced, otherwise it would burst and the infection would kill him.

I gave him valerian root to knock him out, so my task could be done with relative ease. After soaking my knife and his groin in alcohol, I cut open the carbuncle, and blood poured out in a dark red stream that spread around him on the clean linen sheets. The water gland fluid came with it and then the yellow pus began to work its way upward through the deep hole which now resembled a crater.

With boiling water which had cooled, I began to wash off the blood and pus. The bloody rags built up, and I thought it was never going to end. I had never seen someone lose so much blood, and I hoped and prayed that I was doing the right thing.

Once the bleeding stopped, I packed the wound with the crushed peppercorns and garlic that I had made into a paste, and bound it securely with clean bandages.

I kept busy cleaning the room of the blood and the smell. I burned all the linen, and washed all the floors and walls, and opened the window to allow some fresh air in. By the morning, much to my relief, the colour began to return to Nicholas's face, his breathing became regular, and the fever had broken. For the first time in my life I thanked God.

I sent letters to Mary and Fredrick, to warn them what had happened, I gave strict instructions that anyone showing signs needed to be removed and if any bodily fluids escaped they must be cleaned up straight away and not left. Bed linens and clothes to be burned, and bodies to be washed, so the disease didn't spread. I advised them to close the gates of the wharf to stop people entering or leaving. Notices were put up, to inform people to take the necessary steps to prevent further contamination. The city was now in lockdown.

The period of convalescence was long and tedious. Nicholas's eyes were still dull and expressionless; I could never tell if he even knew who it was taking care of him. Each time he looked at me, I hoped for some sort of recognition, but there was nothing.

On the tenth day after he had fallen sick, I sat on the bed wiping his face with a cool cloth, until I realised he was watching me, something in his eyes had changed, as if the fog of fever had lifted. He saw me. A thrill of pleasure ran over me. He smiled at me as I touched his cheek. A single tear slipped down my face.

'Oh, Nicholas…'

'God bless you, my darling…my angel…' His voice was soft, almost a whisper. He turned his head to kiss my hand. I could only say his name, for my throat had become thick until it ached, tears flowed more freely down my cheeks. Nicholas turned his head back around and gave a light sigh and closed his eyes.

Day after day, little by little he began to talk more, only a few words at a time, but that was enough for me. His eyes would follow me everywhere and in them I saw love and gratitude that tore at my heart, and every day I told him I loved him.

17

Royalist rising

It was nearing the end of December, Nicholas had recovered, although not fully. We soon realised that Nicholas and the two other sailors had been isolated cases, or perhaps the quick thinking on my part had prevented the spread of the disease.

The fleet was ready to depart for England, and Nicholas was impatient to leave. It was time to leave Holland and say our goodbyes to our friends, which was terribly painful. This was one of the hardest things I had ever had to do.

Mary cried so hard. I pulled her in for a hug and told her I would keep in touch, and I gave her strict instructions to take it easy and not to listen to all the gossip.

'And look after our little garden!' I shouted out to her, as we departed the Hague.

We approach the docks and the sense of foreboding descended on me like a thick black cloud, my heart was heavy; I knew what would be waiting for us. The Prince of Wales refused to remain in Holland, and no amount of persuading would convince him otherwise, but just maybe our fortunes could turn in our favour. I knew Charles was doomed, but I would fight tooth and nail to save Nicholas.

*

We had returned home to English waters, it felt strange and unfamiliar somehow. I hoped we had done enough to secure the King's freedom, but only time would tell. Nicholas had great expectations, and he started to plan our future: we would go back to Holland to live out our days in relative peace, raise our family, and wait for the day when the prince of Wales would re-take his father's throne, so we could return to England, to Debden Hall, if all went according to plan.

The downpour of rain on the cabin roof woke me from my sleep. I felt a little disoriented, and it took me a moment to get my bearings. Nicholas stirred and murmured in his sleep, he turned and took the quilts with him. Exposed to the cold I got up quickly, and ran for the fur robe and an extra blanket that had been thrown casually on the floor next to my woollen tights.

Then dressed in all three, and feeling much warmer, I bravely walked over to the ship's side portal. The English sky was grey and thick with clouds, the morning had just broken, the sea mist had all but disappeared. Dropping the blanket and robe by the side of the bed I climbed back in next to Nicholas, tugged the quilt from around him and lay back down. I stretched out the sleep from my body, arching my back as my pelvis rubbed up against him.

'Mm?' he said. 'Hm,' he sighed as he gripped my behind and went back to sleep, holding on. Turning around I nudged my bottom closer into his warmth. Even in his sleep his arm circled my swollen stomach, he pulled me even further in, where I could feel the hardness of him. I tried to go back to sleep, but the closeness of him was too much to bear, as my thoughts wandered to other things. I pulled the quilt up over my shoulders and buried my face inside to warm my freezing nose. I wriggled closer to Nicholas for warmth.

'Madam, how do you expect a man to get any sleep, with you moving around, especially whilst your pert little bottom continuously rubs up against me.'

'Oh, you're awake. Sorry I didn't mean to wake you.' A little devilish smile played on my lips.

'Hm, you could have fooled me, wife.'

His hands fell away as I felt him stretch out, he pushed himself into my bottom and I felt his morning glory. Nicholas's hand moved up my thigh, and pushed my shift up to my waist. I moved my hair out of the way so he could kiss my neck.

'Hm.' I sighed in pleasure. He lifted my left leg and placed it over his hip, so he could gain easy access, and I began to turn. 'No,' he said, 'stay still, I want to take you as you are.'

He went back to kissing my neck with his tongue and I felt his fingers enter me. Warm and slick, I was more than ready for him.

'Please, Nicholas, now. I want to come with you inside me...Please,' I said, breathless. He entered me from behind, slowly, both side by side. The pleasure I felt was indescribable as he pushed in and out, and I could feel his ridged contours gliding back and forth inside of me. His fingers caressed my swollen bud. It didn't take me long for my release as I cried out in ecstasy.

*

For the next week, the Dutch fleet hovered just off the coast, we had one hundred ships at our disposal. We had word from France that they will add twenty-five ships to our cause, and they were lying in wait at Dunkirk. Cromwell had yet to arm a loyal fleet, which proved no problem for us.

Under the cover of darkness, Gregor, Alec, Nicholas, and I, along with the Prince of Wales, made our way to Westminster.

The air around us was thick with an eerie fog that rolled off the Thames, it seemed to follow us the further in town we went. I was thankful because it kept us hidden from prying eyes.

The walled city smelt of the centuries old, ugly, stinking and full of decay, but full of colour with a rotten sort of beauty within. The streets were narrow, some paved with cobblestones but most of them not, and down the center or along the sides ran open sewage kennels. Posts strung out at interval stations which served to separate the carriage-way from the narrow space left for pedestrians. I wondered what century they decided to build pavements. Across the streets leaned the houses, each story overhanging the one beneath shutting out the light and air almost completely from the tightest of the alleys. Church-spires dominated the skyline and from my estimation there were more than a hundred within the walls and the sound of their bells was probably a continual music of London during the day. Creaking signs swung overhead painted with red and gold lions, blue boars and the coat of Stuart arms. In Holland it had been sunny and almost warm but here the fog hung heavily, thickened with the smoke from the fires of the soap boilers and lime burners. There was a penetrating chill around us and in the air. During the day I imagined the streets were crowded, vendors strolling along carrying their wares and housewives could almost make all their necessary purchases on her own doorstep.

As the night swiftly descended on us there were few people around. Prostitutes hung in shop doorways bawling their recommendations, not hesitating to grab a customer by the sleeve to urge him down a darkened alleyway.

A drunken satin fop staggered into a sedan-chair and shouted at his liveried footman to hurry on home.

We walked some distance, until we reached another public house. It was tucked down a narrow street hidden between a staggered row of wooden houses.

The sign dangled out on an elaborate wrought iron arm, and, on the front, there was a painted picture of James 1st and underneath it said the King's Head. How ironic I thought to myself.

We didn't enter through the main entrance. Instead, we followed Gregor around the back, and he rapped on the old oak back door with a pattern of knocks, much like Stefan and Nicholas did back at the inn in Durham. The door opened and I followed the men inside.

Candles flickered around the room casting a subdued light. The ale house was empty, but, I mused it would be, in the early hours.

Upon entering the room, I was surprised to see Stefan and about ten other men, some faces I recognised, but some were unacquainted to me. However these were clearly all Nicholas's men, because they all wore his crest upon there cloaks.

'Stefan it is so good to see you.' Nicholas affectionately clasped Stefan's hand as they shook.

'So, you made it across safely then?' said Stefan with a wide smile.

'Yes, no trouble at all, which has me a little worried.' Nicolas's smile slipped from his face.

'We have been keeping regular lookouts and I have a man on the inside, and so far there has not been a whiff of anything amiss, insofar as the king's daily routine of going about the ground unattended has not changed either.'

'Well, let's hope it stays that way, my good fellow!' The prince of Wales's voice boomed around the ale house as he slapped Stefan on the back.

'Shush.' Stefan put his finger up to his lips.' 'There are people asleep upstairs and we don't want to alert anyone of your presence, sire.'

'Terribly sorry, old chap.' The prince took himself off to the bar. 'Come, Mistress Carolina, how about you pour me a nice mug of ale.' I looked horrified at Nicholas; he raised his eyebrows at me. Before I could answer young Alec stepped in.

'No, your Royal Highness…let me do that for you.' Bless Alec, I could kiss him sometimes. He was such a sweet young boy with bright blond hair that was kept short and hidden well beneath a hat, with kind green eyes. A little on the slight side, but he had a hidden strength. I supposed this was one of the advantages of being in Holland with Gregor. We joined Nicholas's men up a large round table, Alec placed a pitcher of Ale and an extra four mugs.

It's good to see my lady,' said Stefan. 'How did you find Holland?'

'I loved it there, although it was colourful to say the least and not just the clothes.' I chuckled. 'It's good to see all of you.' I raised my mug to all of the men, even those I was unfamiliar with.

They all raised their ale mugs. 'To our safety, and getting the King out of England,' I said. 'Here, here.' They all replied in unison.

Once the prince of Wales was seated at the head of the table discussions began. I sat and listened, but made no comment as they made their plans.

The strategy was to create a diversion at Tower Bridge with the Dutch fleet. On the night Cromwell's men were to transfer the King from St James Palace to the Banqueting house, the fleet would sail through the Thames Estuary towards the Tower of London. Once the cannon fire alerted parliament that there was an impending attack, Cromwell would, with any luck, order his army towards the Tower, keeping only a handful of guards around the King.

Nicholas and his men would then attack. If all went to plan, we would all escape on horseback towards the docks at Tilbury. Once on board, we would sail to Scotland to place the Prince of Wales at the head of Hamilton's army, and then safely to Dunkirk, where the King would be transferred to the French naval fleet and then to Paris to live out his remaining life with his Queen.

Then Nicholas and I would sail back to Holland. However, I knew deep down this would never happen. I knew he would be leaving me soon. Would these be our final hours together as I sat watching him with my heart in my throat.

*

The night of the rescue was upon us, I had barely slept the night before through fear and the days leading up to it had affected me more than I had realised. Nicolas and I had laboured so hard to prevent the prince of Wales from coming, and now our only hope was to somehow change the outcome. I feared in my heart that history would not be re-written; no matter how many obstacles we faced, and won, deep down I knew now that victory would forever be out of our reach.

I was dressed as a boy so I could blend in with the men. Nicholas and I had argued leading up to this night and I told him that I was not going to be left behind, despite my pregnancy. I knew it would be risky, but I couldn't bear to leave him. I needed to keep him in my sights at all times.

We rode through the streets of London, towards St James's Palace where we were met outside by Stefan, who had gone on ahead of us to secure the surrounding areas. The Prince of Wales still insisted on coming, and nothing we said would dissuade him. We heard the drums roll, and the signal bells began to ring; the fleet had been spotted. I tried to fight down the wave of nausea, It burned in the pit of my stomach. The fear had become my sickness. The first boom of cannon fire alerted us – that was our signal, and I prayed that the diversion would work.

'How many guards were posted to the King, when he left St James Palace?' Nicholas asked Stefan.

'We counted twenty, but that doesn't cause us any problem, we can out match them.'

'Just twenty?'

'Yes.'

'Good, they should be here in the next ten minutes or so.' Nicholas then turned to me. 'As soon as you see us return from that corner,' he pointed to the road ahead. 'You get the horses in position. But if anything happens you do not wait, you leave, do you understand?'

'Yes,' I whispered.

Nicholas took hold of my shoulders and squeezed gently. 'Promise, Caroline.' His expression hardened.

'I promise,' I whispered, My voice barely audible. I could hardly speak with worry.

'Alec will take you safely back to your parents, and if I can, I shall meet you there.' He drew me close, and I sighed heavily against his chest with a heavy heart.

'Come back to me,' I murmured into his ear. I drew back and he kissed me on my lips.

'Always.' Then he turned and joined his men as they waited in position for the carriage that contained the king.

I heard a whistle, the signal from one of the men to say the carriage was on its way towards us. I was slightly distracted by my fear, and I had a terrible feeling of utter helplessness as I watched Nicholas and his men take down the small army of soldiers that surrounded the King.

The fighting was wild and terrifying, full of calamity and fear, some of the soldiers fled and I thought we had won the fight. Gregor jumped onto the carriage and grabbed the king, and joy burst through me; we had done it! Maybe I had been wrong, maybe I had changed history for the better...

My triumph was soon dispelled by horror, within seconds of them grabbing the King I heard a trumpet sound. Out of nowhere, Nicholas, Stefan and his men were surrounded by two hundred or so soldiers from Cromwell's New Model Army. I sat still, powerless to move my horse, my vision blurred and in that moment, I felt my heart break. It was a small flutter, but it hurt.

Over the noise of musket fire and steel clashing with steel, I heard Nicholas shout, '*we have been betrayed!*'

I screamed, and mounted my horse as I saw the Prince of Wales flee with the help of Nicholas. I heard Nicholas shout, 'Caroline, run!'

I galloped as fast as I could to get to him, but as I passed the prince, he somehow grabbed the reins of my horse and turned me off in the other direction.

'No, Nicholas!' I screamed and turned in my saddle, I looked helplessly on as ten or more armed soldiers circled him. Alec ran towards him, but he was set upon. A sword was thrust into his stomach.

Nicholas screamed, a blood curdling cry, as I watched him charge towards the soldiers. He was taken down with a fierce struggle. I was powerless, I could do nothing. The tears streamed down my face, not only for Nicholas but for the loss off young Alec. I kicked my horse to a full gallop and along with the Prince of Wales, side by side, we made our way out of the carnage.

I knew this would happen; history would always push back…

We rode as fast as we could, into darkness save for the flickering torchlights in the distance. The cold wind rushed past my ears, the night was freezing over, but I didn't feel anything inside, I was numb. I reined my horse in to stop, and turned back towards Westminster. The Prince of Wales must have sensed I was no longer behind him because the next thing I was aware of was the prince grabbing my reins to halt me. What the hell? He pulled up short to my mount and I shook my head at him.

'What are you doing?' A muscle in his jaw twitched, I could tell he was angry.

'I'm going back,' I shouted.

'You cannot go back, you will be arrested!'

'I'm going back to our lodgings; there I will wait for news of Nicholas, and if I can get him out I will.'

'We are undone, madam…nothing will change.' His jaw went slack and he gave a heavy sigh.

My temper flared. 'Who did you tell?' I could tell by his face he was to blame. He looked at me with crestfallen features. 'How dare—'

'Who did you tell?' I repeated my question, I cared not for good manners at this point.

'Marquis and Holland my trusted friends…but they would not betray me.' His face twisted with emotion as the recognition dawned on him.

'You're an idiot, what did Nicholas tell you? Trust no one.' Agitated and angry, if I had a knife on me, I would have plunged it into his heart. 'Holland switches sides on whoever has the advantage at the time…Cromwell…and if you had bloody well listened to me in the first place this would not have happened! Nicholas told you to stay put, but you had to be the martyr, you thought you would ride to save your father and be the hero. I told Nicholas as much, you are both to blame for this mess and it now up to me to get him out. Get out of my sight, turn tail and go back to Holland.'

'How dare you speak to me like this.' His nostrils flared and he went to raise his hand.

'I dare, and I do and if you lay a hand on me it will be the last thing you do.' I snatched my reins from his hand and turned my horse back towards London. 'But don't worry, your highness,' I said dripping in sarcasm, 'In eleven years, you will be coming back to rule, and quite badly I might add.' With that last remark I kicked my horse's flanks and sped back towards Westminster, leaving him in a cloud of dust behind me.

The last remark of the Marquis was replaying in my mind. 'You will have no idea when your fate will find you, but when you do, you'll know it's by my hands.'

His words were no longer a threat.'

18

Trials, tears and goodbyes

I went from one noble's house to another. All those loyal to Cromwell, I begged for an audience as I tried to petition anyone that would hear me. I stood outside parliament every day for nigh on a week, trying to get a glimpse of Cromwell or any one from his parliament.

This appeared futile, I was getting nowhere. I was a woman of little consequence to these powerful men.

I was spat at by one of the soldiers, when I tried to get through the doors of parliament.

'Royalist bitch,' he said before spitting onto the floor by my feet.

All my efforts amounted to nothing, I even tried to become aquatinted with Cromwell's wife Elizabeth, through the lady Ireton, one of my mother's closest friends, but she failed to show up for afternoon luncheon. No matter what I tried, I was unsuccessful. Defeated and exhausted, all I could do was go back to my room at the ale house and wait for news.

It was a few days later that I learned that Nicholas had been taken to Newgate prison. It was a condemned stinking hole, and only used as a debtor's prison, so I was shocked to learn Nicholas had been incarcerated in there. Maybe this was a good thing because I could try and bribe the guards on duty.

*

The floors of the prison were covered with rushes which smelt sour and old. I cringed and tried to keep my arms close to my body so I didn't brush up again the walls.

Rats darted in and out of the corridor, as I walked towards Nicholas's cell. The stone walls were dripping in green mould and black mildew, you could see the build-up of slimy moss, and the odd mushroom that poked up in the damp, dark corners. It was mid-morning, but it was so dark inside it was impossible to tell if it was day or night. The only light came from the flickering of the tallow-candle, which had burnt almost to the wick.

The entire prison lay in an eternal gloom, the windows deep set and narrow, opening only upon the dark passages. Ugly flea bitten cats and dogs roamed the hallways, and they fought with the rats for every shred of refuse. The smell was thick, and so intense it seemed almost tangible.

I hitched up my skirt and mounted a dark stairway, I followed the prison guard. He stopped in front of a door and held out his hand, and I placed a gold coin in his dirty palm. He bit the coin to check its authenticity, then nodded and opened the door to let me in.

'You 'ave arf an hour,' he said, in a gruff voice.

I walked into the room and pulled the hood of my cloak down. Nicholas looked up, surprise furrowed his brow as his eyes bored into me. We ran towards each other; the tears were flowing heavily down my cheeks.

'My god, Caroline, what are you doing here?' he clasped my shoulders and drew me away slightly, his face twisted in pain and regret.

'I had to see you before the trial.' My voice wobbled a little.

'It's filthy here, and I worry about you and the baby.' His eyes swam with unshed tears.

'We are fine, it's you I worry about.'

He pulled me back into his arms, and we clung to each other tightly, I knew this was probably going to be the last time we held each other. I closed my eyes tight, trying to stop the tears from flowing.

'I have tried to petition for your freedom, I even offered a heavy coin, but they will not drop the charges of treason.' I could feel his heart beating rapidly against my cheek.

'Have you word of Stefan and my men?'

I couldn't hold the tears back any longer, I cried so hard I could just about talk. 'Oh, Nicholas they were executed two days ago.'

'How?' His voice broke as he struggled with his emotion.

'Please, Nicholas, you don't need to know.'

'How?' His eyes burned with anger.

'They were hanged at Tyburn,' I said with sorrow.

'Did any of my men survive?' He searched my face for some sign of hope, I could not give any. I shook my head.

'Not one, not even Stefan or Gregor?'

The anguish in his face was so apparent I didn't know what to say, all I could do was hold him.

'We were betrayed,' he said. 'I should have listened to you, I thought I could beat the odds if I knew what was coming. Listen to me, I want you to go home to Debden manor. I have left a will and you and the babe will not want for anything.' He caressed my face and wiped a tear away.

'No, please! Let me see if I can bribe the prison guards, and then we can escape, and sail back to Holland.'

The panic I felt inside was indescribable. Everything was out of control and I couldn't stop it from spinning. Time was getting away from me, and I couldn't turn it back.

'It won't work love, and if you get caught...' He paused for a moment. 'This is my fate. It always has been, but the one consolation in all this mess is you. You have brought meaning, joy and love into my life, and I will live on in our babe.'

'Please stop talking like that! We can run, now....pretend you are dead! I will bring back some herbs to make it seem you have died in the night, and when your body gets put out I will come and get you. Please Nicholas, this can't be the end! What will I do without you? You are my life, my world. I cannot lose you, not ever!' My breath caught in and I couldn't breathe out. The terror gripped my throat, like hands squeezing me tight and not letting go.

'Shush...breathe and calm, my love. All will be well.' He forced a smile.

'No, it won't. You will not survive this and neither will I.'

I collapsed in his arms, and we stayed like this without speaking, just holding onto each other and knowing this would be our last time together.

The bang on the door echoed around the dark, damp room.

'Times up.' I heard the gruff, grainy voice of the guard.

I interlocked my fingers tight, I wouldn't let go, I couldn't let go.

'No!' I screamed, as Nicholas pulled my arms from around his waist. Please, don't leave me, please this cannot be the end of us, I won't let it. Please...' I was drowning in a sea of fear and loneliness, how would I survive without him, I knew I wouldn't be going back to my own time and deep down I knew I was going to live this life without him.

'Caroline, look at me.' He placed his hands either side of my face, and through my blurred vision I could see his eyes, glistening with tears and anguish of his own.

'Stop, enough. I cannot take your tears. I cannot be strong unless you are. Leave London, go to my mother, raise our child and just think that one day we will be together. I will always be with you even in death.' He kissed me one last time.

I love you so much it hurts,' I said, as he released his lips from mine.'

'It hurts me too, love. Now go, and don't ever look back.'

He nodded to the guard to take me.

'No! Nicholas! I'll find you again I promise…' I screamed as the guard pulled me through the doorway. I held onto to the heavy oak frame, I felt my nails break as he pulled me away.

My sobbing echoed around the corridors of the prison, this was wrong, I knew I should be strong for Nicholas, but my heart was broken and there was nothing I could do to stop his death.

*

303

The court room in Westminster was packed for the trial of King Charles and Lord Nicholas Trevilian.

I couldn't leave London, I had to stay.

Charles entered first, he wore a tall hat and around his neck was the blue of the garter from which was suspended his badge of St. George and the dragon, carved in onyx and studded with diamonds. His beard was full, but what I beheld was not the man I remembered from nearly sixteen months ago. His hair had turned grey, and he had aged considerably. He stood in the railed off area known as the bar, and he kept his hat on, so everyone was reminded that there was not one person there who was his equal. Next the door opened, and Nicholas was brought in. He was so handsome, dressed all in black, with a snowy white shirt and jabot. His hair was washed and tied back, his beard neatly trimmed, my heart melted and ached all at the same time. I had changed history, but not in a good way, Nicholas was on trial the same day as the King, and both would be sentenced together.

A young clerk, who had introduced himself as prosecutor Bradshawe, prepared to speak, but Charles rose, and raised his left hand.

'Hold! I would like to know by what authority? I mean lawful. There are many unlawful authorities in the world, but I would know by what authority I was brought thence.' There was no stutter in his speech. He continued. 'Remember, I am your King, your lawful king. I advise you to think well upon it.'

Bradshawe coughed into his hand, and continued.

'You are being tried in the name of the people of England, of which you were elected King.'

'No.' Charles spoke over the young clerk. 'England was never an elected kingdom but a hereditary kingdom for near a thousand years, therefore let me know by what authority I am called hither. I do stand more for the liberty of my people than any that come to be my pretended judges. And if the people were represented by parliament, which court, where is parliament? I see no House of Lords here that may constitute a parliament! You have shown no lawful authority to satisfy any reasonable man. That is your apprehension, Bradshawe, and as far as I am concerned the man below me, Lord Nicholas Trevilian should not be on trial today either. He is not a traitor to England, you all are.'

I watched as the young man became flustered, and he adjourned the court. 'Take down the prisoners,' he stammered.

'The King you mean,' Nicholas corrected the man. Shouts of, *God save the King!* broke out as they were both escorted from the hall.

Bradshawe shouted, 'Justice, justice!' as they were taken away.

It had been a small victory today; Cromwell's lackeys lost their argument, but the following day, the King and Nicholas were back in court.

Bradshawe again asked him to plead, and again, Charles asked by what authority he was being tried.

Bradshawe lost his temper. 'Guards take away the prisoner.'

'The king you mean,' Nicholas said again, in amusement.

The crowd erupted in laughter. 'Take him away too,' Bradshawe ordered sharply.

On the third day of the trial, Charles and Nicholas were both yet again asked to plead. This time it is Nicholas who answered.

'On whose authority? I see no peers, but for my King.'

The young clerk's irritation at the two men was evident, he couldn't control the situation to his advantage.

'Truly, sirs,' Bradshawe addressed both men. 'Men's intentions ought to be known by their actions; you have written your meaning in bloody characters throughout the whole kingdom. Your claims to stand for liberties and privileges of your subjects remain evident.'

As the soldiers moved to escort both men out of the hall, Bradshawe reiterated, 'Remember, you're both in a court of justice.'

Charles commented coolly, 'I see before me a power.' Only then did they both rise to take their leave.

My body was numb, my head was pounding by the time I got back to my lodgings; the pressure of the trial was growing. The ministers ranted and raged from the pulpit, against the sin of killing a king.

The Scots, French and Dutch ambassadors pleaded for Charles life, and that of his fiercely loyal subjects. They made veiled threats about what they might do if the King was to be executed. Charles was, after all, king of the Scots, the uncle of the King of France, and father-in-law of the now Prince of Orange; I'd had word from Mary that Frederik had died not long after we had departed. At least now Mary would be left alone, and whispers of the court will be behind closed doors rather than out in the open.

On the morning of Saturday 27th January, Charles was brought back into Westminster, along with Nicholas. A trumped-up charge was brought to the attention of the judges, that upon the King's orders Nicholas had urged his men to kill unarmed citizens of Leicester.

'That's a lie!' Nicholas stood in outrage.

'Be silent!' Bradshawe glared at Nicholas. Charles tried to speak, but he was cut off. Bradshawe, dressed in red robes, reminded the court that Charles and Nicholas had been brought before them on a charge of treason, and other high crimes that were carried out in the name of the people of England.

I was so angry; I couldn't contain myself as my voice rang out from the gallery.

'Not half, not even a quarter of the people of England! Oliver Cromwell is the traitor!' I shouted above the ruckus in the room. Unbeknownst to me, my comment would go down in history.

'Which whore said that?'

One of the guards in the gallery tried to drag me out. Nicholas knew it was me, and in temper he jumped over the bar and ran towards the gallery.

'Get him!' Bradshawe screamed, and the whole place was in uproar. Guards swarmed Nicholas, as I tried desperately to get to him. Both of us were detained; Nicholas was sent back down to his seat, and I was escorted from the hall. I screamed at the guards to let me listen, and they agreed. I stood by the doors, so I could hear the court.

Bradshawe spoke. 'I give you one last opportunity to acknowledge the jurisdiction of the court, and speak in your own defence.'

I heard Charles ask that he be heard in the painted chambers, before the Lords and Commons. The time had come at last to negotiate, or so Charles and Nicholas thought. But in asking to see the Lords, as well as the Commons, he was again denying the supremacy of the commons. I waited for the sentence to be handed down. The hall had gone quiet, so I could hear a lot clearer.

'Charles Stuart, tyrant, traitor, murderer and public enemy, and as such you will be put to death by severing your head from your body. Nicholas Trevilian, you are a traitor to your country and the commons, you did but side with Charles Stuart and do his bidding, you will be put to death by severing your head from your body. I heard the court stand.

'NO!' I screamed and fell to the floor, whereupon I was carried out and dumped on the steps of Westminster.

I wrote home to both my parents and Nicholas's mother, I pleaded with them to stay away, and I told them that after the execution I would make the necessary arrangements for Nicholas to be brought home.

I received a knock at the door a few days later, a soldier stood in the doorway. 'My Lady.' He inclined his head. 'Can I help you?'

He handed me four letters, written in Nicholas's hand and addressed to me, my father, his mother, and our unborn child. I thanked the soldier, and closed the door.

I couldn't think straight, my soul felt empty and lost, but I promised Nicholas I would be strong. Fate had a way of throwing us together, and now that fate was going to tear us apart.

In the days leading up to the execution I often wondered if the other Carolina had switched places with me. Was she in the future? Of course she's not, it's me now. Too many thoughts and questions ran around in my head, none of which could be answered. I didn't want to read my letter, but I had to know what it said.

I opened the letter and looked at his smart handwriting, knowing this would be the last time I would ever see it again.

My Darling Caroline, my Lina, my love,
This is the hardest thing I have ever had to do, to say goodbye. Death is not the person that dies, death is on the person that survives. You have brought so much joy to my life, something which I would never have imagined, I know in my heart that we will see each other again, so know this: I am not frightened, I go to my death with the knowledge this is not the end, which we both know to be true. Look on this as another chapter gone in our lives and I shall be waiting for you in our next adventure. Go, live out your days in peace and comfort, and raise my child with the loving care you have shown me. I will always be a part of you through my son or if I'm lucky to have a daughter just like her mother, full of spirit and love. Every day I spent with you, even though it was only for a short while, 'twas enough to last me and I am content going to my grave knowing this. So, my darling be strong, live your life to the fullest and never regret anything.

Your loving husband
Nicholas

And always remember, it is to live that requires courage, not to die.

I lost count how many times I read Nicholas's letter, over and over, but a part of me had to be brave. Despite the sadness, I also felt angry towards Nicholas, he sealed his own fate with the Marquis and looking back now I knew I would never have been able to save him.

My stomach growled; I had no desire to eat but I must think of the wellbeing of our baby. Food was brought up and I sat alone at the table wishing things were different. My days dragged along, I just sat in the room staring into nothingness, whilst I waited for the day of the execution. I was pining for a man that I would never see, hear, or make love to again. I felt the baby move for the first time. It all became too much to bear, as I collapsed on the bed and sobbed until my tears ran dry.

*

The late morning of the 30th January 1649, standing in the gardens of Banqueting House, I cut a solitary figure. The minutes seemed to speed along at such an alarming pace.

My head was down, with silent tears rolling down my cheeks waiting for the inevitable. I felt out of control, the fear and frustration at not being able to stop this was beyond words, but I knew deep down in my soul that I could not stop the wheels of time. A warm hand on my shoulder disturb my thought, I turned and looked into the eyes of my father, John Sackville.

'Father.'

He held out his arms, and I walked into his embrace.

'I could not let you do this on your own my child.'

I could feel him stroking the back of my head, giving comfort.

'I'm trying to be strong, but I can't.' I sobbed, 'I need him, Father, I cannot live without him. Please help me. He is my life, my soul.'

'I have tried, my darling, I have been in London for a few days and I have pleaded with Cromwell and his lackeys, but they will not shift in their views. They still see Nicholas as a threat.'

'Nicholas knows it is futile now, and he would be willing to live quietly with me and our baby. Can we not try to reason with them again, but together, for the sake of his child.' Surprise fleeted very briefly across my father's face.

'Hear me, daughter there is nothing we can do. Nicholas has accepted his fate, and he wishes for me to return you henceforth, back to Debden Manor. He does not want you to see this.'

'I'm sorry, but I'm staying, if I can't be with him, at least I can be with him until the end. I want to be the last thing he looks at. Do this for me, please?'

'If that's what you wish my darling, but be strong for him. Do not break down.'

'I promise.' I nodded silently at my father. I glanced up towards the sky and prayed.

Don't let him suffer, make the strike quick and true. I said aloud in my head.

*

We made our way towards the scaffolding that was shrouded in black, and pushed ourselves through the crowds of people to get to the front.

'Have these people got nothing better to do?' I looked around in disgust.

'It is a wicked world, Lina; people love to watch this and unfortunately they bear no compassion for the accused loved ones. Are you sure you want to do this?' he squeezed my hand in comfort.

I wanted to be there for Nicholas. I wanted him to see me strong, and standing with him until the very end. It was a façade, because I was crumbling inside, but I didn't want his last memories to be of me sobbing, and being dragged away, in Newgate prison.

'No, I'm here until the very end.'

My father held my hand strong and firm, I seemed to take comfort in this, it gave me the strength to stand tall.

Big Ben chimed. One o'clock; the end is nigh. My stomach hollowed in fear.

Nicholas walked out onto the block. The block itself was scarcely more than a hewn log on the ground, eighteen inches long by only six inches in height. Nicholas would have to lie flat.

'Have you any last words?' the bishop asked him.

We stood almost opposite him, he saw me, and his eyes glistened with tears. I looked up and we nodded to each other and smiled. I mouthed *I love you.*

He nodded and mouthed *I know, I love you too.* He spoke loud and clear. 'Carolina, my wife, my angel, my lover and my soul, I will see you soon and Lord you gave me an incredible woman and I will love her beyond my death.'

I shouted back, keeping my voice strong and full of love. 'I love you and I will find you again, I promise.'

Nicholas took off his cloak and handed his wedding ring to the bishop, and he whispered something in his ear. The bishop nodded and turned to me. He walked forward, leaned down as I approached him, he handed me Nicholas's wedding ring.

I glanced up at Nicholas never breaking eye contact. He laid down flat and put his head on the low block. My mouth went dry, I could barely swallow. My heart hammered fiercely in my chest, my breath came in short, sharp gasps.

I had no time to think before the axe fell clean. I screamed and ran towards the block. The despair swallowed me whole, my husband was no more, ceased to exist.

The executioner held up Nicholas's head. 'Behold the head of a traitor.'

'I lunged at the man and screamed, 'Put his head down, leave him be!'

I heard a noise in the distance, something like a wild animal's cry, and I realised that wail was coming from me.

'Get the stupid whore away from here!' The executioner pushes me away.

My father tried to pull me back. I pushed past the guard who went to grab me. I heard my father shout from behind me. 'Lina, stop!'

I slipped on something wet, Nicholas's blood. My clothes were covered with it. Hysteria overcame me as I knelt in the pool of his blood. My hands were drenched.

The gut wrenching loneliness overwhelmed me as I bent my head. I clutched my stomach and cried with despair. Then through my blurred vision I saw an image, I was looking back at myself through the red stream of scarlet. It no longer looked like me. Gone was the puddle of blood and in its place was a clear image. It was almost like looking into another mirror.

Confusion creased my brow as I touched the image before me, then I fell forwards just like before. Even as I lost consciousness I heard my father call my name in the distance, as the memories of Carolina's future pushed through my mind.

Images of their son, Nicholas, so like his father. I watched him grow from a baby to a handsome man, I saw him marry for love, with a beautiful wife and four children. But what of Carolina?

I pushed my mind through the images, further into the future. Carolina was old, seventy-seven. She had never re-married, and she died as she had lived: loved. She had lived a full and happy life, but her heart had never really recovered. Nicholas's fate I'd known, deep down, could not be changed. Time was brutal, it always had to end this way. History, time, or fate, whatever you call it, will always push back no matter how we try to change the story. The images of Carolina's future faded to blackness, as I watched her die with her family around her.

*

A flash of light penetrated through my subconscious and I opened my eyes. I was standing in an open meadow full of colourful flowers. The fragrant aroma surrounded me;

it filled my nostrils. I breathed in deep and closed my eyes.

'Caroline.'

The whisper I'd heard in the wind spoke to me again, and I opened my eyes. Nicholas stood in front of me and I knew this was heaven. My heart pounded in my chest; I was with him again. I tried to step closer, but I was being held back.

'Nicholas,' I screamed. I held out my arms as he tried to pull me towards him, but some unknown force held me back.

A voice behind me whispered. 'You will never be allowed to stay together, even in death.'

What had I done wrong? Then I fell into darkness.

*

'Wake up.' The voice said as my body was rocked from side to side. I tried my hardest not to wake but the voice got louder and the shaking harder.

'Please wake up! Father has told me to come fetch you. The Heathen army has been spotted at the banks of the Deben; they will soon be upon us!'

I opened my eyes and gazed around at my surroundings; confusion and fear overwhelmed me.

'Where am I?'

About the author

Victoria Short was born in Epping and raised in Loughton, Essex. She now lives in Suffolk with her husband and her two teenage children.

In between writing she works in the film industry making stories for the screen.

After writing her debut fiction novel, 'Our Story, Coming Home, Victoria pulled together her late grandfather's WW2 Logbook 'A Stokers Log' The British Pacific Forgotten Fleet.

To keep up to date on Victoria's writing you can follow her on social media.

www.facebook.com/VLShort
www.twitter.com@VLShort
www.victoriashortjames.wordpress.com

Printed in Great Britain
by Amazon